Alpha's New Beginning

KIMBER STONE

Charlotte,

You are a beautiful soul, I am lucky to have a friend like you! Happy Reading!

Love
Kimber Stone xxx

Copyright © [2024] by [Kimber Stone]

All rights reserved.

No portion of this book may be reproduced in any form without written permission from the publisher or author, except as permitted by U.S. copyright law.

I am so thankful for the amazing people I've had the privilege of meeting throughout this journey. I need to thank my wonderful editor Marc for all his hard work getting this book ready for print. You're a pleasure to work with and always keep my spirits high. Another huge thank you needs to go to my Fairy Godmother Leah; you're one of a kind and I couldn't have done this without you!! My family and friends who have been supportive through everything, I can't tell you how much that means to me. Knowing I have you all in my corner makes me want to work harder to make you all proud.

When you have a dream, you've got to grab it and never let go.

-**Carol Burnett**

Prologue

Xander

One week, it had been one week of darkness and loneliness. The day after Daniel's talk with our mate Amber, I casually mentioned he needed to mate and mark her as soon as possible. It seemed Daniel didn't like my tone or my constant insisting that we do it right away, so the jackass blocked me. I couldn't believe it, I was the other half of him and he had the nerve to block me. I still knew what was going on, thankfully. I could communicate with Amber's wolf, Lana.

My sweet Lana has been keeping me up to date on all of Daniel's moves. I tried reaching out to Daniel multiple times but he just shoved me deeper into the back of his mind. I knew Amber tried to reason with him, he simply told her he needed to concentrate on establishing himself as Alpha and didn't have time to deal with my shenanigans.

To say I was hurting would be putting it mildly, the nerve of this guy; how could he be an alpha wolf without a wolf? Maybe I could have asked the Moon Goddess to pair me with a more grateful human.

I was starting to go stir crazy only having myself to talk to day in and day out.

I had an idea though. I was going to ask Lana to tell Amber that I was getting weak, by not connecting with Daniel. Hopefully, he would be scared of losing me forever and would drop the block between us. I had it all planned out. I just needed to wait until Lana reached out to me.

While I waited, I let my mind wander to Daniel and everything that had happened in the last week and a half. Maybe I was wrong in pushing him to mark Amber. He had just lost Annabelle after all, he also found out his father tried to kill him as a child. He then had to fight his psychotic father to the death to become Alpha of his former pack. Maybe I was the jerk in all of this? Damn, the solitary confinement was making me go soft. I needed to get out of it quickly.

Chapter One

Chapter 1

***A**mber*

Waking up wrapped in Daniel's arms the morning after we talked made me happier than I cared to admit. I knew his heart wasn't ready to love again, getting my hopes up was a dangerous thing. I was emotionally teetering on the edge of a cliff at the moment. Finding my mate, losing my father, finding out I was a Luna all in a day was a lot.

If Daniel couldn't bring himself to love me, if he rejected me, it would be the end of me. I was falling for him and I didn't know how to stop it. I was choosing to be cautiously optimistic for the time being. The day passed slowly and a bit oddly. Daniel seemed distracted and agitated, his beautiful hazel eyes kept shifting to the blue eyes of his wolf, Xander. I tried to ask him a few times if everything was OK. He just brushed it off as his wolf being a pain in the ass. I could see as the day progressed Daniel got more and more agitated. It all came to a head as we were getting ready for bed, he suddenly yelled out.

"For Fuck's sake, Xander, ENOUGH!"

This scared the hell out of me and I jumped a good foot off the ground. Daniel profusely apologized for scaring me. He looked haunted as he turned around announcing he had work to finish, then went back to his office. I was worried I had done something to upset him, but Lana reassured me the outburst had nothing to do with me and everything to do with Xander.

I went to bed feeling only slightly better about the situation. I had trouble falling asleep that night. I tossed and turned for a few hours. When I fell asleep I had a terrible nightmare about losing Gabriella and woke up in a cold sweat. Once I calmed myself down and realized it was just a nightmare, I looked over to Daniel's side of the bed, it was cold and empty. The clock on my bedside table said it was five thirty in the morning. Had Daniel not come to bed yet, or did he just wake up that early? *"Lana, are you sure Daniel isn't mad at us?"* I hated sounding like a needy mate, but I was worried.

"I'm positive that Daniel's earlier outburst had nothing to do with you, he's got a lot on his shoulders right now, and Xander had been pestering him all day, trying to take over and mark us."

"Oh, seriously? No wonder he was so upset, he's not ready to commit to marking me! Last night, I told him he could take the time he needed, I guess Xander had other ideas." I sighed and scrubbed my hands down my face in frustration. This could set us back in a major way.

"Amber, I reached out to Xander earlier after the outburst, he's doing OK, but Daniel put a block up between them. Xander is annoyed but thinks Daniel will come around soon enough. I can still communicate with him, so don't worry."

I thanked Lana for explaining the situation to me. I tried to go back to sleep without any luck. I was worried about Daniel. Fighting with your wolf was never fun, we were a team that needed one another to function properly. I was unable to fall back asleep before the sun came up and a new day began. I decided to get up even though it was still very early, so I crept over to Gabriella's room to check on her. She was sleeping peacefully as I looked down on her lovingly, no matter what today would bring she would be my spot of sunshine. The day was much the same as yesterday, Daniel was cranky and irritable. He had to hunt down a handful of men that were still loyal to Alpha Francis, and wanted to cause trouble for us. These men were quickly taken care of by Daniel, Justin, Olivia and Alpha Arnold.

I found out later from Olivia that Daniel never shifted during the fights, because he refused to remove the block with Xander. After supper, I tried speaking with him about unblocking Xander, but he just told me he didn't have time for Xander's antics.

We went to bed every night, pretty much all week in silence and when I woke up Daniel would already be gone. He had training or meetings; always something that kept us apart. I felt useless, since we hadn't established when I would take over as Luna yet. Olivia's mother, Angela, hadn't come out of her room since the day my father died, so getting any Luna training from her was not going to happen. Margot, her sister, was bringing her meals and making sure she didn't do anything crazy. Thankfully, I had Gabriella, who kept me busy and kept me smiling. It broke my heart some days seeing Daniel with her. He was so sweet and tender, but I could see the pain in his eyes every time he looked at her. It was obvious how much he missed Annabelle. I prayed to the Moon Goddess that one day I could be enough for him.

We made it to the end of the week and were lying back to back in our bed. I knew Daniel wasn't asleep, and I desperately wanted to ask him if I was enough, if he even wanted to give us a chance anymore. This week felt like a giant wedge had formed between us, and that any hope I may have had, that first night falling asleep in his arms, was fading fast.

I couldn't bring myself to say anything, so I willed myself to fall asleep. I woke up after another nightmare, this time about my father's death. I rolled over looking for solace and comfort from Daniel. However, I was met with an empty, cold bed. I pressed my bedside clock, and it lit up the darkness, showing me it was two thirty. Where could he have gone?

I made the decision to get out of bed to go look for him. I went to his office first. I listened at the door for a moment before I knocked lightly. I waited but got no response. I wondered if he was even there. I heard nothing from where I stood, so I decided to take a chance and went in without being invited. What I found in his office broke my heart.

CHAPTER TWO

Chapter 2

Daniel

I woke up the morning after I spoke to Amber with her wrapped in my arms. I couldn't help the smile that spread across my face and the warmth that radiated through my chest. I knew it wouldn't be long before I was ready to make her mine. I just needed to process my grief a little longer and get myself sorted as Alpha of the Onyx Crescent. I needed to get up but I didn't want to ruin this perfect moment. *"So then, don't move, stay with mate and mark her."* Xander's smug voice broke through my happy moment.

"You know very well I'm not ready to mark her yet, Xander, we hardly know each other and I haven't fully grieved for Annabelle. Also, marking her now while she's asleep without consent would be an asshole move."

"Maybe, but if we don't mate and mark her soon we run the risk of losing her completely. I'm sure she wouldn't mind being marked now, I feel it in my bones that we need to mark her today."

"Don't push me Xander, I won't let you bully me into doing something neither of us are ready for. You heard her last night. Amber is willing to wait for me to be ready, and will give me the space I need, while still being there for me."

Xander was about to say something else but I cut him off by putting up a block. He'd managed to put me in a sour mood. I gently removed my arms from around Amber and got up to start my day. Any warm fuzzy feelings I had when I first woke up were now gone, reality hit me as I prepared for the plethora of meetings I had that morning. I had to figure out who was still loyal to my deceased father, and who we could train as warriors, since we pretty much lost all the ones the pack had during our challenge.

Even though I had put up a block, Xander still managed to push through multiple times that day, and tried to take over every time he saw Amber. It was exhausting constantly fighting him for control. He wouldn't stop pushing me to mark Amber, screaming and yelling at me that he had a right to his mate, and it was his turn to be happy. I spiralled more and more as the day went on. By bedtime, I had just about all I could take from Xander and exploded at him. I didn't even realize that I had yelled out loud until poor Amber jumped out of her skin, as she was getting into bed.

Before going over to Amber, I pushed Xander as far as I possibly could into the back of my mind, and put up a solid block. I needed space from my crazy wolf; a day or two for me to think and deal with all the bullshit. I had too much piled up on my shoulders at that moment. I quickly made my way over to Amber and apologized to her thoroughly. She accepted but I could see the hurt and confusion in her eyes. This broke my heart. The last thing I wanted to do was hurt her, she was so understanding. She was also my sister's best friend, which meant if I hurt her I'd most definitely have to deal with Olivia. That thought terrified me. Olivia was a strong, capable alpha female who wouldn't hesitate to dump me on my ass again if I hurt her best friend. I respected both women too much to hurt either of them, I needed to get myself and my wolf under control.

I wished Amber a good night and went to my office to work on a few last things before bed. I worked later than expected and didn't have the heart to risk waking Amber up by going to bed. I decided to just sleep on the couch in my office. If I was being honest, it was cold and hard, nothing like the soft bed I had upstairs. The bed with my beautiful mate waiting for me, her luscious vanilla/coconut scent filling the room. I felt Xander pushing against the block and made sure to push him back, so he stayed where I put him. I fell asleep rather quickly dreaming of Amber and the life we could have. My dream quickly became a nightmare when I saw Annabelle in my dream crying, asking me how I could replace her so easily. I woke up at five am in a cold sweat, saddened by my nightmare. I decided to go to the gym and let out some stress.

I was so tired from hardly sleeping, and exhausted from my fight with Xander the day before. I had no patience and was unusually grumpy all day. Alpha Arnold commented on it and I just brushed it off as needing to get the traitors under control. Olivia, Justin, Alpha Arnold and myself went after the group of troublemakers and took care of them that afternoon. I didn't like killing, but these wolves were nothing but trouble and would have stopped at nothing to make our lives miserable. Since Xander was blocked, I couldn't shift, which was as infuriating as it was dangerous. Olivia tried to convince me to let Xander free, but I told her to please mind her business, I would handle my wolf. Xander needed to be taught a lesson and if I gave in now I'd never hear the end of it. What I had wanted most at that moment was to hold Amber and let her scent calm me.

I went looking for her before supper and found her with Gabriella. Seeing them together made my heart swell with joy. I was so lucky that Gabriella would have such a strong, caring woman to help raise her. I went to them and lovingly took Gabriella into my arms as I took a long inhale of Amber's scent. I instantly felt calmer and more at peace. I smiled at Gabriella and the smile I got back was the same as Annabelle's. I had a moment of sadness, but overall I was happy that I would always have a piece of Annabelle with me, that would shine through Gabriella. I enjoyed my time with Amber and Gabriella immensely.

When supper was called, I was crestfallen that we would have to be around others, and our private family moment was over for now. After supper, Amber shyly approached me. I was happy she wanted to talk to me, but that quickly changed when I realized what she wanted. She was trying to convince me to set Xander free, but I brushed her off. I felt like a massive asshole, I saw the pain in her eyes but she didn't understand. If I let Xander out, he would take over and make me mark her. I had to protect her from him at all costs, until we were ready to mate and mark. I thought of telling her but chose not to. What if she blamed herself for my wolf's foolishness? I would feel even worse than I already did.

The week seemed to drag on, it was much of the same boring crap day in and day out. I would have meetings, Alpha training and actual warrior training. Then, I would work too late, sleep poorly on my office couch, wake up grumpy and sore. Wash, rinse, repeat. I felt like I hardly got to see Amber. It was partially my own fault, as I was intentionally staying away at night to protect her. Sleeping in the same bed as her, knowing I couldn't touch her yet would have driven me mad. So, I threw myself into my work even harder.

My favourite part of the day was the warrior training sessions that Olivia and Amber were running together. I couldn't help but be impressed by my mate. She had incredible fighting skills. I was a very lucky man. I realized just past mid week that I was falling for her, irrevocably. It wasn't just the mate bond doing its job. I realized I missed her if she wasn't in the office with me. I loved her beautiful smile, her infectious laughter, her quick wit. I loved how she cared about everyone, making sure we had all the things we needed during meetings, pointing out flaws in our logic and, most of all, I loved how much she loved Gabriella and took such good care of her.

Once Friday rolled around, I was a complete mess. I was agitated, and just wanted to hold Amber all night and never let her go. I planned on telling her there and then about my feelings but ended up chickening out. I heard her lightly snoring and decided to go get some more work done. I didn't get much work done that night. I spent most of my time staring into space, and thinking about what Amber's reaction would be to the confession of my feelings to her. I was starting to get sleepy, before I made my way to the couch. I took a framed photo out of my desk drawer. The photo was of Annabelle, Gabriella and myself that we had taken not long before she had passed. I went to sit down, looking long and hard at the picture. I sent a prayer to the Moon Goddess thanking her for pairing me with Amber. I also thanked her for giving me Annabelle, for the time I was lucky enough to have her. "Annabelle, I know you told me to move on and be happy. I am ready to do that now. You will always be in my heart. Thank you for the memories." I blew a kiss to the heavens as I slowly slipped into sleep holding the photo frame. I planned on telling Amber first thing in the morning how I felt and maybe, if I was feeling nice I would let Xander out of confinement.

Amber

I walked into the office and saw Daniel sleeping on the office couch. That hurt; he'd rather sleep on a cold, hard couch than in the same bed as me. What instantly shattered my heart though was what I saw when I got closer to him. Daniel was holding a family picture of himself with Annabelle and Gabriella. It was clear to me now that I was never going to be good enough for him, he clearly missed his old chosen mate and could never get over her. I didn't blame him, he had a life before everything got turned upside down. I made the choice at that moment that I would let him reject me. Lana started to whimper in my mind.

"I'm so sorry, Lana, I know how much you wanted your mate, but I can't compare to the woman he lost, and it's not fair for me to live in her shadow for the rest of my life."

"Amber, you need to fight for our mate. Maybe he was just having a moment of mourning. You never know. What about Gabriella? If you let him reject us, we'll never see her again."

I choked back a sob, she was right. I would never get to see Gabriella again if he rejected us. I was so confused and hurt at that moment, I needed space to think and figure out my feelings. Suddenly, I knew the perfect place that I could do that, and no one knew about it; I could be alone to lick my wounds in peace. I couldn't bring myself to do it face to face, so I chose to write Daniel a note. I let him know that I needed to do some thinking alone. I apologized for disappointing him. I knew I could never measure up to Annabelle. I said I would be back in two days after I cleared my head. I put the note on his desk and before I left, I covered him with a blanket - he looked cold. I gently placed a kiss on his cheek. As I did, he stirred slightly, which made me hold my breath.

Luckily, he didn't wake up. I took one last look at him and quietly left his office. I ran back to my room and changed into some jeans and a sweater, I packed a backpack with a few essentials and headed off. The secret cabin my father owned deep in the back of our pack lands, was perfect for what I needed. I just wanted to be alone and think of what I really wanted to do. Once I'd figured it out I would come back and face Daniel. I tiptoed into Gabriella's room and gave her a kiss on the top of her head. She smiled in her sleep and it melted my heart.

I was going to miss that little girl the most if I decided to let Daniel reject me. A lone tear slid down my cheek which I wiped away quickly, before it could land on the baby and wake her. I told her to be a good girl while I was gone, and I would see her soon. I quietly snuck out of the pack house and took off running for the north side of the pack lands. I was numb at this point from my swirling feelings, so the early morning chill didn't bother me much. I had about a half-hour run until I reached the cabin. This was going to be a rough two days.

Chapter 3

Olivia

I woke up wrapped in Logan's arms. I smiled up at him in awe. I couldn't believe this gentle, kind, funny, gorgeous man was my mate. I had never in a million years imagined myself mated. I couldn't help my smile as I memorized every inch of that man's face. I was scared to breathe because I didn't want to ruin such a peaceful moment. It had been a long time since I had any peace in my life. We still had a long road ahead of us in that department.

My father was removed from power only the day before and Daniel replaced him as Alpha of Onyx Crescent. The issues that remained were: that we had lost all our ranked wolves, Daniel had no idea how to be Alpha and we still had traitors in our midst. The thought of all the work we still had to do before we could be truly at peace, made me groan internally.

"If you continue staring at me any longer you may start to bore holes in my face." Logan smirked as he cracked one beautiful blue eye open at me.

I had been so engrossed in my own thoughts that I hadn't noticed when Logan's breathing had changed, his words startled me and I jumped. "You scared the hell out of me." I admonished him.

"I would never scare you on purpose. How about you let me make that up to you?" He smiled sensually as he rolled on top of me and planted a smoking hot kiss on my open mouth.

"Please don't tempt me, Logan, there is nothing I want more in this world than for you to make it up to me. The only problem is, I promised Daniel I would help him sort through our father's office this morning and help him track down the rest of the dimwits that were loyal to that asshole."

Logan groaned as he rolled off of me, but held me close so I couldn't run away. I looked up at him in time to see disappointment still present on his face, before it lit up with a huge smile that was just for me. It killed me, because that smile did things to my lady bits; I was very close to saying fuck it and just staying in bed all day with him. Instead, I chose to do the responsible thing and promised I would make it worth the sacrifice later.

"I am going to hold you to that promise, my love." He whispered in my ear before taking my earlobe into his warm mouth and sucking on it. This caused lightning and tingles to shoot through my body.

"Hey! that's not playing fair," I cried foul at his actions.

This set Logan off into a fit of laughter, which I couldn't resist and in turn I burst out laughing as well. We laughed until our sides ached and a knock was heard on my door. I knew it was Amber before she spoke, wanting to let me know that Daniel was in our father's office, waiting for me to start.

"Well, duty calls. Let's get this over with as fast as we can, so we can come back and make it up to each other." I winked at Logan as I bounced off our bed and headed for the bathroom.

Fifteen minutes later, we were both dressed and knocking on the office door. Daniel bid us to enter. As we walked into the office, it took us a moment to find poor Daniel. We eventually spotted him sitting at the desk half hidden, by the stacks of paper scattered everywhere, and giant piles of ledgers that were stacked sky-high on the corner of the desk. The ledgers were obscuring our view of him. I was shocked by the state of the office: our father hated clutter and disorganization. This made me smile and chuckle to myself. I hoped he was seeing this from Hell, and dying a little more. Sure that was mean to think, but that man deserved nothing less. I asked Daniel how long it had taken him to re-arrange the office to this lovely state. He stopped reading the document in his hand and looked at me puzzled for a moment, before registering what I was talking about.

"You're asking about this mess? I didn't make it! I came in here this morning and this is what I found. I've been randomly picking up papers for the last half hour trying to make heads or tails of them all."

I had asked the question in jest. I hadn't expected that to be the answer. Knowing someone or multiple people had ransacked the office prior to either Daniel or I getting in there, was troubling to say the least. What were they looking for? What did they find? I scrubbed my hands down my face in frustration. This was going to take a lot longer than I had hoped, and the make-up fun I had promised Logan was looking farther and farther away.

As if he knew exactly what I was thinking, he looked at me with a shit-eating grin on his face. "Guess you should have taken me up on my offer earlier," giving me a wink and an air kiss to add insult to injury.

I was about to respond to Logan when Amber walked in with coffee and fresh pastries. He was a lucky man. I chose coffee over violence at that moment. Amber sat next to Daniel and started going over a stack of papers that hadn't been touched yet. I voiced my questions to everyone - between sips of coffee and bites of a muffin. Amber looked up from the page she was holding, and said that they had asked the same questions themselves earlier when they saw the state of the office. Daniel held up a paper he was reading, and mentioned that it looked like part of the pack's deed. He had only managed to find three other random papers that looked to be part of the deed. He couldn't tell if the rest were taken or still scattered around the office.

"The deed? What would they want with the deed?" That was a troubling question that I wasn't sure I wanted the answer to.

"Honestly, Olivia, I don't know. We've got one hell of a mess to sort through here, and a lot more questions than answers."

Daniel said this more harshly than I was expecting. I looked at him with concern and saw his eyes bouncing from his own hazel eyes to his wolf, Xander's blue ones. I found that odd but chalked it up to the stress of being the new alpha. Maybe they were disagreeing on how to solve this mystery. The afternoon dragged on, and by the end of the day we were no further ahead in our quest to find answers. Daniel was just getting crankier and crankier until finally he called it a day, and we all went our separate ways.

Logan and I made it to our room and we were both too exhausted to even bother with anything we had discussed that morning. We threw ourselves into bed and both fell asleep rather quickly. The last thing I remembered was Evie bitching at me, that I was wasting her best years by not jumping on our mate every chance we could. I had no energy left to argue with my sex-addicted wolf, so I just ignored her and went to dream land.

We woke up the next morning and found Daniel in quite a horrid mood. I wondered if he and Amber had fought the night before. I truly hoped that wasn't the case; he was my brother but she was my best friend, and I would kick his ass into oblivion if he hurt my sweet Cupcake. I tried to broach the subject with him several times but he just brushed me off, so I let it drop. We had more important things to deal with.

Justin and Alpha Arnold had found a stronghold of my father's remaining loyal men, not too far away from the pack house. We made a plan and headed out as soon as we were ready, to take care of them. The plan was that we were going to keep at least three men alive, to get information from them. That plan went to hell when Daniel refused to shift, and we ended up killing all but one dimwit. Even the one we kept alive was barely hanging on, we took him to the pack hospital as soon as we got back and we left Justin to watch over him.

I cornered Daniel on the way out to ask what the hell he was thinking by not shifting during a fight that big. His answer was that he had a fight with Xander and was blocking him. That answer confused and concerned me. Daniel promised he would unblock his wolf in a few days, once he cooled his heels. I could tell he wasn't happy with our conversation, so I chose to drop the subject and left him to go clean up.

On my way to my room, I ran into Amber with Gabriella. The baby was so happy to see me. I gave her a kiss on her soft silky hair. I was a hot mess and didn't want to get blood or dirt on the baby. I wasn't going to say anything about what happened, but I knew if the roles were reversed I'd want to be told. I let Amber know what happened earlier with Daniel not shifting during the fight. She was shocked and dismayed by what I told her. She hugged Gabriella tighter and told me that Daniel had been angry since yesterday, and she wasn't sure what to do, or if she could even do anything to make it better. My heart was wrenched for my best friend. I knew how much she wanted to make her bond work with Daniel, but I also knew my brother needed time. I reassured her the best I could and went back to my room to shower.

I hadn't seen Logan all day and he wasn't in our room once I got out of the shower. I was so tired from the fight that I ended up passing out until the next day. I woke up wrapped in Logan's arms, which made me happy. Sadly, before I could make myself and Logan happier, we were summoned to the office.

The rest of the week passed in much the same fashion. We had meetings and I was teaching multiple warrior classes a day with Amber. I barely remember seeing Logan most days, but each morning I'd wake up in his arms. At least I knew he still loved me despite our lack of intimacy. I was glad I had one less thing to worry about, because everything else kept me deep in worry.

Daniel grew angrier and angrier as the week progressed. Amber seemed to withdraw more and more, but kept a smile on her face none the less. We borderline lost the dimwit twice, but our doctor worked some miracle and he survived. Not that it did much good. It seemed we had kept the lowest man on the totem pole. He knew practically nothing. The only bit of information he gave us, which was our silver lining out of the whole ordeal, was he confirmed we hadn't killed all the men. There were still about half a dozen left at another unknown location. That was both a win and a loss for us. Knowing we still had people to hunt down who were likely going to cause us trouble, was demoralizing.

I went to bed overly tired again, planning on having a heart to heart with Daniel in the morning. I wanted to find out what was actually going on, so we could all get on the same page and work as a proper team. I fell asleep with an uneasy feeling in my stomach and had many nightmares in the first few hours I tried to sleep. That left me feeling unsettled and not looking forward to what tomorrow had in store for me.

Chapter Four

Chapter 4

Justin

The week we spent at Onyx Crescent passed rather quickly. Poor Daniel had a lot of work to do as the new alpha. His cockroach of a father had left him quite the shit show to clean up. Three days ago, I helped Daniel, Olivia and Alpha Arnold get rid of about a dozen problematic loyalists, who were trying to avenge Daniel's psycho father. We found out later that there were still more hiding somewhere else, which would require yet more work to find them. As much as I wanted to help Daniel, it was time for me and Melissa to head back to Jade Moon later today.

I had a new position as Alpha to take over, since my father had met his own demise at the beginning of the week. Now that my pack was free, I would be able to officially claim my mate, Melissa, and we could start our life together, finally. I knew today was going to be tough for her. She had to say goodbye to her brother since he would be staying at Onyx Crescent with his mate, Olivia. Logan was also my best friend, so leaving him behind was a tough pill for me to swallow. I'd always had plans that I would make him my Beta once my terrible father was gone. Now, I wasn't sure what I was going to do.

First things first, though, looking at Melissa sleeping peacefully in my arms. I smiled at how cute she was, with her hair a wild mess across the pillows, drool pooled at the corner of her lips, and the cutest little kitten snore coming from her. I couldn't wait to wake up to this every morning for the rest of my life. People could call me crazy, but I found this ridiculously sexy. My cock twitched at the thought of Melissa splayed out on the bed all dishevelled and moaning my name. I reached down and gave my rock-hard cock a squeeze to relieve the pressure that was building. What did this woman do to me?

I had just woken up and just by looking at her I knew I needed to be inside her. I gently ran my nose up the side of her neck and nipped at her earlobe playfully, making her stir slightly. I then kissed my way back down her neck and ended up at her marking spot, which I gently started to suck on. This seemed to have the desired effect as she let out a sweet, seductive moan, which was music to my ears. I didn't relent, and swirled my tongue around her marking spot until she finally opened her eyes, with a beautiful smile forming on her lips, just for me.

"What a way to wake a girl up, I could get used to that." She winked at me as she stretched lightly next to me.

"Oh, there are plenty of other ways I thought of to wake you up."

"Oh, really? You'll have to show me, I'm intrigued." Melissa purred at me while cupping my cheek.

She didn't have to ask me twice. I outlined her jaw with the back of my fingers and let my hand trail down her neck, under her night shirt and lightly traced her left nipple. She shivered, and I watched as her pert pink nipples hardened almost instantly from the contact.

I continued my journey down her torso until I could feel the heat radiating from between her legs.

"Someone is an excited little kitten this morning, you're already getting ready for me!"

"I'm always ready for you, Alpha, you're so strong and sexy!" Her husky voice was dripping with want and need.

Melissa and I loved to role-play. We enjoyed playing the roles we both carried out in the pack, but in an over-exaggerated manner. I was the strong Alpha and she was my sweet, sexy little omega that needed me to save her and ravish her. It was enjoyable since we had to be so secretive back home, it was, in a way, mocking our predicament. It always made us laugh, since neither of us are the stereotypical alpha or omega. She knew exactly what she was doing by calling me her Alpha. I slipped easily into character and ordered her to strip for me.

"That's right, my little omega, I have very important Alpha duties to attend to today, so be quick and strip. I need to see that tight, little body and sweet, delicious pussy of yours, before I have to go."

"Yes, Alpha, I hope I didn't disappoint you by sleeping in so late. Let me make it up to you."

Melissa quickly threw off her night shirt, revealing her beautiful naked body beneath. My cock was so hard it was sensitive against my boxers, as she reached over and pulled it out gently. She licked her lips as she locked eyes with me. Next thing I knew, my cock was sliding down her throat. I wasn't expecting that and let out a loud moan. I could feel Melissa's lips curl into a smile around my manhood. This woman was a siren, she knew all the right moves to turn me into putty in her hands. She expertly swirled her tongue from base to tip, then back down again, all while sucking with a force that would make a vacuum jealous. My eyes rolled into the back of my head, the sensations this woman gave me were out of this damn world. Melissa took my balls into her hand, massaging them until I knew I couldn't hold on much longer. I told her I was going to cum and she stopped what she was doing instantly.

"Ah, ah, ahhhhh, Alpha, you can't cum, yet! I still have more of a job to do." Her bottom lip pouted.

My heart nearly stopped at her words. I was so close. What was she doing? This sly little minx had just taken our game to a whole new level. I watched as she straddled me and slowly, almost painfully, slipped my cock into her dripping pussy. This was completely new. Melissa always lets me eat her out first. She knew how much I loved tasting her and pleasuring her; she was growing more confident and brazen. This turned me on even more. I gripped her hips tightly and surged upwards, causing her to cry out. I couldn't help the need to pound my cock into her, her moans and cries of pleasure spurred me on even more. I could feel her orgasm building. I sat up and latched onto her left nipple, sucking hard on it. That seemed to be what she needed as her breath hitched and her walls clenched around my cock, she was so tight I felt like I was about to cum at any second.

Unfortunately for me, though, I wasn't going to be lucky enough to have my release. There was a furious pounding on my door. A frantic Olivia shouted my name, begging me to open the door. The pounding startled Melissa and she jumped off my cock as if it were on fire. I groaned in frustration. What the hell kind of timing was that? I was so close to releasing, how could this be happening right now?

"Justin, please open the door, Amber has gone missing! We don't know where she is and Daniel is beside himself. We think someone may have taken her from the pack house. Please come quick, we need your tracking skills."

If she only knew the irony of asking me to 'come quick', I so nearly did and still wanted to. Melissa shocked me then by opening the door to Olivia. I had just enough time to throw the blankets over myself. She had put her night shirt back on while I was busy bitching to myself and I hadn't noticed her going to the door. Olivia burst into our room with worry plastered all over her face and stains from the tears she had clearly been shedding.

"I know it's early, and I'm so sorry to have barged in like that. You are the only decent tracker we have here, and I don't know what to do. Daniel discovered she was gone and was losing his mind."

"Give me a minute to get dressed, and I'll meet you down in Daniel's office momentarily."

"Oh, thank you so much, Justin, we owe you one."

She left quickly to return to Daniel's office and Melissa closed the door behind her. I wagged a finger at her and asked why she opened the door without warning me. She just smirked at me and burst into laughter. Well, I guess that was the end of my morning fun, it was time to get up and help out.

Chapter Five

Chapter 5

*A*mber

I woke up with a splitting headache. I rolled over on the small twin bed to check the time on the bedside table. It was nine thirty. I had slept later than I had planned. The pressure increased in my head and I suddenly realized it wasn't a headache, it was Olivia pushing with all her might against the barrier I had put up. I guess they found the note I left. I felt guilty that I hadn't told my best friend I was leaving. I knew she would have convinced me to stay. I didn't like the thought of her worrying about me, but I couldn't stay. After what I saw in Daniel's office the previous night, I knew I didn't belong in his life.

"Amber, are you sure that's what you saw? He could have just been grieving. Saying a last goodbye?"

"Come on, Lana, you saw the same thing I did. He was holding that framed photo of himself, Annabelle and Gabriella as if it were the most precious thing to him."

I shook my head to try and ease the pressure. Was I overreacting? Maybe Lana was right? I scrubbed my hands down my face in frustration. Last night I was so firm and set in my decision. Why was I wavering and second guessing myself now? I was getting very frustrated and anxious. The incessant pushing in my head wasn't helping. I wished Olivia would have given up already and just let me be. I thought about lowering the block and telling her I was fine, but I was sure after seeing the note I left for Daniel, she had questions and that's why she was so persistent. I decided I would get up and go for some fresh air. There was a beautiful little stream two minutes away. The tiny cabin was stifling and I needed to move before the anxiety swallowed me whole.

By the time I made it to the stream, the pressure in my head was as good as gone. Olivia must have realized I'd speak with her once I was back, and had given up. I exhaled a giant sigh of relief. I felt like I was being selfish, but after the week I had just endured, I needed time to cool off and get my head on straight. Why did I feel so guilty though? I was never the type of girl to live for other people and worry about what others thought of me. Was it because Daniel was my mate? The damn mate bond made you feel so different about normal simple situations. Before Daniel, if a lover lost interest that was fine, ciao, bye! Rejection wasn't an issue for me. Now, with the mate bond, though, it's a whole different story and I don't like feeling vulnerable.

"What if we made a list of pros and cons about telling Daniel to reject us?" Lana offered gently.

I dove to the bottom of the stream and came back up floating on my back, staring blankly up at the white fluffy clouds in the blue sky. I thought about what Lana suggested and agreed to make a pros and cons list. It didn't take me long to come up with a list off the top of my head. Being honest with myself, the cons strongly outweighed the pros of rejection. The only pro was it allowed Daniel to live with the memories of Annabelle in peace, from my jealousy.

"Is that really living though, Amber? He won't be happy living with a ghost and memories, when he had his true mate right in front of him."

Lana sounded quite annoyed at my flawed logic and I had to agree with her. I didn't think Daniel would be happy living with memories that would eventually fade over time. The one sticking point on my cons list was I would never get to be with Gabriella again. I loved that little girl so much and felt like I would die if I had to say goodbye to her for good. I burst into tears at that point. I felt so helpless, I didn't want to lose my future family and happiness. Yet how do I get over this heartbreak?

"We need to go back, tell Daniel what we saw and how it made you feel! If he is anything but sympathetic and understanding about how you're feeling, then I will push forward and reject him for you!"

Lana was so matter of fact about what we needed to do. It filled me with a restored sense of hope. I knew it could be a dangerous thing, but at that moment I needed to cling to that small speck, or I would fall apart. I hoisted myself out of the stream and dried off in the sun for a little while, before I decided to head back to the cabin. As much as I just wanted to sprint back to the pack house, I knew myself, and I still needed a day to work up the courage for the talk I had to have with Daniel. I was also a woman of my word. I said two days in my letter, I wasn't going to go back on that now.

I walked back to the cabin feeling lighter than I had in the past week. I was virtually back at the cabin when I heard what sounded like footsteps nearby. I stopped and listened. What if Daniel or Olivia had come looking for me and found me? I was so careful to block my scent when I left, I assumed finding me would be next to impossible. I waited for what seemed like forever, holding my breath, but no one appeared and I didn't smell anyone. It was probably just an animal, or my imagination. I walked into the cabin and my breath hitched. There, sitting at my little table dwarfing everything in the room, was a well-built, middle-aged man who had a very dangerous aura emanating from him.

"Ah, Luna, so glad you made it back. I'm Greg, I've been waiting to speak with you. Have a seat. That's an order."

Daniel

I woke up wrapped in a soft warm blanket. I smiled to myself, knowing it must have been Amber who covered me in the night. I stretched and sat up with a yawn. I looked at the picture frame in my hand and said one final silent goodbye to Annabelle. I knew she would be happy for me, and it was clear I would be well cared for and loved. A movement to my right caught my attention and startled me. I hadn't realized I wasn't alone in my office, a young omega was at my desk stacking papers and rearranging the chaos. I stood up quickly, which in turn startled her and the pile of papers in her hand went flying everywhere. I rushed over to help her pick up the papers.

"I am so sorry, Alpha. I didn't mean to wake you. I was told to bring you breakfast but there was no room on your desk to put it. I thought if I just moved a few piles around and re-stacked other piles, then you'd have room to eat. Please don't send me to the dungeon for punishment."

I stopped picking up the papers and stared at this young girl, of no more than fifteen, in horror. "What is your name?"

She audibly gulped and started to shake uncontrollably. This worried me terribly. What did that monster do to his pack members? This poor child was terrified of me and it broke my heart. I asked her name again in a gentler tone, she looked up at me with giant doe eyes and stammered out her name in a barely audible whisper. Her name was Claudia. I then asked her age and she let me know I wasn't far off my original guess. She was fourteen.

"Listen to me Claudia, I could never hurt a child like yourself or even any innocent adult for that matter. I don't know what my father did to pack members, but I can promise you I would never send you to the dungeon for punishment. I'm not like him!"

I saw the tension leave her jaw and shoulders, Claudia visibly relaxed and we finished picking up the papers, which we placed on a pile on the corner of the desk. I thanked her for bringing me breakfast and for helping me rearrange my desk. I had to admit it did look better. Claudia bid me goodbye and headed out of my office as Olivia was walking in.

"Good Morning, Daniel, how did you sleep? Where's Amber?"

Olivia was looking around the office for her and looked crestfallen when she didn't see her.

"I'm not sure to be honest, I fell asleep on the couch, I'm guessing she must have covered me and went back to bed. I'll go check on her soon. I need to discuss something with you first."

Olivia gave me an odd look when I said I had slept on the couch, but agreed to sit down and listen to what I had to say. We sat facing each other. I told her what had just happened with Claudia and what she had said to me. Olivia blanched at the part about the dungeon. The look of horror in her eyes mirrored my own.

"That despicable son of a bitch, if he wasn't dead already I would kill him."

"So, safe to say you didn't know this was going on?"

"Obviously NOT!!!! He was horrible to the omegas and I always tried to ease their discomfort, but I sure as hell didn't know he was doing that to them. I would have put an end to it myself a long time ago, Daniel."

I believed her from the look of sheer rage on her face, she had gone from white to beet red. I asked Olivia to compile a list of all the omegas in the pack and I would personally go see each and everyone to apologise. They needed to know I wasn't the monster my father was, I needed them to trust me. Once that was done, I wanted to set up counselling for them all. Clearly, there was trauma.

"Speaking of apologies, Daniel, you need to go wake Amber up and apologise!"

I looked at her dumbfounded. "What do I need to apologise to Amber for? I didn't do anything wrong."

"Oh, yes you did, you slept on the couch in your office. I'm willing to bet that wasn't the first time this week?! How do you think she felt being left alone all night in bed? Amber will never say she's hurting, but I know my best friend and you, not wanting to be with her, would most definitely crush her."

The look she was giving me reminded me of when she kicked my ass that fateful day in the forest. I was such a dumb ass I didn't think of it that way. I'd really screwed up. I had been sleeping in my office all week. I facepalmed myself and got up quickly to go check on her. I got to our room and it was empty, no sign of Amber and the bed was made as if she hadn't slept there last night. I went back to my office and told Olivia she wasn't there. Olivia tried to mind-link her but came up against a block.

"That's really weird. Amber would never block me, something is not right. Let me try again."

Olivia tried to link Amber for over half an hour, with no luck. She linked multiple pack members asking if they had seen her. All of them answered the same. They hadn't seen Amber since last night. I went to check Gabriella's room and found my daughter sleeping peacefully, with no sign of Amber. I was beginning to panic. Where was she? Olivia was pacing my office when I got back and I knew she was feeling the same panic I was. Something bad had happened to Amber, and it was all my fault.

Chapter Six

Justin

I walked into Daniel's office ten minutes after Olivia had come banging on my door, ruining any fun I was having with Melissa. The scene that I was faced with worried me slightly. Daniel was pacing a hole in the carpet on one side of the desk and Olivia was creating a lovely crop circle on the other side. They were both so engrossed in their own thoughts they didn't even notice I was in the room with them. When I cleared my throat, they both jumped a good foot in the air, Olivia letting out a little scared squeal.

"I'm sorry, Olivia. I didn't mean to scare you. I didn't realise how serious this situation was, seeing you both now is making me worried."

"I didn't think it was that serious either, Justin, except I can't reach her by mind-link and Amber has never blocked me, in all our years of friendship. I just have a bad feeling something happened to her."

I scrubbed my hands down my face, this was going to be a long day if we couldn't find Amber. I needed to get a team together and work out a tracking map. As I was making the plans in my head, I noticed out of the corner of my eye that Daniel had gone stone stiff and started to shake. I walked over to him and put my hand on his shoulder, he turned with wide eyes and just shook his head back and forth uncontrollably.

"No, No, No." Daniel kept repeating loudly. I gripped both of his shoulders and tried to shake him out of whatever trance he was in. Olivia even ran over screaming his name. Try as we might, nothing seemed to work. Olivia motioned me to step back. Once I was cleared from in front of Daniel she stepped forward and slapped him. I'm not talking about a small little tap either. I'm pretty sure this slap resonated across the pack house - I had to remember to ask Melissa later if she heard it. Suffice to say I'm glad Daniel's head was well attached to his body or else it would have flown long and far. This tactic seemed to have worked though, as Daniel blinked rapidly, and held his cheek immediately.

"OUCH! What the fuck, Olivia? That really hurt. Why did you need to slap me so hard?"

"You were stuck in a trance yelling NO, over and over. I needed to snap you out of it quickly. What the hell happened to you?"

"Not what happened to me Liv, I think something just happened to Amber. We haven't completed our bond but I could feel her emotions through it. She was terrified and paralyzed by fear. I then felt a jolt of pain, before you hit me, and now I can't feel anything. We need to find her!"

Daniel had tears brimming in his eyes as he told us what he felt while in the trance. I felt really sorry for him. If anything like that were to happen to Melissa, I would go feral. Olivia was shaken to the core as well by Daniel's words. Amber was her version of Logan to me and I wouldn't survive without my best friend. We couldn't waste any more time, we needed to get moving. I linked a few of the men that I had brought, who were still on site. Once they arrived, I asked Olivia for a map of the pack lands. We went over every square inch of the map, I split it into quadrants and I designated groups to scour all the quadrants simultaneously.

"Listen guys, there is a chance we won't find anything in this search. I want you to be prepared for that possible outcome. Before we all go out there, could it be that Amber was just overwhelmed by everything going on this past week, and needed a break? Could she have gone to another pack to visit family, or a friend's house?"

The look Olivia shot me with after my last statement was one that said I had crossed a line. I wasn't sure what that line was so I tried to backtrack, but she cut me off really fast.

"No, Justin, she wouldn't have just left like that without letting someone know where she was going. Amber has no other pack or family to go to. I am the closest thing to family she has left now."

Daniel looked at Olivia like a wounded puppy but refrained from saying anything. Given the mood Olivia seemed to be in, that was the best decision he could have made. With that being said, we wrapped everything up. I sent my men out and told them to link me with updates. I teamed up with Olivia and Daniel; we were going to search the north side of the pack lands. Once we were in the woods, we fanned out and began searching every cave and crevice that we saw. I just happened to look over my shoulder and I saw Olivia suddenly stop dead in her tracks as if she had been struck by lightning. I ran towards her when I saw how pale she had gotten. I prayed to the Goddess that she hadn't found Amber's body. As I got closer to her, I saw that there was nothing there. I was confused, so I had to ask her what was wrong.

"What is it, Olivia? You look like you've seen a ghost. Did Amber link you?"

"Goddess, no she didn't, but I think I know where she may have gone! When we were really young, she told me about a secret cabin that her father owned. No one, not even Amber, was supposed to know about it, but she had overheard her father speaking about it once with her mother before she died. If Amber needed to think, she might have gone there."

"That's a great lead! Did she tell you exactly where it was located?"

Olivia shook her head and looked crestfallen. "She never knew exactly where it was herself. As a little girl she only pointed in this direction and said somewhere over there. We'll need to go out as far as we can, to the back of our land and see if it's there."

We all agreed and took off towards the northernmost border. About twenty minutes later, the outline of a small building came into view. Daniel took off at a sprint shouting Amber's name. Olivia and I followed not far behind. What we found was not promising. The door to the cabin was open and hanging by one hinge, we knew Amber had been there by her strong scent in the small room. The state of that room, however, was shocking. It looked like there had been an epic battle. The room was tossed and there was blood splattered on quite a few surfaces. Amber's blood and the blood of at least one other wolf could be detected. This scene set Daniel off into a tirade. He was furious that someone would hurt his innocent mate and even more upset that he hadn't been there to protect her. I walked over and grabbed him by the shoulders.

"I know it's upsetting, Daniel, but freaking out like this isn't going to get her back. We need to keep our heads in the game and think quickly. Everything looks fresh, so they must not have left that long ago."

"Justin's right, time is of the essence right now! I know seeing she's hurt is upsetting, it's bothering me too. I know my Cupcake, though, and she most definitely put up a good fight, and didn't go quietly. Judging by the amount of the other guy's blood, she did more damage to him."

Olivia's comment seemed to mollify Daniel and he calmed down enough for me to let him go. We did a quick sweep around the tiny room and I noticed a pad of paper and pen in the middle of the table. I called Olivia and Daniel over to read it. What we read sent waves of confusion and chills through all three of us.

GIVE ME WHAT IS RIGHTFULLY MINE OR YOU WILL NEVER SEE YOUR PRECIOUS LITTLE LUNA AGAIN! MEET ME IN 48 HOURS WITH THE DEED AT YOUR EASTERN BORDER FOR THE EXCHANGE.

GREG

Amber

I regained consciousness and tried to look around. It was pitch black, my vision was still slightly blurry so I couldn't make anything out. I had blood dripping down my face and I was in chains. I fought against them for a moment but to no avail, I was well tied. I attempted to reach out to Lana and she wasn't responding. This was bad. Very,

very bad! It got even worse when I heard that deep, gravelly voice in the darkness that sent a shiver of terror down my spine.

"Well, well, well, look who's awake."

Chapter 7

*A*mber

"Well, well, well, look who's awake."

His deep, gravelly voice sent a shiver down my spine and instantly made me want to vomit. I had never felt a more powerful or evil aura in my life. I refused to make eye contact and turned my back to him. I had nothing to say to this monster. I made myself very clear at the cabin.

"If I were you little Luna, I wouldn't turn your back to me, if you ever wanted to see your friends and family again."

I continued to ignore him. If he thought threatening me was going to do anything, he had another thing coming. I did not negotiate with terrorists and, as far as I knew, this man was one. When I walked into the cabin and saw him sitting at the table dwarfing everything in the tiny cabin, he instantly made me uneasy. The man was large, imposing and had an edge of danger to him. The first words out of his mouth were an order for me to sit. I take orders from no one. I'm not a dog. He wasn't my Alpha or my friend. I had no reason to listen to his orders. He refused to tell me his name when I asked.

"I am the one true Alpha." Was all he said to me. That made me snort and laugh in his face. He didn't like that very much. I saw his jaw tick as he clenched his fists. He told me I would soon see what he meant, and I would regret my insolence.

Mister Grumpy was still threatening me to turn and face him as I continued to ignore him. My luck finally ran out and he grabbed the length of the excess chain and yanked it hard. This made me spin around and fall off the bench I was sitting on. I hit the floor hard. That was going to leave a mark for sure, especially since Lana was nowhere to be felt. I was essentially human, and the sudden burning and ache in my knees reminded me of this.

"I have a task for you, little Luna. If you want to avoid any more injuries, I highly suggest you be a good girl and comply. I need you to make a video for me to send to that mate of yours. He must be missing you terribly by now."

A bitter laugh escaped my lips before I could stop it. "He doesn't even know I'm gone or that the cabin I was in exists, so I highly doubt he knows you have me or cares."

"Tsk, tsk, little Luna, a mate always knows where the other is. My men have confirmed he found my letter. They say he was highly upset and distraught. They could hear his roar a few miles away. You might have even heard it if I didn't have to knock you out."

"Stop calling me little Luna, I am NO LUNA! Do you see a mark on my neck? You have the wrong girl. I will not make your stupid video and I don't believe you for even a second that Daniel found your letter."

"Aha! Daniel, thank you for giving me his name. Always good to know the name of your opponent, before you take back what belongs to you, and get rid of the trash."

Shit, shit, shit, I hadn't meant to give up Daniel's name. I let my emotions get the better of me. When we were at the cabin he told me he needed Daniel's name to write him a friendly letter, but I refused. He had gotten mad and threw everything off the table, breaking glass and causing a holy mess. I took the opportunity to attack while he was distracted, writing the note. I grabbed a chunk of glass and attacked him. I was able to get a few good shots at him hitting his main arteries. He bled quite heavily but he was a fast healer, faster than any wolf I had ever seen before. He got a few dirty hits on me as well. I won't lie, they hurt like hell but I kept going at him. That was until he let out his aura to full capacity. It was suffocating and stopped me in my tracks. He wasn't just strong, he was also evil; the darkness in his soul was clear as day and it scared me shitless. Before I could recover my wits about me, I got knocked over the head and was rendered unconscious. Next thing I knew, I was waking up in whatever this dark room was, chained and wolfless.

"Well then, little Luna, since you won't help me, you are of no use to me right now. I highly suggest you don't cross me again or you won't be around much longer."

For a large man, he moved very quickly. I didn't even have time to hit him with a comeback before I felt a needle puncture my neck. I cursed as I fell back into darkness, silently praying to the Moon Goddess that someone would help get me out of here.

Olivia

We were all rooted to where we stood in the tiny blood-soaked room, our jaws hung low as we read and re-read that letter at least fifty times. What the hell did this Greg character mean by taking back what was rightfully his? The three of us kept looking at each other with the same question in our eyes. I even asked Evie if she had any clue what the letter meant. My wolf was as clueless as we all were. We stood there for what felt like forever until Daniel broke the silence with a mighty roar. I had never heard such an angry, pain-soaked roar before. I walked over to him and gave him a tight hug, he clearly needed it.

"She's gone, Liv, I hadn't even told her how I felt, and now she's injured and kidnapped. I may never see her again. I have no clue who Greg is and I know even less about what he meant by taking back what's his."

"It's going to be OK. I know you're scared but I need you to be strong for Amber. We'll get her back, if that's the last thing I do. We have to figure out what deed he's looking for. Do you think it's our pack's deed?"

Daniel shook his head and shrugged his shoulders, our pack's deed would make sense, but why did this creep think he owned our pack? There were so many questions and very few answers. I was trying to figure it all out when Evie cut into my thoughts.

"Olivia, do you remember the other morning, you and Daniel found papers that looked to be part of a deed document. However, the deed wasn't found; could the people who ransacked the office have been looking for it and left when it wasn't located?"

"Ooooh, Evie, that isn't a terrible theory. I will speak with the guys and we'll have to investigate a little further into this. Thank you for your help."

"You can thank me by jumping on that delicious mate of ours when we get home later."

Evie gave me a wink and stepped back before I could say anything. It was hard to tell if she was kidding or not. She knew how much Amber meant to me. I wasn't resting or doing anything else for that matter until she was home safe. I focussed on the task at hand and got the boys' attention. I told them Evie's theory and they agreed it was worth a deeper look into. We only had forty-eight hours to figure this out before meeting with Greg. Not that we would ever give up the deed to the pack, but we needed to try and figure out why he thought he could have it. I grabbed the note off the table and told the boys to hurry up. We needed to get back to the pack house.

We hauled ass back and within half an hour we were sifting through papers on Daniel's desk. Justin had called his men back to the pack house, and they were helping us sort through the piles as well. Logan came in after a short while. I explained everything that had happened, what we had found and as I finished my story he pulled me tightly against his chest. A sob caught in my throat, and I had to push away before I lost it completely. Logan looked a bit hurt but he understood my reasoning. I needed to keep a clear head to get Amber back. I didn't have time to fall apart.

We worked as a well-oiled machine for about two hours, but still came up completely empty-handed. The only thing of interest that Logan found was a note from Amber, telling Daniel that she needed time to think and would be back in two days. So, I guess she did technically run away without telling me, the realisation made my heart clench. Why wouldn't she tell me? I knew she must have had a damn good reason and I looked forward to hearing all about it once she was home.

"Amber's note must have gotten mixed into the piles, when that young omega, Claudia, tried tidying my desk for me." Daniel sighed as he scrubbed his hands down his face.

"You don't think the omega was working with Greg and hid the note on purpose, so we couldn't find Amber in time, do you?"

We all stopped what we were doing and looked at Justin, that was quite a loaded question honestly, but I had known Claudia since she was a little pup. She was kind and very shy, doing something malicious like that that wasn't in her wheelhouse. Not to mention, she loved Amber and had no affiliations to my father's loyalists, and we assumed they were the ones who had ransacked the office. I told Justin as much and he dropped the idea, it was just an unfortunate accident that the note got mixed into the other documents.

By supper time, we hadn't found anything useful. We were discouraged to say the least. More so, when Justin announced that he and Melissa had to go back to Jade Moon. Daniel tried to bargain with him but to no avail.

"I need to get back to Jade Moon and settle a few things of my own, but I will come back in time to go with you to meet Greg. I will also bring more back up with me, since we may just need it."

Daniel agreed, since he had no choice in the matter. We would spend the next two days trying to figure out this mystery as best we could. I prayed to the Moon Goddess that Amber was OK wherever she was, and that she was staying strong. This was going to be a long forty-eight hours.

Chapter Eight

Chapter 8

Justin

Leaving Onyx Crescent wasn't easy, I knew how desperate Daniel was for the extra set of hands and eyes to figure out this mystery. I didn't have a choice though. No one knew my father was no longer in the land of the living. I had to go back and let the pack know I was now the Alpha of Jade Moon. We didn't have an official Beta. My father believed he was the only wolf important enough to be ranked. Therefore, we had an 'unofficial Beta', who took over if ever my father and I were both away from the pack, like in this instance. After my father's passing, I didn't want to cause any drama back at home. So, I called Richard and let him know I needed him to step into his Beta roll for the week, since my father's trip would be longer than expected. Melissa and I got into my car at around seven and we hit the road home. The drive was pleasant as we drove happily holding hands.

"Are you nervous about becoming Alpha, my love?"

I turned my head and smiled at Melissa, kissing the top of her hand which was intertwined with my much larger one. "No, my love, I am not nervous at all! I've been waiting for this moment for a very long time. With you by my side, we will make this work."

"Oh, Justin, are you sure you want me by your side as Luna? I'm just a nothing omega. I don't want to cause you any trouble, you've had more than enough of that with your father."

"There is no one else on this planet that I would want to lead with! You are far from being nothing, you are my everything Melissa. You are my peace, you always have been through all the insanity my father caused."

I saw the tears shimmering in her eyes, it broke my heart into a million pieces knowing my asshole father caused her to feel this way about herself. I would spend the rest of my life cherishing her and proving why she is the best choice to be by my side. She had been pivotal in the last two weeks in helping Olivia and baby Charlotte. Melissa showed more grace last week at Onyx Crescent than most Lunas who were born into the role could ever. I told her as much and watched a small shy smile spread across her face. We drove the rest of the way back in comfortable silence.

Once back at the pack we went up to my father's office, and I linked Richard to meet us there. He seemed extremely relieved to see me back. I requested a report of what went on while we were gone. He seemed hesitant at first to say anything in Melissa's presence. I let a low growl out in his direction and told him that he had better get comfortable with his future Luna, or it would be a rough ride. We watched him squirm for a bit, but he was a smart man and continued our conversation without missing a beat. Nothing went out of place while we were away, so I was happy not to have to deal with anyone for the time being.

I was about to tell Richard about my father's demise when a sudden idea hit me. My father had everyone on edge, the fact he was gone would greatly improve the well being of all our pack members. However, I didn't want to have to explain what actually happened to him, it could end up going to the werewolf council and I didn't want any trouble for Logan. Instead, I was going to use this Greg situation to my advantage. My father would die 'a hero in battle'. I would use the term 'hero' very loosely. It would be the perfect way to explain his demise, keep whatever shitty legacy he had and usher me in as the new Alpha. I knew my loyal men would never say otherwise to my version of the story. I told Richard that I would need to head back to Onyx Crescent in two days' time to meet up with my father. I informed Richard that my father had sent me back to check up on him. This sounded exactly like my father so I knew there wouldn't be an issue. Melissa subtly shot me a confused side look but kept her face blank. Richard sighed with what could only be described as the weight of a hundred men on his shoulders. I knew what he was thinking, so I told him he was doing a great job and I appreciated all his help.

By that point, I'd had enough, so I dismissed Richard, telling him to enjoy the next two days all to himself and we would touch base before I left again. He bid Melissa and I good night, leaving the office quickly before I could change my mind. Once the door was closed, Melissa turned to me with an arched eyebrow.

"Where did that story come from? I thought you were going to tell Richard what happened and tomorrow tell the pack you're the new Alpha?"

"I had a better idea, my love. If we tell everyone what went down, there will be an investigation and I don't want there to be potential trouble for Logan."

Melissa gave me a thoughtful look and nodded for me to continue. She reached out and squeezed my hand, which I knew was her way of saying thank you for watching out for her brother.

"So, after we face off with Greg we will report my father's death to the council as a tragedy of the conflict. I'm hoping there will be no fighting, but I have a bad feeling this guy is trouble and there will be. In the case of a battle, it would benefit us greatly. My father would have an official cause of death that would keep his legacy intact and we could be sworn in as Alpha and Luna hassle free."

Melissa smiled at me with a look of awe and wonder on her face.

"How did I get so lucky to have such a smart man as my mate?" Her last words were purred in my ear as she leaned in for a hug, her warm body pressed against me making my cock jump.

My mind went back to earlier in the day when I got screwed out of my spectacular finish. I grabbed Melissa tightly against me and walked her backwards towards the door. I crashed her back into it and locked it as our lips crashed into each other. The kiss stole my breath away with how hot and needy it was. Both of us needed the other more than air at that moment. Melissa moaned into my mouth and my cock turned into a hard rod of steel, painfully trapped in my pants.

I could swear Melissa was a mind-reader. The next moment, she dropped to her knees and undid my pants in one quick motion, my pants pooled at my feet and my cock sprang into her face. Melissa looked up at me through her lashes and licked her lips, like someone who was starving would look at a giant steak. Before I could say anything, she had her hot little fist wrapped around the base of my shaft and was lightly pumping at a delicious pace. I let a feral moan leave my lips, which spurred her on more as my cock disappeared down her throat. The feelings this woman was giving me were intense, my head began to swim as I felt her tongue swirl from base to tip over and over.

I could feel my climax building. I knew she could tell as well because her suction got stronger and so did her grip on the base of my cock. The pleasure was so intense I partly wished I was the one with my back against the door for support. As I reached the peak of my pleasure, Melissa reached down and squeezed my balls, giving them a nice little twist tipping me over the edge. I came fast and hard. I heard Melissa sputter a little bit, but she managed to take it all down. Only one small drop of cum dribbled out the side of her mouth, which she licked up with a smile on her face. I had to brace myself on the wall for a moment to catch my breath. I shakily helped Melissa up off her knees.

"You really enjoyed doing that, didn't you? My sexy little minx."

"You know I would do anything for you, my love. I hope that made up for this morning?"

"Absolutely it does. I couldn't ask for anything better to end my day with."

Melissa winked at me and unlocked the door, giving me a moment to pull up my pants. I shut off the office lights and we headed up to our room. I was really going to enjoy having my own office, that was one hell of a way to christen it. I knew I had a lot of work to do in the coming days, but I was going to have fun doing it.

Chapter Nine

Chapter 9

Justin

I woke up holding Melissa in my arms, as she snored peacefully. A smile split my lips as I bent down to kiss the top of Melissa's head. I looked down at her long smooth neck that was currently bare without a mark. A pang of sadness went through me, my mark should have been on her a long time ago.

"Don't beat yourself up, Justin. Your father made it impossible to safely mark our mate. You know there is nothing more I've wanted since we discovered Melissa was our mate. We won't have to wait much longer."

"I know you're right, Mason, it just breaks my heart that I haven't been able to claim Melissa as she deserved."

I loved that my wolf was the calm voice of reason between the two of us. I was just excited about starting my life with the woman I loved. Melissa was strong, caring, funny and brilliant. It didn't hurt that she was also the most stunning woman I had ever laid eyes on. That wasn't the mate bond talking either. I've had a huge crush on her since we were young pups. When it turned out we were mates, I was over the moon; Melissa was equally as excited mixed with a bit of fear. It broke my heart but I understood why she was fearful. My father was one of the worst Alphas around, hating anyone he deemed beneath him.

Besides my father, Logan was the one we had been most nervous about telling we were mates. Since their parents had died, he was always over protective of his baby sister, and knowing how my father was he would worry himself to death. Luckily, when we told him he was overjoyed that we were mates, he could see how head over heels I was for Melissa, he knew I would never let anything happen to her.

I wanted to go through stuff in my father's office, so I gently extracted myself from the bed and Melissa's warmth. A slight frown passed across her face as she lost my presence. I quickly tucked her in and I watched as she snuggled down into the bed. I got dressed and made my way down to my father's office. I wasn't looking for anything in particular. I wanted to understand his day to day and how he kept the pack running.

I spent a solid hour opening drawers, rummaging through files and ledgers. Nothing very interesting came out of it. In fact, everything was a little too squeaky clean, which left me with an uneasy feeling. I scrubbed my hands down my face and pounded my fist on the desk in frustration. The force of my fist hitting the desk caused a panel to open on the underside of the desk.

Behind the panel there were 4 buttons. I found that quite intriguing and pressed the first one, which opened the far wall of the office. What the hell was my father doing with a secret room in the wall? I got up quickly and locked the office door, I did not want to be interrupted. I walked up to the opening carefully and looked inside; what I found left me completely speechless.

Amber

I started to come out of the fog again. I didn't know how long I had been out for, or where I was, for that matter. I could tell I had been moved because it was brighter, and where I was lying was much softer than before. I still couldn't reach Lana, which worried me terribly. Where was my wolf? Would she ever come back to me? I was taken out of my thoughts by pain burning through my wrists as the shackles were yanked firmly.

"Time to wake up, little Luna, you've been out for far too long and I need you to work now."

That voice really made my skin crawl. I opened my eyes slowly and glared up at Greg who was hovering over me. I looked side to side and saw I was in an empty room chained to a bed. In front of the bed there was a camera on a tripod, which confused me even more.

"I see by the look on your face that you are wondering what's going on. Well, you see little Luna, I need to send a message to this Daniel of yours. He needs to know that I'm not fucking around and he had better give me what I want. Since you aren't willing to cooperate, you leave me no choice but to take what I need from you."

My blood ran cold at his words, as the door across the room opened and another large man entered with an evil glint in his eyes.

"You see, little Luna, my buddy Leo here is going to help get what I want out of you, all you need to do is lie there like a good girl and it will all be over shortly."

I began to fight against the shackles and curse them both out. All that earned me was more pain, and laughs from the two dangerous men. Leo, as he was called, came and stood next to the bed as Greg went over to the camera and pointed it at the bed. I looked up at Leo and told him he could go to hell, and if he touched me I would make sure he died slowly and violently. He told me I was very funny as he elongated his claws.

Greg yelled action, and before I knew what was happening, Leo had shredded my shirt off my body, slicing my chest in the process. Blood was dripping down my body. Without Lana, I would heal slowly like a human and most likely scar. I struggled against the shackles again in a final attempt to free myself. I yelled at Leo to leave me alone, but all that earned me was a slap across the face with claws out, as he climbed on top of me and licked me from my cheek to my belly button. My stomach rolled and I felt like I was going to be sick. Leo had gotten down to my pants and had started to remove them from my body as I thrashed under him. He backhanded me, which made my head spin. I begged him not to do that. I promised him and Greg I would behave, and get Daniel to give him anything he wanted. That didn't work, as Leo gave me a disgusting grin and ripped my bottoms to pieces. Leaving me naked and shivering on the bed as I bled. I heard Greg snarl. "If you ever want to see her in one piece again, you better get me what I asked for."

Next thing I knew, Greg was calling for Leo to get off of me. He let out a frustrated growl but listened. He leaned down and told me he didn't like an audience anyway, but not to worry, he'd be back to rock my world soon. This was too much for me and I threw up all over myself. Both men laughed and left the room together. Leaving me naked, bleeding and now covered in my own vomit. I burst into angry tears. How could this happen to me? I begged the Moon Goddess for this to be over and for me to get out alive.

Olivia

I woke up early and decided to go into Daniel's office, to see if I could find any clues to who Greg was, or try to find the deed itself, so we could make sure it was secure. As I approached Daniel's office, I saw Claudia coming out of the office and closing the door. She hadn't seen or heard me so I tucked myself along the wall. Claudia looked quickly around the hallway with a terrified look on her face and started walking quickly away. Unfortunately for her, she wasn't paying close attention and slammed right into me as I stepped into her path.

"Care to tell me what you were doing in Alpha Daniel's office, Claudia?"

"I...I...I...I...I"

She stammered with a look of sheer terror on her face and then fainted. I was able to catch her before she hit the floor. I linked Daniel to come to his office immediately. I told him I may have found our culprit, and I wasn't happy about this new development. What could this little scared omega have to do with some psycho that kidnapped my best friend? It was confusing, to say the least, but I planned on getting to the bottom of it.

Chapter Ten

Chapter 10

Daniel

My mind was a mess. I felt like I was drowning and didn't know which way was up or down anymore. Life without Amber was bleak and I felt lost, like a pup chasing its tail. I had gone through a roller coaster of emotions in a very short period of time. If I didn't have a heart attack I'd be surprised. I waited for a witty come back and was met with nothing but silence, as I sadly realized there would be none since Xander was still blocked. That too was weighing heavily on me, not having my wolf to talk things through with left me feeling empty inside. I was doing the right thing, wasn't I? Xander needed to be taught a lesson for pushing me to mark Amber. Although, maybe if I had marked Amber sooner or at least told her how I felt, all of this horrible scenario could have been avoided. Amber wouldn't have run away and she would be in my arms right now. I tried to fall asleep as I clutched her pillow to my chest, breathing what little scent of hers it had left, deep in the fabric. After tossing and turning for what seemed like hours, I finally fell into a nightmare riddled sleep.

All I saw around me was blood, it was dripping from everywhere. I could hear Amber screaming for help, begging me to find her. The sequence would then change to Annabelle asking why I couldn't save either of the women I claimed to love. This left me devastated as the scenes and sounds just kept replaying over and over. Finally, I opened my eyes to a familiar place. I was in the garden of our Moon Goddess, Selene. I looked around slightly disoriented until I caught sight of her in the distance. I watched as she glided towards me with a look on her face I couldn't quite decipher. It left me with an uneasy feeling in the pit of my stomach. The closer she got, the clearer I could make out the look in her eyes and I was slapped hard by the disappointment I saw there.

"I...I...I can explain, I didn't know she would be kidnapped and put in danger. Please tell me she's OK?"

"Hush now, Daniel, I summoned you here not just to talk about Amber. You have a bigger issue at hand and it needs to be addressed immediately."

Her usual light, friendly demeanour was replaced by a heavy sorrow with an undercurrent of anger. As I tried to guess what she could be alluding to - I was racking my brain - I noticed a figure crouched behind her legs.

"Xander, you're here buddy?"

"Now, I'm your buddy?" He scoffed and lifted his nose towards the sky in indignation.

"Of course you're my buddy! You'll always be. I just needed to teach you a lesson. You had to understand where I was coming from."

"A lesson? You call shutting your best friend out of your life for over a week, teaching them a lesson?"

Xander began to growl at me as anger and hurt flashed in his eyes. Before I could say another word, Selene cut us off.

"That's enough fighting from the both of you! You're two halves of the same whole. I hand picked you both for each other and I expected you both to act better than what I've seen. Xander, you pushed Daniel too far with your need to mark Amber, and Daniel, you took the blocking too far. One or two days would have sufficed."

I looked down at my feet sheepishly. I knew she was right. I kept him blocked out of spite, pride and sheer stubbornness. In the end, it hurt both of us. I knew without my wolf I was weak, I really needed him to help me figure out how we were going to save Amber. I looked over to Xander, who was lying down at Selene's feet with his ears flat against his head and tail tucked between his back legs, looking as remorseful as I felt. I knew Xander would never be the first to say anything, so I swallowed my pride and decided to put an end to all of the nonsense.

"Xander, I am sorry I left you blocked for so long. I was struggling with everything I was dealing with and having to learn as a new Alpha. I took the blocking too far out of spite and that wasn't right. Because of that, I may have cost us our mate."

My voice trembled and cracked as I said my last bit, Xander looked at me with sadness and let out a small whimper.

"I'm sorry, too, I should never have pushed you to mark mate when you weren't ready. I just had a bad feeling in my bones that we needed to be connected to her. It seems I was right..."

Xander trailed off, as Selene looked down at him with a pointed look and cleared her throat.

"You know I'm sorry, that's all I'm trying to say! Can you please unblock me when you wake up and we can figure out how to get mate back safely?"

I smiled at Xander and walked over to him. I knelt down and wrapped my arms around him. I gave my wolf a big hug, pouring all my love, sadness, fears and regrets into the hug. Xander tried to wiggle free at first but then realized he wasn't getting free, so he just let me hug him. He pulled back and licked my face, which made me laugh out loud, breaking the tension in the air. I hadn't felt this light hearted all week. At least one thing had been fixed in my life, now onto the fifteen million other issues that needed to be solved.

"Thank you, Daniel and Xander, for working out your differences, it truly broke my heart to see you both miserably sad and alone. You will need to work together to bring Amber home safely. I am sorry, my child Greg is causing so much harm. He will be swiftly dealt with once he's returned to me."

I blinked up at Selene, understanding clearly what she was saying. I didn't like having to kill other wolves. However, Greg took my mate, my Luna, and clearly injured her from the blood bath we walked into. He needed to pay, and pay dearly he would. I asked Selene if Amber was still alive. She told me yes she was but she was in great danger, and we needed to get to her as soon as possible. I asked her where we could find Greg and she told us that, unfortunately, she wasn't allowed to meddle anymore than she already had. I was crestfallen that she couldn't help me anymore but grateful that she had given me a chance to right my wrong. I said as much to her and next thing I knew I was in my bed again blinking up at the ceiling. I scarcely had time to register that I was awake before I got a link from Olivia. She was urging me to hurry to my office, she had caught the culprit and I needed to come right now.

I jumped out of bed without thinking and took off towards my office. I took down the block with Xander as I ran. He didn't have time to say anything to me as I made it to my office. I skidded to a stop as

I saw Olivia standing near the couch holding an unconscious Claudia in her arms. I watched as she placed her down on it.

"What is the meaning of this? What happened to Claudia? Where is the culprit you were speaking of?"

Chapter Eleven

Greg

I had watched that little Luna run around the pack without a care in the world. I knew she was going to be my target. How else do you bring an Alpha to his knees? She was his everything. Or at least that's how it was supposed to be. Finding out she had disappeared overnight was infuriating. It took me half a day to track her down. When I did finally track her down, she put up one hell of a fight. That little Luna gave me a run for my money and inflicted quite a bit of damage on me. I was highly impressed by her skill level. In a sick way, it turned me on. I was beginning to think after all this was over I would make her my Luna, that clueless new Alpha wannabe didn't deserve her. From what she said, it didn't seem like he cared for her anyway.

I hadn't had a Luna since my fated mate decided to cross me all those years ago. She made her choice and I saw out her punishment. Did it hurt when she took her last breath? Of course it did, but I was built stronger than that and came out just fine on the other side. Some called me soulless and a monster. They weren't wrong. I've had many bed warmers over the years but none have piqued my interest quite like this small, feisty she-wolf. She was spunky and full of fire. I knew we'd be a great match once she came to terms with the demise of her first mate.

When I saw she wasn't going to cooperate with me, I decided to bring in the big guns to scare her a little. My right-hand man, Leo, wasn't quite as scary as me, but he was high on the list. The way she fought him and defied him made me instantly hard. They were so engrossed in their banter that they never noticed, not that I cared to hide it. If I wanted something, I took it. No one dared to defy me. Something in me snapped though, when I saw Leo rip my little Luna's clothes off her body. He was meant to scare her and rough her up a little, that was it.

That was crossing the line. He was touching what was mine and I would be having none of that. I called him to get off of her. He hesitated, which enraged me. No one defied my orders. My wolf, Samson, was foaming at the mouth and trying to push forward to teach Leo a lesson. I managed to stay in control and get us out of the room. I noticed that Leo had whispered something to my little Luna before he turned to retreat, and it made her stiffen with fear. I was going to have to find out what he said to her.

"That's one sexy, spunky little minx you've got in there, old buddy. Once you're done with her, I will have to take her off your hands for some fun."

"You will be doing no such thing, Leo. That little minx is the key to my new pack and I will be needing her for quite a while longer."

It took everything in my power not to let Samson's voice blend with mine. I didn't want Leo to know my hand just yet, now that he showed me his. If he heard my wolf getting involved, he would want a piece of her just to spite me. He may be my right-hand man, but I didn't trust him as far as I could throw him. I took the chance to ask him what he had said to her. I saw him stiffen slightly as he started to chuckle, and shot me a pure bullshit answer. He said he had told her he had fun playing around with her. I didn't believe for a second and neither did Samson.

"We must protect our little Luna, get her out of there. Don't let Leo know where she is."

"I'm way ahead of you Samson, that fucker won't be getting his paws on what is mine. I found her, I will keep her."

I chuckled with Leo so as to not arouse suspicion. I told him I had work to complete. I needed to get that video we had just created over to the Onyx Crescent, to make sure that Alpha Daniel knew we meant business. Leo said he had some things to attend to and was on his merry way. The moment he rounded the corner, I linked my head omega, I told her to come tend to my guest. She would need fresh clothes and to be transported to the secret room inside my bedroom closet. Only she knew of its existence and I trusted her explicitly. Knowing my little Luna would be tucked away safely from Leo made me a happy man. I congratulated myself on catching Leo before who knows what could have happened. I walked into my office and set to work preparing the tape for Alpha Daniel. Taking him down, getting my new pack and stealing his mate was going to be my greatest coup to date. I couldn't wait.

It took me two hours to prepare the video and have one of my men take it to Onyx Crescent. I had checked in with Marie, my head omega, and she assured me my little Luna had been taken care of and was settled in the secret room. I had made sure to have that room built as a panic room of sorts for my fated mate. In the end, it was me she needed to be afraid of. Who would have thought? I laughed to myself, remembering the look on her face as I squeezed the life out of her. The melodic crack of her neck still rang through my mind and gave me chills of contentment. No one crossed Greg Pagano and got away with it, my little Luna would learn that quickly. I closed up my office and headed for my room. I wanted to have a chat with my little minx, I locked my bedroom door and set the alarm. I didn't want any intrusions, I headed for the closet and moved the faux wall, scanning my retina and giving my fingerprints as directed. The wall gave a little beep and slid open. Inside, I could see her sitting on the edge of the bed. Marie had only tied shackles to her ankles, she was getting soft in her old age. The moment my little Luna spotted me her face darkened, she crossed her arms over her chest and looked towards the wall.

"Oh, come now, little Luna, is that any way to greet your saviour?"

"My SAVIOUR? Are you on drugs? You kidnapped me, beat me, had one of your henchmen beat me and strip me, and now you're calling yourself my saviour? I think NOT, and STOP CALLING ME LITTLE LUNA!"

It took everything in me not to burst out laughing, she really was a feisty little thing. Sitting there glaring at me and yelling at me as if that would phase me at all. Her low growling was making my cock twitch in my jeans like crazy, I had to readjust myself as I got closer to her. I sat next to her on the bed. I wanted to touch her so badly but knew I couldn't show my hand so fast. She needed to get used to my presence and see that I was worth being with.

"Alright little Luna, if you don't like me calling you that, how about you tell me your real name?"

"NEVER, you don't need to know my name. I won't be here much longer."

"Suite yourself. I will just have to keep calling you little Luna, and don't get your hopes up my dear, you will be here for quite a while longer."

I got up and started moving towards the door. She could sit there and pout for all I cared. As I was about to leave the room, I heard a faint whisper. If I wasn't an alpha werewolf I wouldn't have heard it.

"Amber."

"Ah well, nice to meet you Amber. I still like little Luna better, but at least I can switch it up. As you know, my name is Greg and it's a pleasure to be your saviour. Thanks again for that wicked performance this afternoon, it's really going to help me get what I want."

I saw the tears of anger well up in her eyes as she turned her back completely to me. I chuckled and left the room, closing the secret door and putting everything back to the way it was. I was so excited to have Amber close to me. Now I could see her anytime I wanted. The next few days were going to be very interesting.

CHAPTER TWELVE

Chapter 12

Justin

I walked quickly over to the office door to lock it. I couldn't afford to have random people walk in while I was investigating the secret room. Once I heard the lock click, I let out the breath I hadn't realized I was holding. I carefully crept towards the open wall, scared of what I would find inside. My mind was spinning at the possibilities.

"We're Alpha's, there is no need to be scared. We will face whatever is in that room head on!"

"I love your optimism, Mason, but you do remember our father was a psychopath, right? There could be Goddess knows what behind that door. So you better believe I am scared shitless."

I loved that my wolf was fearless, but this was an unknown situation that our father was involved in. I couldn't share his bravery no matter how hard I tried. Once I reached the opened wall, I gave it a slight push and slowly moved inside. What I saw made my jaw drop. Floor to ceiling monitors, I had found my father's secret control room. He hadn't been kidding when he said he had the entire packhouse bugged with hidden cameras. I looked at each screen, my blood turning to ice the more I saw. The main hall had a camera, the kitchen, the dining hall, to name a few. Even on my side of the Alpha wing. Finally, I came to the last screen in the bottom row. That was the one that really pissed me off. There on the screen I saw Melissa, in my bed, still snoring away. That sick twisted bastard had a camera in my room. So he knew about Melissa and I, meaning he was just waiting to use that information to hurt me. I clenched and unclenched my fists in anger as my nostrils flared.

*"Calm down, Justin, there's nothing we can do about it now. The man is **dead**."*

"Good riddance! I only wish I could bring him back to life, so I could get the satisfaction of killing him myself with my own two hands."

I sat down in what appeared to be the controller's chair, hoping to calm myself down slightly. I had such an intense rage burning inside of me towards that monster, that I just wanted to smash all the screens that were hidden in this tiny room. I knew I couldn't though, I needed to keep the room intact and comb through all I could. My father was up to no good with this room and I had to find out what it was. I stopped and wondered if my mother had known about this room before she passed? Did she condone the spying? Questions I would never get answered but couldn't help but think about. How different would life have been had she been alive. Would my father have been such a monster? I always wanted to believe it was her death that drove him to be the way he was, but we'd never know.

It didn't take long before I was fully immersed in the videos. My father had a file on the control screen that held hours upon hours of every single camera in the packhouse. I noted that some dated back years. These were mainly from the camera in my room and the Alpha wing. This meant that all the time I thought I was smoothly hiding things from him, he knew what was really going on. This made my head spin just thinking about it. I felt like I barely scratched the surface when I suddenly heard Melissa's beautiful voice in my head.

"Are you OK, *my love? It's been several hours and I've been worried about you. Jenny reached out to Mason when I went to the office and found the door locked. All Mason told Jenny was that you found something horrific your father left behind and you were trying to process it."*

"Please come back to the office, Melissa, I will unlock the door for you and show you. I am so sorry if I worried you. I swear I've only been here for half an hour."

As I said the last part, I rubbed my eyes and focused them on my watch, which said 2:30 pm. That couldn't be it? Could it? That had to be a joke. I could have sworn it was still early morning. I thanked Mason for reaching out to Melissa's wolf, Jenny, when they came looking for us. I would have hated to think she was looking for us in a panic.

I got up swiftly and went to the office door. As soon as the lock clicked, Melissa pushed open the door and threw herself into my arms. She gave me a long, tight, bear hug and made me promise to let her know next time something came up like that. I apologized again and promised her I would try my best not to worry her. I made sure to lock the office door once more. That earned me a questioning look from Melissa. I took her hand and told her to follow me. It was at that moment she noticed the wall was open, the expression on her face changed instantly to bewilderment.

"Just wait, sweetheart, you haven't seen anything yet!"

I pulled Melissa into the room behind me and her eyes widened to the size of dinner plates, her jaw hit the floor and she had to blink multiple times, as she took in the sight of all the monitors in front of her. I nearly laughed at her reaction, since I felt mine had been the exact same, but I refrained out of respect.

"Justin, what the hell is this? Your father wasn't lying about the packhouse being monitored?"

I watched as her facial expressions changed from screen to screen, when finally she got to our bedroom, her face drained of all colour and she started to shake slightly. I was afraid she might pass out but she regained her composure quickly and looked at me questioningly. I nodded my answer to her silent inquiry. He knew! The whole damn time, he knew and he was playing some sick twisted game. Melissa looked lost in thought at that moment, as if trying to digest everything she had just learned.

"Listen, he's gone, my love! We may never know what he was planning with the information he knew and kept to himself. I'm OK with that! You get to be my Luna and we can now be a couple proudly without fear. He can't hurt us anymore."

Melissa nodded and gave me a small smile, then reached out to squeeze my hand. I knew she was going to need some time to come to terms with what we now knew. My father had access to all our intimate and private moments, he knew we were together. I couldn't bring myself to tell her I'd come across many of our sexy videos while searching the logs. I knew that would embarrass her to no end. We walked over to the control chair and Melissa clicked on the file from the day of the challenge. We saw Logan and I leaving with our men for the challenge, clearly hearing our plan. Watching this video made me grit my teeth. I couldn't believe he had been spying on us all this time. Another video clip a bit later caught my eye. It was of my father rushing out of the packhouse with his gaggle of men. I clicked on the video. We hear him shouting to his men to hurry up and not to screw this up for him. His life depended on a clean execution of this plan. Melissa and I looked at each other quizzically, we then heard my father's cell phone go off and he answered it in a meek tone.

"Yes, we're on our way now! Just make sure you're standing by to swoop in and claim your new pack and land. Yes, it's going to work. I promised you it would work. Yes, I know what you'll do to me and my pack if it falls through. OK, goodbye."

I had never seen my father so flustered and nervous before. He took a giant gulp of air after hanging up the phone and wiped sweat from his brow before continuing to bark orders at his men. Melissa was the first to speak; asking who the hell my father spoke to, before I could answer that I had no clue, one of his men in the video gave us the shocking answer.

"Alpha, why are you letting Greg do this to you? We can take him."

"GREG!!!!" Melissa and I both shouted in unison. We never heard my father's answer as they walked out the front door of the packhouse. At that point, I didn't care, we had solid proof that my father was involved and potentially invited this psycho onto our lands. I needed to get this information over to Daniel and Olivia as quickly as possible. We needed to figure out who Greg was and time was running out. We were due to leave to go back to the Onyx Crescent by the end of the day. The meeting with Greg was the next morning. Time was short and we needed to move quickly. Just then, Melissa snapped her fingers, grabbed my hand and pulled me towards the door.

"We own the largest and most extensive record library in the States. We will find out who Greg is."

Goddess I loved this smart, sexy woman! We locked up my office and took off running to the records room. Time to hunt down Greg!

Chapter Thirteen

Chapter 13

Olivia

After I laid Claudia down on the couch gently, I backed away and turned to Daniel to answer his question, as he shot me a dirty, confused look.

"The culprit, my dear brother, is right there passed out on the couch. I saw her sneaking out of the office, she then ran into me head on. When I asked her what she was doing, she panicked and passed out."

The confused look Daniel gave me would have been comical if it weren't for the seriousness of this situation. I scrubbed my hands down my face in frustration, I wanted my best friend back safe and sound. I couldn't understand what this tiny teenage omega could have to do with her being taken.

"Liv, how could this tiny young thing have anything to do with Amber's kidnapping? No one knows Greg, it doesn't make any sense to me."

"I know Daniel, I've known Claudia since she was a newborn pup! I don't understand it either, but I'm hoping she will be able to explain it all away somehow."

As if on cue, Claudia began to stir, both Daniel and I turned towards her, ready, to get to the bottom of all the troubling questions. Once her eyes were open and she saw us, she sat bolt upright with a shriek and began stammering.

"I...I...I...I didn't do it...he made me do it...he said he'd kill her if I didn't do it...but I couldn't do it...I swear I couldn't...I... I...I...please don't hurt me."

"It's OK Claudia, take a deep breath, please. Alpha Daniel and I aren't going to hurt you, we just want to understand what's going on and how you connect with the kidnapping of Luna Amber."

I saw Daniel wince out of the corner of my eye when I said Luna Amber. He knew he fucked this up majorly and would have a lot of groveling to do. For the moment, my main concern was Claudia and who was threatening to kill who. I walked over, sat down next to her gently and put my hand on her shoulder to help calm her down. Claudia stiffened beneath my touch for a moment but then relaxed. She had always been an open, easy-going, happy child. To see her as scared as she was now sitting beside me was really upsetting.

"Let's start from the top, Claudia. What were you doing in the Alpha's office? We can't help you if we don't know what's going on."

"You won't get mad at me and imprison me? Or kick me out of the pack?"

The tears I saw shimmering in her eyes broke me. I looked up at Daniel and he looked as horrified and saddened by her questions as I did. I motioned for him to answer her, since he was the Alpha. Daniel knelt down in front of Claudia and gently took her hand while clearing his throat awkwardly.

"Claudia, I made you a promise the other morning, didn't I? I promised you I was nothing like my father. I would never hurt you or banish you for telling the truth. It's very important we get answers from you now. The pack is in grave danger and so is our Luna. You are the only one who can help us."

Claudia slowly nodded as she squeezed Daniel's hand for strength. She took a deep breath before launching full force into the story. Just when I thought I had heard every possible evil thing there was, Claudia managed to shock me. She told Daniel and I how she ended up in the office earlier in the week. She was in there to find and get the deed to the pack. Not only that, but she was supposed to poison Daniel's breakfast so he would fall gravely ill and be easy to overthrow. I watched as the colour drained from Daniel's face at that admission. Claudia had as well and started to cry and shake, she swore up and down she could never do such horrible things to her Alpha. I calmly asked her why she was there in the first place, if she would never do those things. She told us that her mother's brother, Henri, was one of my father's supporters. He had kidnapped her mother, Rita, after he and some other men had failed to find the deed while ransacking the office. He forced Claudia to search for the deed. He had told her they had been close to finding it but were interrupted by us going into the office. Henri told Claudia if she didn't retrieve the deed and poison Daniel he would kill her mother.

Now that I was thinking about it I hadn't seen Claudia's mother, Rita, since the day my father died. I asked Claudia if she knew where her uncle was and she shook her head. She said he was sneaking into her room to demand updates, then he would disappear until the next time. I gave her a grim look and urged her to continue with her story.

"The other morning I had found the deed that Henri asked me to get, I found it right before Alpha Daniel woke up and scared me. I dropped the rest of the papers I was holding and then pretended I was making room for his breakfast tray. I'm very sorry, Alpha Daniel, I lied to you."

"It's OK, Claudia, I understand why you had to do it. I'm not pleased, but I get it. I never felt sick though, so I need to ask what kind of poison you gave me? Also, if you found the deed, why did you come back to my office?"

Claudia looked sheepishly between Daniel and I.

"I couldn't go through with poisoning you, Alpha, you were so kind. I removed the poison capsule when you had your back turned to fix a pile of papers. I also couldn't give the paper to my uncle, no matter how much I wanted to save my mom. I didn't feel right betraying the pack that way, so I snuck back in earlier to put the deed back. It's the last sheet in that second pile to the left. I figured you'd find it yourselves eventually."

I got up quickly and searched the bottom of the second pile to the left, as Claudia had said, low and behold there it was. The deed to Onyx Crescent. I was happy Claudia was telling the truth. I couldn't believe her uncle was such a lousy piece of shit, using her like that. I returned to the couch and gave her a big hug.

"Thank you for being loyal and putting it back. We also thank you for your honesty. I do have one more question though. Why did you hide Luna Amber's letter?"

Claudia hugged me back tightly but pulled back with a confused look on her face.

"I never saw any letter from Luna Amber, I only saw a lot of official documents, nothing else. Maybe it was in one of the piles that got knocked down by accident?"

"I believe you Claudia, I remember you accidently knocked a few piles over when I scared you. Do you happen to know if your uncle is working on his own? Or is he working with anyone?"

"Thank you for believing me, Alpha. My uncle isn't smart enough to plan things, he is a follower. He said that Greg would be very pissed off if I didn't find the deed."

Before Daniel or I could say anything, we heard a loud gasp from the office door. I turned to see my Aunt Margot with wide eyes, mouth agape and colour draining from her face.

"Did you just say Greg? I pray to the Goddess I heard you wrong."

Amber

I had nothing but nightmares, Daniel walking away from me, telling me I would never be good enough to be his Luna. I would then hear the chilling laugh of Greg, telling me I belonged to him now. I longed for Lana, I needed her guidance so desperately. I woke up with a start after one particularly rough nightmare, with the feeling I was being watched. I rolled over to see Greg sitting on a chair leaning over the bed staring at me like a creeper. I jumped away from him on the bed and kicked out my left leg, making a connection with Greg's jugular. He hadn't been expecting me to kick like that, he fell back coughing and sputtering with a stunned look on his face.

"Y...y...yo...you...you're a feisty little bitch, aren't you my little Luna?"

He was having trouble catching his breath and coughing horribly. His face was red with embarrassment and started to contort in anger. I couldn't care less if he got angry, he deserved it. He then did something I was not expecting, he started to chuckle in amusement.

"Oh, my little Luna, we're going to have so much fun together, you and me."

"There is no you and me, you psycho. Next time I catch you watching me sleep like a creeper, I'll do more than kick you in the throat."

Greg stopped chuckling at my words and his face slipped back into the blank mask he wore much of the time. I had pissed him off. Good! However, he scared me to death when he pounced on the bed and pinned me down in one swift move. I tried to struggle but he was much too heavy for me to even budge an inch. Without Lana, I only had human strength and it was no match against an Alpha. Greg bent close to my face and licked my cheek, which made me want to vomit instantly.

"Don't forget little Luna, I own you! I can do whatever I want whenever I want, to you. For your future well being, I suggest you be a good girl and remember that."

I was about to retort when he got off of me with another laugh and walked towards the door shooting me a skin crawling wink. I was starting to feel like I was falling into a pit of despair, when out of thin air, so faint I all but missed it:

"Don't worry, Amber, we'll get out of here!"

Chapter Fourteen

Chapter 14

Amber

Was I hearing things? Had I finally snapped and gone insane? Was that really my sweet wolf coming back to me? I was so terrified that I was having another nightmare that it took me a minute to say anything to her.

"Lana, is that really you?"

"Yes, Amber, it is really me! I am so sorry I left you like that. Whatever concoction that psychopath filled you with sent me into another dimension of sorts. I've been fighting tooth and nail to get back to you."

She sounded so tired. I felt really bad for her. I had so many questions, concerns and plans to go over with her. That would all have to wait because at that moment a huge wave of relief swept over my entire body. It was so intense I started to cry uncontrollably and shake. I had the other half of my soul back, I would have my full strength and quick healing back. I'd be able to fight Greg and get myself out of here. All of it was too much for me at that instant and caused me to break down.

Lana kindly talked me through it, and poured as much comfort into me as she could. I could sense her weakness and it really pissed me off that he did that to my once strong, proud wolf. Greg would pay for everything he'd put me through, if it was the last thing I ever did.

"I promise you, Amber, we will find a way out of here. I need to caution you though, it's not going to be easy. Greg is a very dangerous wolf. We will have to proceed with caution."

This wasn't news to me, I could feel how dangerous he was by his aura. I needed to let Lana rest and regain her strength, so we could come up with a plan. I was lost in thought when the door to the little room I was being kept in opened. This startled me, as I wasn't expecting Gred back so soon. Instead, I saw his head omega, Marie coming through the door with a nervous expression on her face. I was about to ask her if everything was OK when the answer was given to me.

"Well, well, well, you're quite hard to track down, my dear. Look at you all fancy and free in your VIP room. Thank you Marie, I won't be needing your services anymore."

I winced as Leo sliced Marie's neck, she gasped as the blood gushed out of her and she hit the floor. I didn't know the woman from a hole in the wall, but she had been the only decent person to me this entire time, so I felt bad for her. Fire burned in my eyes as Leo stepped over Marie's twitching body and started to stalk towards me. I knew I had nowhere to go, I was trapped and Leo knew this as well. An evil glint shone in his eyes as a smirk lit up his deranged face. I had to play this cool or he was going to have his way with me - I was completely at his mercy.

"Do you have enough strength left Lana to partially shift when the time comes?"

"I do! The moment that fucker gets too close, we will shred him and send him back to Hell."

I was so happy to have my feisty wolf back, I tried to buy myself some time to think by asking Leo what he thought he was doing. Greg had clearly chosen me, since he was the Alpha, Leo needed to fall in line and behave. This seemed to be the wrong thing to say I saw anger flare up in Leo's eyes, his jaw started ticking and fists clenching.

"Greg is NOT THE BOSS OF ME! I am my own wolf. If I want something, I will take it! I don't follow others or rules."

By this point, he had made it to the edge of the bed and grabbed me by the throat. I knew struggling was pointless and would only cause me damage. Instead, I was stiff as a board and stared Leo down. He leaned in and started peppering kisses down my shoulder and collarbone. It took every ounce of strength I had not to shudder in disgust, knowing the type of prick he was, he would think I was enjoying it. I warned him not to do that again or else.

"Or else what, princess? There's nothing you can do, you are wolfless and at my mercy. No one is coming to save you."

He began to laugh gleefully like he had won some sort of prize. Little did he know I had my wolf back and we were about to make him regret all his life choices. I asked Lana if she was ready, she assured me she was. Leo leaned down and started to go for my breasts. That is where it was going to end for him. I told Lana "NOW!", she elongated her claws and with one quick swipe we ripped Leo's throat out. He stumbled back with a look of shock and horror on his face, clutching his throat. I fell onto the bed covered in his blood.

"I warned you not to do that again, asshole."

I didn't have much time to gloat to myself as a loud roar shook the entire room. A very angry and crazed looking Greg came flying into the room. He looked over at Marie on the floor, then at Leo, who was on his knees about four feet from the bed bleeding out all over the floor. His eyes finally made their way to me on the bed. He looked concerned at first, but then an approving, proud smile brightened his face. What a sick fuck this man was. Was he actually enjoying this gruesome sight? He stopped to check Marie and shook his head.

"Damn, I really liked this one, she did a good job. It's going to be hard to find a replacement."

He continued over to Leo, expanding his aura, making his half dead form waver.

"As for you, you backstabbing bastard, I'll see you in Hell."

With that, he swung his arm and took off Leo's head. It landed unceremoniously at the foot of the bed. That was it for me, I turned and threw up. Greg eventually made it over to me on the bed.

"Ahhh, my little Luna, I knew we belonged together! Look at you taking care of trouble when it comes looking for you."

He reached down and picked me up, throwing me over his shoulder like a potato sack. I let out a squeal in protest and began to pound his back as he walked towards the door. This seemed to have no effect on him whatsoever.

"Easy now, my little Luna, I like it rough. We don't have time for any of that right now. We have to get you washed up and changed. We have a date with your Alpha Daniel, to get our pack in a few hours! I need you to be all clean when I present you as my new Luna."

Justin

Melissa and I ran into the archives like our lives depended on it. Well, in this case, the lives and pack of our friends depended on it. We didn't know who Greg was or where he was from. Hell, we didn't even know how old he was. We knew this was not going to be an easy task, it would be like finding a needle in a haystack. We made a quick judgement call to start looking into the birth records from five years before my father was born, just in case he was older than my late father. I took the first year and Melissa took the volume for the next year. We worked in tandem for hours.

"Any luck, my love? I've got nothing in this log book. I'm beginning to think this man is a ghost or Greg is an alias name."

Melissa gave me a sad look and shook her head, letting me know she had nothing either. I scrubbed my hands down my face in frustration. We needed to leave to get back to Onyx Crescent in only a few more hours, we needed to find something soon. As if the Moon Goddess herself heard my plea, Melissa shouted and startled me.

"Oh, my Goddess, I think I found him! Listen to this, Justin: *On July sixth, a new pup was born to Alpha Magnus St. Pierre of the River Hound pack.* They make no mention of a Luna? That's strange."

I had found it odd as well, but I urged Melissa to continue reading.

"*The new heir to the River Hound pack was named Greg St. Pierre. He was bigger than most pups at birth and was said to make many people uneasy right from the start. People stated it was like he was born from the pits of Hell.*"

I saw the chill run down Melissa's spine, she looked up from the log book with an uneasy expression on her face. She said she didn't want to read anymore and asked me to come finish the page. I obliged her request, took the book from her and continued to read the paragraph. It seemed that our buddy Greg was strong from the get go, almost unnaturally so. If he didn't get his way, he would bludgeon the omegas who were tasked with his care. By the time Greg turned five, he had killed a dozen omegas and three other pups from his nursery school.

I looked up at Melissa in horror. Neither of us could believe what kind of sick psychopath this man was from such a young age. The article went on to say that at eleven years old, Greg and his father had a disagreement during Alpha training, and Greg ended up murdering his father, Alpha Magnus St.Pierre, in cold blood. Thus becoming the youngest Alpha on record. The article ended with people's accounts of the tragedy. They stated they had never seen so much blood in one place, and the young Alpha stood there covered in his father's blood, revelling in the carnage. I dropped the book onto the table as if it had burned me.

"We have to get back to Onyx Crescent immediately! Daniel and Olivia need to know what they're dealing with! We need to get Amber out of his clutches quickly."

Chapter Fifteen

Chapter 15

Olivia

I watched as my Aunt Margot blanched and began to tremble. Her reaction to hearing Greg's name was concerning to say the least. She walked further into the office as if in a daze and sat down on the couch next to Claudia. It took several minutes before the fog lifted and she was able to look at each of us, as if seeing us for the first time. "Alright, is someone going to tell me what the hell is going on, and why Greg's name is being thrown around this office?"

Daniel and I looked at each other sheepishly, we hadn't really spoken to anyone except one another about what was going on. Margot had been taking care of our mother since the day of the challenge, it was just like we forgot she was there. I took a deep breath and launched into the whole sordid tale; from discovering Amber was gone, to finding out she was kidnapped by Greg, to this exact moment we found out the extra information from Claudia about pack members helping him out.

Margot scrubbed her hands down her face and looked at us with a very grim look. I turned to Claudia and asked her if she had any more information. She said that was all she knew. I asked her to please go relax in the library until we had finished speaking with Margot. She was going to get a new room, but I didn't want her where her uncle could find her in the meantime. Claudia agreed, and gave us all a little bow as she exited the office. I turned to Margot then, and asked how bad this really was.

"I'm not going to sugarcoat this. Greg is an absolute psychopath. He used to go to school with your father, mother and Alpha Renato. I remember he used to bully them all terribly. Your father was left bloody and bruised on many occasions. I also had the horrible luck of stumbling upon his pack when Francis banished me from Onyx Crescent. Had I realized that was his pack, I would never have stopped. I was trapped there for weeks. The man took great joy in torturing me. He thought I was a spy and wanted me to crack. He got bored eventually and released me to the dungeons. I got a lazy guard one night who hadn't locked my cell properly and I ran so fast, never looking back."

"Oh, my Goddess, Margot, I am so sorry you had to go through that." I stared at Margot with my mouth open.

Margot gave me an apologetic glance and continued, "I honestly had never been so scared in all my life. It got even worse though. While I was there, he killed his Luna with his own two hands. Snapped her neck."

I couldn't believe what Margot had just said. I was shocked and now more terrified than ever for Amber's safety. I knew I wasn't alone in my sentiment as I looked over at Daniel and he was shaking. Xander was no doubt trying to take over, he was fighting back so hard he had beads of sweat running down his face. I reached out my hand and took Daniel's. I told Xander we were going to get Amber back, he just needed to let Daniel think and not fight him. That did the trick as Daniel stopped shaking and let out a giant breath that he had been holding.

"Margot, do you have any insight into how we can take Greg down? Does he have any known weaknesses? Anything that could give us the upper hand?" I had a feeling there was nothing, but I had to take the chance and ask my aunt.

"Honestly, Liv, if he did, they were very well guarded. The man is a beast!"

"Your aunt is right, Olivia!! Greg is more terrifying than any of us could have ever thought."

We all whipped around surprised by Justin and Melissa walking into the office with concern plastered all over their faces. Melissa closed the door behind her and walked over to where we were. Justin proceeded to tell us what he and Melissa had learned from their archives. The more they spoke, the more nauseated I got and by the end Evie was pacing nervously in my head. What the hell were we going to do? This monster was coming to our pack later today to quote-unquote, take his pack back, whatever that even meant. Justin seemed to read my mind as he added that he had found his father's secret recording location, and had seen a video of Renato calling Greg to meet him at the pack on the day of the challenge. He said he was ninety-nine point nine percent certain his father had brokered this whole mess. He looked down at his shoes in despair.

"Justin, it's not your fault! You are not your father. The fact you're here with all this information is amazing, and we cannot thank you enough." I reassuringly squeezed his shoulder.

Justin didn't get a chance to answer as there was a knock on the office door. I knew before it opened that it was Logan. Evie had brightened up and was wagging her tail in excitement. I ran over and threw my arms around Logan's neck. I felt like I hadn't seen him in so long and I really needed his support at that moment. He wrapped me in his strong arms and hugged me so hard it felt like he would crack me in half.

"Oh, he can break us in half later in the bedroom." Evie purred like the horny wolf she was. I reminded her now wasn't the time. I ignored Evie as Logan let me go and produced a flask stick from his pocket. I gave him a curious look and he shrugged his shoulders.

"Daniel, a messenger left not long ago, he brought an envelope with this inside and told me to give it to my 'soon-to-be-ex-Alpha'."

My blood ran cold at that message, that meant it could only be from one person: Greg. Daniel stepped forward, thanking Logan for bringing it to him, and took the flash stick. Daniel looked at all of us and asked if we could leave him alone as he needed a moment alone. We all agreed and headed out of the office, it worked out perfectly for me as I wanted some alone time with Logan, to try to decompress. I took one last look at Daniel feeling slightly guilty for leaving him and told him I was only a mind-link away if he needed us. He gave me a small sad smile, and thanked me before I ran for the hills.

Daniel

Everyone filed out of the office as I asked, Olivia hesitated for a moment giving me a reassuring look and letting me know she was only a mind-link away. Margot was the last one remaining and went to close the door, she looked me dead in the eyes and told me she wasn't going to leave me alone. I wanted to argue with her but

I didn't have the strength so she stayed. I sighed as I walked over to my computer and inserted the stick. I was nervous about what this contained and told Margot as much; she came over putting her hands on my shoulders for support. I didn't realise but I was holding my breath anxiously and what we saw next made us both freak out.

Xander roared loudly in my head, there was no stopping him this time, he took over instantly and shifted right at my desk. Margot swore as she ran to the door to block Xander from leaving the office. It took several tense minutes of Margot fighting my angry wolf and telling Xander he needed to be calm, think straight, and reserve his energy if he was going to take Greg on and stay alive. My aunt was surprisingly strong and was able to keep my wolf in check much to my relief. Margot and Xander stared each other down until finally he let me shift back. I fell to the office floor naked and sobbed uncontrollably over what I had seen on my computer screen. Margot ran over to the couch to get a blanket to cover me, as I wailed.

"How could he do that to my sweet Amber? Margot, they stripped her, she was chained naked to a bed, covered in blood and bruises. Who knows what they did to her. This has to end NOW! Greg needs to die!"

"I know it's shocking, Daniel, it breaks my heart they did that to her and I agree he needs to die; but I need you to calm down first. You need to be level-headed before you face him, right now you're going into shock."

I closed my eyes and took a deep breath, as I shook violently. Margot was right, I needed to have a clear head before facing off to Greg. If I got hurt or killed, I would fail my sweet mate and leave her stuck with that psychopath. Margot dragged me to my feet and guided me to the couch, she gently pushed me to sit and told me she'd be right back. I was grateful she had stayed.

Greg

Amber punched, kicked and struggled with all her might while she was thrown over my shoulder. I thought she was absolutely adorable, she actually thought she could hurt me without her wolf. Samson was growling in my head that I needed to take her and mark her now, but I shooed him away. My little Luna deserved to have me do it right. She would get a grand ceremony, and when I took her for the first time it would be magical and she would be into me as much as I am into her. Samson called me an idiot, but I paid him no nevermind.

We had made it to the bathroom by then. I placed Amber down gently on the counter and she looked up at me with such venom in her stare. We were going to be one hell of a strong power couple. I turned on the shower for her and told her to strip and get clean. She folded her arms and looked her nose up at me. I warned her that she could get in the shower on her own accord or I would gladly strip her and shower her myself. Her head whipped around and if looks could kill I think I would have been dead, those dagger eyes she threw me were intense.

"You wouldn't fucking dare!"

"Oh, don't tempt me my sweet little Luna, we will have more time to play another day. Right now you need to get cleaned up, so we can go see your ex and let him know we own his pack now; and I own you."

Amber opened her mouth to refute my claims, but I took my shot and leaned forward, silencing her with my lips as they crashed into hers. She struggled and pushed against my chest with all her might. I was still stronger and held her tightly against me as my tongue sought hers. She tasted so sweet my head was swimming with lust. I heard her gasp as she undoubtedly felt my cock harden against her leg. It was a beautiful moment, until it wasn't and the taste of blood filled my mouth. The smart little bitch had bitten my tongue with all her might.

Chapter Sixteen

Chapter 16

A mber

It all happened so fast, I went from being thrown over his shoulder, to sitting on a bathroom sink to having this asshole's tongue shoved halfway down my throat. My self-preservation kicked into high gear and I did the only thing I could think of at that moment, since he was too big for me to move. I bit his tongue as hard as I could. The metallic taste of his blood was now in my mouth and it took everything in my power not to wretch. I felt him jerk back, I braced myself for the violence I knew was coming my way. When a few seconds passed without anything, I opened one eye. When I saw the devil himself laughing, I was so confused.

"That really fucking hurt, little Luna. I'll give it to you, you're a smart little bitch. Now get your sexy ass in the shower before you make me do something you'll regret."

He emphasised that last part with a growl that left no room for argument. I had also felt him get hard against my leg when he kissed me. I did not want any of that so I obliged. I swallowed my pride and stripped, bolting into the shower hoping the steam would block his view of me. Lana whispered to me faintly to breathe and not to let go of hope that we could get away from this monster. I showered as quickly as possible. When I was done, he was still standing outside the shower holding a towel for me. I begrudgingly took it from him.

"What am I supposed to wear? My clothes are soaked with blood. I can't leave here in a towel."

"As much as I'd love to see you in only a towel or nothing at all, for the rest of the day, I agree. No one else gets to see my woman that way, but me. Come."

I hesitantly followed him into what I correctly guessed was his bedroom. I did not like being in that vulnerable position: stuck alone with him in a room wearing only a towel. He had made no secret of the fact that he was delusional and thought I was his woman. The thought of being his woman made my skin crawl; that was not going to happen ever in this lifetime. Lana let a small growl resonate through my head.

"NEVER, we belong to Daniel and Xander. If this fucker touches us again I will kill him."

I agreed with Lana to keep her calm, but the mere mention of belonging to Daniel made me wince. If he didn't want me before, he sure as hell wouldn't want me after this whole ordeal. The fact he hadn't come to save me was more than enough proof that I wasn't important to him.

"Stop! I'm the other half of your soul and I know what you're thinking. We had no clue who this guy was or where he came from. Daniel would be in the same boat, needing to figure out where we are. That takes time."

"Well, Daniel doesn't need to worry about it since it seems we're going to him, according to the asshole over there."

I let out an audible sigh which made Greg turn around and look at me with a sharp eye. I didn't want him suspecting I had Lana back, so I shot him a dirty look and asked him where the clothes were. I was getting cold and wanted to be dressed. He chuckled and threw a handful of clothes at me.

"You're about the same size as my original Luna, so these should fit nicely."

Great, he was giving me his dead mate's clothes, just my luck. I needed to tread carefully so I didn't end up like her. A chill ran down my spine as I turned away from him to put the clothes on. It took every shred of power I had to not burst into tears as I put on this poor woman's clothes. Lana talked me through it and I thanked the Goddess she was able to get back to me. Now I wouldn't feel so alone.

Olivia

I ran for the hills after my aunt Margot shot me a look for dragging behind and feeling guilty. Margot was effectively scarier than my own mother, I wasn't going to question her. Daniel knew he could mind-link me, that was good enough. I chose instead to think of the alone time I was about to get with Logan, Evie started to purr like a kitten in my head. It felt like it had been an eternity since Logan and I had spent more than five minutes together.

We walked into our room and as I was locking the door, Logan grabbed me around the waist and spun me in his arms. I wasn't expecting this and let out a little squeal. He buried his nose in my neck, drawing in a long breath of my scent. A shot of electricity ran through me down to my toes. I had missed Logan so much, right now I needed him to help me forget everything. I ran my hands through his hair, gently massaging his scalp. This earned me a deep moan which I felt in my core. Logan kissed and sucked on my mark, which made my knees turn to jello and a moan escaped my parted lips. He looked down at me with a sexy smirk on his face, his eyes were dark obsidian, letting me know Norman was pushing forward.

"I need you to help me forget everything for a little while. Could you do that for me, love?"

My answer came with Logan picking me up, carrying me to our bed and placing me gently on the edge of it. I anxiously reached for his belt buckle, but he took a big step back and wagged his finger at me. I arched an eyebrow at him and he gave me the sexiest smile in return, that made me wetter than I already was. He began swaying his hips as he unbuttoned his shirt. I giggled uncontrollably at the realisation that I was getting my own personal striptease. By the time his boxers hit the floor with his cock bobbing in my face, I was a panting hot mess. Evie was screaming at me to let her out so she could worship our mate as he needed to be. I blocked her because I only had eyes for the sexy specimen in front of me, and had no time for her antics. I got up from the bed, licking my lips. As I got to him, I went down on my knees looking up at him through my lashes. Asking permission to have a quick snack; permission was granted. I started by licking pre-cum off the head of his cock. I felt a shudder of pleasure go through his body as I licked him from top to bottom in one go. I slowly made my way back up, teasing him as I swirled my tongue along the sensitive underside of his cock. I enjoyed the moans he was making and relished the gasp he let out as I sucked his entire member into my mouth in one go. I was a few bobs in when he pulled out of my mouth. I looked up at him confused and disappointed.

"It's not about me right now, it's all about what I need to do to make you forget. Remember?"

"But, I was enjoying making your knees weak and hearing you moan."

"There will be plenty of time for that after! But for now you're mine." His last words were a growl that spread heat through my entire body. Logan ripped my shirt into shreds, which startled me. He was never the take-charge type. Logan made fast work of the rest of my clothes, leaving me naked in front of him. He ran his hands all over me before settling them on my ass and lifting me up. I instantly wrapped my legs around his hips, grinding on his gorgeous cock that was now pinned against my wet pussy and our stomachs. Logan crashed his lips onto mine in a hot sensual kiss that made my head spin, his tongue fought for dominance with mine and was winning hands down. As we kissed, I was grinding harder on Logans' rock-hard cock. The friction was wonderfully delicious. I felt my climax building and I couldn't wait to get myself off. Before I was able to reach my release I lost contact with Logan as he put me down in the middle of the bed.

"Wrists together and over your head, now."

I blinked up at Logan confused for a moment before coming to my senses and obeying him. I liked this version of my man more than he could ever imagine. I just about fainted when, next thing I knew, he was locking my wrists to the bed with handcuffs. He smiled at me, which made me swoon. As he bent down to kiss me, he took a blindfold from behind a pillow and fastened it to my eyes. All I could do was be in the moment and enjoy the sexy ride. His warm breath fanned down my throat towards my breasts, leaving goosebumps the entire way. I gasped as he sucked my left nipple into his hot mouth, gently biting and sucking as he massaged my right breast. He released my left nipple and moved over to give the right side the same attention. Logan continued his mission down my stomach with sweet little butterfly kisses, as I couldn't see anything. All my other senses were on high, I felt like a spring that was being wound up ready to bounce off the edge of the earth.

"Spread your legs for me, show me that gorgeous pussy of yours." Logan's husky voice made me do the opposite and press my legs together chasing that wonderful friction, but he cleared his throat and tapped me on the outside of the thigh. I obliged by spreading my legs wide for him.

"That's my good girl!" His voice was like liquid silk, I felt my juices dripping out of me as he hoisted my legs over his shoulders. He kissed my inner thighs, leaving love bites and driving me insane. I was trying to guide his mouth to where I wanted it to be, after multiple love bites he finally made it to my pussy. He licked me from slit to clit, my hips bucked as he circled my clit with his Goddess-sent tongue. He anchored my hips down with one arm as he inserted two fingers into my dripping pussy. He started slowly building a steady, rapid-paced rhythm. He plunged his fingers into me non stop as his tongue worked my clit into a frenzy, I could feel myself getting close to the edge. My stomach muscles were getting tighter with each lick, just when I thought I was about to burst he pulled his fingers out and stopped paying attention to my clit. I whimpered at the loss of all the wonderful feelings.

"Logan, what's going on?" He never answered me, instead he released the handcuffs and flipped me over onto my knees. Before I knew what was happening, I heard the smack and felt that glorious sting of leather meeting skin. Logan had found my crop collection and had completely surprised me by using it for the first time. I had to say I was very impressed, he came off like a pro. I didn't have much time to think as another smack came down onto my other ass cheek. I let out a deep moan, the pleasure this was giving me was on a whole new level. Logan unleashed a good half dozen amazing spanks. He had me delirious with pleasure. I was waiting for another round of spanking, but I felt the head of Logan's hard cock at the entrance to my pussy instead. In one swift move he pushed into the hilt, the stretch was glorious and I pushed back, begging for more. He wrapped my hair around his fist and pulled me up so our bodies were flush against each other. He began pumping at a wonderful pace, pinching my nipples every few strokes. He was building me up for an even bigger explosion than before. I could feel every ridge of his cock as it pounded my soaking wet pussy. I was getting close when Logan reached down to rub my clit, and that sped up my trip over the cliff. All it took to send me into euphoric heaven was him whispering "Come for me" and biting his mark. I don't think I had ever cum like that in my life. My pussy squeezed him so hard he screamed out my name, filling me with his seed. We both collapsed on our sides panting for several minutes. My head was spinning from the intensity of everything. Logan removed the blindfold before wrapping his arms around me. He whispered into my ear as we both drifted in and out of consciousness.

"What a good girl you were! I can't wait to do that again."

Chapter Seventeen

Chapter 17

*E*vie

I was so happy our mate had broken out of his shy shell. I wanted to take that wild stallion for a ride myself, but Olivia kept being selfish and pushing me back. Now was the perfect time, with her relaxed and not paying attention. I hadn't had a chance to connect with my man physically yet. So I reached out to my sexy Norman and told him I was about to rock his world; I needed him to push his human back as well. He was a bit hesitant at first, but I was able to persuade him. I counted to three and we both thrust our respective humans into the back of their minds and took control of their bodies. I threw up a block so I wouldn't hear Olivia arguing with me, sat up and straddled Norman, giving a mischievous smile.

"Hello, my sexy mate! I couldn't let those silly humans have all the fun. I wanted a piece of my man, too."

Norman gave me a sly grin that instantly made me wet. I lifted myself up and slowly, teasingly slipped Norman's hardening cock into my tight pussy. I worked my way to the base where he let out a loud moan. I twisted my hips, slowly squeezing his cock with my walls. The look of ecstasy that was on his face made me pick up my pace.

"Easy does it, my sweet, I won't last long if you do that. I want to enjoy every moment of this."

He grabbed my hips and slowed me down to a painfully restrained pace. To make up for the change in tempo, I made sure to twist and clench every time I hit his base. I reached back and firmly grabbed his balls, tugging them and rolling them in my hand. I felt the electric shock go through his body at that motion. Next thing I knew, Norman stood up, still inside me and I wrapped my legs around his hips instinctively. With quick strides, he made his way into the bathroom and turned the shower on. Stepping into the warm spray, he crashed his lips into mine, making me dizzy from how passionate it was. By the time we stopped for air, I didn't know which way was up or down. I was brought back down to earth when my back was pressed into the cold tiled wall of the shower. Norman pistoned his hips, plunging his throbbing cock deep inside me over and over again, making me cry out. He bent his head down and licked the water droplets that were cascading down my breasts. My nipples hardened instantly as he sucked them into his warm, wet mouth, rolling them around gently between his teeth. I felt my orgasm building, but I needed a different angle to take me over the edge. I gently slid his cock out of my dripping pussy and bent over the shower bench, giving him a wink over my shoulder. Norman looked bereft for a moment at the loss of my tight, hot pussy, but was quick to understand what I was after. He gave me a sly grin as he bent down and licked my pussy from the slit up.

I wasn't expecting his mouth to find my clit when it did, but I didn't mind the extra pleasure that coursed through my body. I moaned like a 'good girl' for Norman and was rewarded by a nice firm spank to my right ass cheek. He teased me mercilessly until I just about lost it all over his face, but right before I reached my goal he kissed my ass cheek and stood up. I was breathing heavily and begged him to fill me with his cum. He kneaded both of my ass cheeks simultaneously, then ran his left hand up my spine. He reached the base of my head and wrapped my hair around his fist, giving himself something solid to hold onto. He lined himself up with my slit and pushed all the way in. I cried out as I was filled by his hard, thick cock. Norman went wild at that point, pounding into me at such an intense speed, that I started seeing stars. Before I could say anything, my orgasm hit me like a freight train. My knees buckled but he caught me in his strong arms, still pounding away until he let out a half moan, half howl of pleasure as he filled me with ropes of hot cum. Both our legs were shaking from the intensity of our climax. He gently kissed the back of my neck and cradled me until I could stand again on my own.

"Thank you, my love, that was amazing. We should probably give control back to our humans. I can feel Olivia pushing against my block. I don't know what is going to happen later today, but I want you to try and stay as far away from the main fight as possible, please."

"Yes, Logan is rather pissed off at the moment. Wherever you are, I will be my sweet. I promise I won't throw myself into any dangerous situations unnecessarily, but I need to be close to you so I don't lose my mind."

I nodded and gently kissed Norman one last time before giving Olivia back full control. To say she was pissed was an understatement, but I didn't care, she'd get over it. I wanted time with my mate and they weren't giving it to us, so I took matters into my own paws. Olivia said we'd discuss it later and blocked me while she and Logan finished showering and went to get ready for the show down with Greg.

Daniel

Margot was gone less than five minutes, she walked back into my office with a change of clothes for me, since Xander had shredded what I had been wearing previously. Margot turned to let me get dressed privately, she went to sit at my desk with two cups of tea she had also brought back with her. Once I was dressed, I went and sat across from her at the desk. She handed me the cup and told me to have a drink. I instantly started sputtering and gagging, it wasn't tea.

"Goddess, Margot, what the hell is that? It tastes like antifreeze for a car."

"It's whisky, or at least it's supposed to be. Your father never did have very good taste in anything."

We both put the cups down and she apologized for her failed attempt at a good stiff drink to knock me out of the shock I seemed to be in. She looked me straight in the eyes and asked me the one question I was dreading, 'Why did Amber leave?' I looked down at my feet in shame and explained how I may have been unintentionally ignoring her and sleeping in my office all week. Margot's eyes narrowed and before I knew what hit me, she had gotten up and smacked me upside the head.

"Dumb ass, your relationship was new and needed to be nurtured. Why would you ignore her and sleep in your office, Daniel?"

"OWWWW! That hurt Aunt Margot. I didn't do it on purpose...I was stressed, trying to figure out all this new Alpha bullshit. She never told me she felt neglected."

That was the wrong thing to say as Margot began pacing beside my desk mumbling to herself and scrubbing her hands down her face, before turning to look at me again with dismay in her eyes.

"Daniel, please don't tell me you think that's a valid excuse? Amber is your fated mate and found out you had a chosen mate and child before her. From what I saw, she was taking it all in stride. How could you think pushing her away would give you a happy ending once the dust settled? She obviously felt like she wasn't good enough for you. Leaving to safeguard her heart from being broken anymore. She didn't need to tell you anything, you needed to include her and make her a priority. You're supposed to be a team."

I hadn't thought of it that way. I looked at Margot, helplessly. I had fucked up royally and may never get to see Amber again to tell her how much I actually cared for her. My mind was going a hundred miles a minute and I was so worried about her. I missed Amber terribly and I knew if I ever got her in my arms again I'd never let her go. Margot finally settled on the couch and I went to join her, we spent a few hours discussing everything. I was about to ask Margot if she thought I had a chance of fixing this, if Amber ever came home, when suddenly the air cracked with electricity and we heard a deep, booming voice that echoed from outside.

"Oh, Daniel, I'm home!! Come on out here and hand over what is rightfully mine!"

Chapter Eighteen

Chapter 18

Daniel

Margot and I ran to the window and looked outside. What we saw pissed me off immediately. There was Greg standing in front of the pack house with a cocky shit eating grin on his face. Beside him stood Amber wearing a blindfold and shackles around her wrists and ankles. Next to her stood a terrified-looking young woman. Margot squeezed my shoulder to help calm me down. I'm thankful she did or I would have shifted and jumped out the office window with no hesitation. I knew that I needed to be level headed and think of a proper strategy, if I was going to get Amber back safely. Greg looked up at the window we were in and sneered at me.

"I don't have all day, little boy. Are you going to get down here and give me my pack? Or do I have to take it back the hard way?"

I turned to look at Margot, and all she could do was shake her head, we had to go out there. That was the first step. As I turned away from the window, Olivia and Logan came busting into the office.

"Is that Greg yelling like a mad man out front?" Olivia looked shaken as I nodded in confirmation.

"Daniel, he's HUGE and his aura is suffocating all the way from where he is outside. He seems very unnatural, Evie is even freaking out."

My sister's wolf was fearless and confident. Hearing that Evie was freaking out did nothing to settle my already frayed nerves. Xander seemed to have a different approach, he didn't care about Greg's aura or how unhinged he seemed. All Xander wanted was his mate back safe and sound in his arms.

"Olivia, grab the deed from my desk, we will go out there and deal with this jackass."

"DANIEL, you aren't handing over the deed to our pack! I won't let you do that."

"Relax, Liv, I have no intention of giving him the deed. I will only pretend to hand it over so he gives us Amber, then we will attack him and take him down."

"We hardly have an army, Daniel. Who is going to attack him besides us?"

"We don't really need an army, Liv, he's here by himself with a scared young woman and Amber. Besides, we have Justin with his men, we also have Alpha Arnold with a few of my old pack members who are still here."

"Is he really only here with Amber and that girl? We don't know for sure, Daniel, he could have a thousand men hiding somewhere to attack us on a whim."

The look Olivia gave me was one of scepticism and fear. I wished she would trust my plan the way I did. I was just going to have to show her that everything was going to be OK. We headed out of the office and saw Justin waiting for us at the front door with his men. I told him to come with Olivia and I outside to meet Greg. His men would wait inside with Logan and Margot for my signal to come out and attack. Justin agreed and turned to Melissa, telling her he loved her and to stay safely in the packhouse. I had linked Alpha Arnold in the meantime, and told him to stand by for instructions to attack from behind. He was staying in a cottage, in the village outside the packhouse yard. He would have the advantage of surprise. We were about to go out the door when Margot spoke quickly.

"I will not go out there and fight him. I'm sorry, Daniel, that man terrifies me and I know he'll recognize me. I'd rather stay here if things go sideways. I can help everyone in the packhouse, I am of better service behind the scenes."

"I understand, Margot, and I think you're right. Please help our people if anything happens to us."

We nodded at each other in understanding. I took a deep nerve-calming breath, squared my shoulders and puffed out my chest before heading outside. Justin and Olivia flanked me as we walked over to where Greg was standing, the force of this man's aura was almost crippling. It took a lot of energy to force ourselves forward and we were all three alpha's. What the hell was this man? He was not natural, that was for sure. I started to feel slightly nervous and warned Xander to be careful, there was a lot on the line.

"Don't worry about me, I've got this under control! I want our mate back, this giant overgrown monkey doesn't scare me." Xander could barely get that last part out as the aura got more intense, but we had made it face to face with Greg. I wasn't interested in him though. I looked straight at Amber, searching her body head to toe and needing to see if she had any fresh injuries. I was going to let Xander tear this bastard into a thousand pieces. My inspection was interrupted by Greg's deep, gravelly voice.

"Eyes on me you puny, worthless little turd. So nice of you to join us, I was beginning to think I'd have to kill your Luna over there and burn down the entire pack." He chuckled in a dangerously maniacal way that sent a cold shiver down my spine. I now understood why Margot stayed inside. I pretty much wished I could have as well. I looked over at Olivia, who was trying to stay calm and looked to be having trouble against his aura as well. I linked her to show Greg the deed. She nodded and held up the paper.

"Is this what you were looking for? Give me back my Luna and the deed is yours!"

"Now listen here, champ, do I look like I was born yesterday? Do you think I'm going to fall for the oldest trick in the book?"

"There is no trick, give us back Amber and the paper is yours." I noticed Amber flinch and stiffen when I said her name. This concerned me. Had he done something to her that she didn't recognize it was me speaking? I thought she would have tried to come to me. She must be waiting for the right moment.

Amber

Greg insisted that I be shackled and blind folded to get to Onyx Crescent. He left no room for argument, so there I was outside my packhouse standing like a fool. The future Beta turned Luna, who couldn't avoid capture. I was failing and hadn't even officially taken over either role. I was humiliated and heart broken, I felt Lana pouring love and calm into me. Lana was still lying low so Greg wouldn't know I had her back, we would need the element of surprise eventually to get rid of this asshole. I realized halfway to the pack that I wasn't just travelling alone with Greg, there was someone else with us. I asked and was told I needed someone to attend to me while I was shackled, so he brought along one of the pack omegas. I felt so bad that yet another innocent life was being dragged into this because of me. I asked her name in an attempt to connect with her. She quietly answered that her name was Zenah. She sounded around my age or possibly a little younger. That realisation didn't make me feel any better. I needed to behave in order to save Zenah as well as anyone else we might cross paths with. While Greg was busy arguing with Daniel, I felt Zenah lean forward and whisper in my ear.

"Luna Amber, I will protect you and help you escape."

I instantly flinched and stiffened when she said that, could I trust her? Was this some kind of joke or test? I asked Lana what she thought and Lana felt Zenah was genuine and could be trusted. My mind started running at a hundred miles an hour. I didn't have time to come up with anything concrete, as moments later the blindfold was ripped off my eyes, causing me to be blinded by the bright light. I became dizzy and disoriented, I felt Zenah's firm hand on my back holding me up. I appreciated her presence more than she knew. I blinked a few times and eventually my vision returned to normal. I saw Daniel looking at me with sheer terror in his eyes and Olivia didn't look much happier beside him. I wasn't sure what was going on as I had stopped listening to the exchange once Zenah had whispered to me. Greg's voice was the next thing I heard as he turned to face me.

"Nothing personal, little Luna, I will make this up to you later I promise, if everything works out."

What in the world was he talking about? I didn't have long to wait for an answer as the next thing I knew my feet were leaving the ground, his large hand had wrapped around my neck and hoisted me off my feet in one swift movement. I shrieked as he squeezed my neck. I started to see spots as I heard him tell Daniel.

"I warned you child, you didn't listen, now her death will be on your hands. Hand over the deed or I'm snapping her neck in: 10...9...8...7..."

I started to struggle and gasp for air as he applied more pressure. What the hell was he doing?

Chapter Nineteen

Chapter 19

Margot

Hell was standing outside our door, and I felt terrible that I had literally sent my family out to be eaten by the big, bad wolf. I knew myself though, I would freeze in panic and be of no use whatsoever. Being inside, watching everything unfold, I could get everyone from the packhouse to safety if needed. I called Logan and Melissa over to where I was standing by the small window. There was something very important I needed them to do for me.

"Listen, you two, I know you don't want to leave your mates, but you must do this for them. If Greg wins he will take over the packhouse, anyone who has Daniel or Olivia's scent will be targeted, including the two of you."

"Margot, I'm mated with Justin and I'm not marked yet, so he would never know or come after me!"

"He would, Melissa. Greg hated Justin's father and wanted to rid the world of him. Greg will know Justin as Renato's son by his scent.

Sadly, you may not be marked, but you carry Justin's scent all over you. You're a walking target, my dear."

Melissa looked at me in dismay. Logan, being the ever loving and protective big brother, wrapped his arms around Melissa in a comforting hug. I loved that Olivia had found such a wonderful and protective mate. That was why I needed to get him the hell out of the packhouse.

"We don't have much time, as much as I have faith in my niece and nephew. I've seen this fucking evil monster at work and they won't stand a chance against him. I need you to go upstairs and fetch Gabriella from her room and my sister, the former Luna."

They both looked at me with questions written all over their faces about why I was mentioning my sister. I sighed and shook my head.

"My sister is the former Luna and Daniel's mother. Greg would want nothing to do with her, he would want to remove anything and anyone connected to Daniel. It would not be safe for her to stay here, you need to go out the back with Gabriella and my sister. About half a mile through the woods there is a small road. I went this morning and stashed a car there for emergencies. Follow the road and it will take you back to Jade Moon."

"What about you, Margot? If Greg had captured you before, wouldn't he recognize you by sight or scent? You would be in great danger as well."

"Logan, I appreciate your concern but I had my scent changed years ago by a witch friend after fleeing his pack. He would never recognize my scent, and I am very good at being in the shadows. He would never know I was here. I need to stay behind to help Amber, she is going to need me. Please hurry and go before anything bad happens."

Melissa and Logan looked at one another briefly and nodded, heading upstairs as quickly as their legs would take them. I was glad that I was able to convince them, now all that was needed was for Daniel, Olivia and Justin to survive this walking mountain of death. I looked out the window and was shocked at what I saw. The next thing we knew, Daniel was roaring and Justin linked his men to charge into battle. Oh, that was not good. I sent a prayer to the Moon Goddess to watch over and protect all those brave wolves.

Amber

The air was getting harder and harder to force through my lungs. I was begging Lana to come forward and get us out of this situation. Unfortunately, she wasn't strong enough yet and couldn't fully shift. I wasn't going to make it much longer. Struggling was useless. The more I did, the tighter Greg squeezed. I could hear Zenah trying to negotiate and reason with Greg, which seemed like she was talking to a brick wall. He was unyielding, I felt my life slipping away, something needed to be done quickly. Just as I thought, all hope was lost. I heard Daniel roar out in anger. I saw him shift and come charging at Greg and I. Behind him I could see other men racing out the front door of the packhouse shifting as they ran. Greg clearly wasn't expecting Daniel to act and was caught off guard. He haphazardly tossed me to the side. Zenah thankfully caught me before I hit the ground.

My head was spinning as the oxygen rushed back through my lungs and was now freely flowing throughout my body. Zenah dragged me away from Greg quickly and produced a straight pin from her pocket. With nimble fingers, she used the pin to unlock the shackles that bound me. I looked up at her with relieved and thankful eyes. I was about to thank her, profusely when a twisted, evil-sounding snarl was unleashed. We looked over to see Greg in a half-shifted state, surrounded by our wolves. One was brave enough to jump at him, but sadly Greg was bigger, faster, stronger. He grabbed the wolf and tore him in half. I looked away before I threw up. It was all my fault. Any more deaths today were on my hands and I wasn't sure I could deal with that. Zenah helped me stand and was urging me to take off far and fast. I was looking around for the best escape route. All we kept hearing were yelps of pain and growls of anger.

Suddenly, I heard one terrible yelp that sent pain radiating through my soul. I looked over and saw that Greg had Daniel by the throat, other wolves, including Olivia, were charging at him to help. The air around us suddenly became electric and all the wolves froze where they stood, either on the ground or in mid-air. I found I even had a hard time moving my body. I looked at Zenah and asked what the hell was happening.

"You didn't know this about Greg, Luna Amber?"

"Know what Zenah? I was kidnapped and tortured for two days. I don't know the man from a hole in the wall."

She looked sheepishly down at her hands before looking back up at me to explain.

"Greg is a hybrid. His mother was a powerful witch who was burned at the stake not long after he was born. She claimed he was pure evil and tried to remove him from this life. She said she knew he was a mistake. However, the former Alpha did not take kindly to this as Greg was his future heir. He had her killed instead. It's poetic justice that only a few years later, as a young boy, Greg murdered his father in cold blood. I guess his mother was right after all. However, that was of little consolation, since the rest of us were left to suffer at the hands of that demon, thanks to the former Alpha's ignorance."

I looked at Zenah in complete shock. I couldn't believe what I had just heard. This was much worse than I had first thought and I knew we were all in grave danger. Daniel being the one who was in the most danger at that very moment. We could all hear the bones in his neck starting to crack. I couldn't let my mate die like this. We still had a lot to figure out. My poor sweet Gabriella deserved to grow up with her father. I made a snap decision that I wholeheartedly hoped I didn't come to regret in the long run. I looked at Zenah with a very serious expression.

"I know you don't know me very well, but do you trust me?"

"I know in my heart that you are pure light and will protect us all. You are the one who will save us from this evil. I trust you."

"Perfect! Then don't stop what I'm about to do, I have a plan." I turned away from a perplexed Zenah and slowly, painfully started to move towards Greg and Daniel. I was using all my energy to fight against the magical hold Greg had over the packyard. I walked for what seemed like forever before I got close enough. I saw Daniel starting to thrash less and looked like he was about to take his last breath. The panic that coursed through me gave me the determination I needed to take those last steps and make it to Greg. I took a deep breath, centering myself for what I was about to do. I reached my hand out and cupped his cheek. Leaning in, I pressed my lips to his in a burning kiss.

Chapter 20

Daniel

Seeing that monster with his hands around my mate's delicate neck, choking the life out of her, made Xander snap. I let out an enraged howl, letting Justin know it was GO time for his men. I shifted instantly and went after that giant piece of shit. I was happy to see I had caught him off guard. From the look on his face, he clearly hadn't thought I was going to do anything. It seemed he thought I was weak. I was more than happy to prove him wrong and put him in his place. As I got to Greg and Amber, he tossed her aside like a piece of trash, pissing me off even more. The young woman that had come along with them caught her. I let out a sigh of relief that she was safe for the moment and turned my attention back to Greg. He gave me a sinister smirk that made my hackles go up. I was about to jump him when suddenly one of Justin's men flew through the air right at Greg. The most ungodly sound came out of Greg as he half shifted. It was a gruesome sight to behold. He grabbed Justin's man mid air and tore him in half.

"Fuck! Daniel, this man, is not fully a wolf. He has a disturbing aura, we need to be very careful or we will end up like that poor bastard."

"NOW you're scared, Xander? This guy is just a giant overgrown monkey, we can still take him."

I couldn't believe that, after all the big talk Xander had been doing, that he was now going to chicken out on me. Greg was all brawn and no brains. If I calculated correctly, I could get a few good hits on him and take him down. Our group converged on Greg and we had him surrounded. He looked helplessly around at us. He knew he was outnumbered. We all sprung into action lunging at him.

Before I knew what was happening, the air crackled with an insane amount of energy and I couldn't move. No one could. I looked around and we all seemed to be frozen in our spots. In one swift move, Greg leaped forward, and grabbed me by the throat, hoisting me into the air. I realized very quickly how screwed I was. I tried to wiggle free but my body felt weighed down and lethargic. Greg put an immense amount of pressure on my neck, so much so we could hear my neck starting to snap with horrible cracking sounds.

"Daniel, we're never going to be able to tell mate how much we love her, or kiss those beautiful soft lips."

"We're not dead yet, Xander, please don't give up. I will fight until our last breath if it means we get to hold Amber once more."

"We are on our last breath..."

My vision started to swim and spot. Xander was right, this was the end. No one could move at that moment, so we had no chance of rescue. The dizziness was starting to ramp up, when out of the corner of my eye I spotted Amber fighting against the pressure and making her way over to us. My heart swelled with pride that my sweet Amber was so strong and was fighting to come save me. That feeling of pride faded very fast as I watched Amber reach up and plant a heated kiss on Greg. I blinked in disbelief as my mate kissed her kidnapper; Xander was growling and cursing in my mind.

I watched as Amber wrapped her arms around his neck, deepening the kiss, pressing her body against Greg's. Greg was momentarily stunned but quickly threw me to the ground, and wrapped both arms possessively around Amber. He hungrily lifted her off the ground as he shifted back into human form. Amber wrapped her legs around his hips. He stood there butt naked, passionately kissing my mate. I died, I must have died and gone to hell. This couldn't be real. However, looking around at everyone's shocked and disgusted faces, I knew I was very much alive and this was in fact happening.

The insane pressure around us seemed to dissolve instantly and Olivia ran to my side. "Oh, my Goddess, Daniel, are you OK? What the hell is going on? Why is Amber kissing that fucker? Do you think he brainwashed her?"

"I don't know, Liv, I just want her safely back in my arms, I need to get her away from that monster." Xander was howling in pain from Amber's betrayal. I couldn't believe this was happening. I was convinced Greg did something to Amber to make her forget who she was, or like Olivia suggested, maybe he brainwashed her into thinking she loved him. There was no way my sweet Amber would hurt me like that. I knew I screwed up, but not bad enough to warrant that.

Olivia helped me to my feet and Justin handed me a pair of shorts to cover up. I watched as Amber slowly slipped down Greg's naked body in a teasing manner and heard her let out a little giggle, which made me throw up in my mouth. Greg looked at us victoriously and stalked towards us, surely to finish the job he started. I braced myself ready to fight or die trying to get Amber back from his deranged clutches. He was only a few feet away from me when Amber stepped in front of him, putting her hands on his chest and looking up at him with big puppy eyes.

"Please don't kill them, I can't stand the thought of any more bloodshed today. You've won the pack and my heart. Banish their pathetic asses. IF they dare set foot back on your land, then you can go ahead and kill them. I won't stop you."

Greg looked down at her with tenderness, this made my blood run cold and bile rise in the back of my throat again. He considered her plea for several moments. "Your wish is my command, my little Luna. I will spare these useless wastes of space. BUT, if they dare set foot on my territory again they will die."

"Thank you so much, my sexy Alpha!"

Greg growled in appreciation at Amber calling him her sexy Alpha, as he planted another kiss on her. I instantly threw up. I couldn't believe this was my current situation. I had no clue at that moment that it was about to get a whole hell of a lot worse.

Amber

Calling Greg my sexy Alpha was the nail in my coffin. I felt my soul leave my body. Lana was so angry at me, screeching so loudly I couldn't think straight. I had to block her. She didn't agree with my plan. She was trying to get me to come up with another idea, but watching Greg about to snap Daniel's neck, I couldn't allow it to happen. This was the only plan I knew would work, there was just one more step to prove to Greg how 'authentic' I was. I was dreading this last step more than anything and hoped that one day Daniel would understand. I turned around after Greg's lips left mine. I was cringing so hard on the inside I needed to steel myself not to vomit. I faced a perturbed looking Daniel with a cold, detached look in my eyes. This was the only way it was going to work.

"I, Amber Small, reject you Daniel Stevens! I have found a real man, someone who isn't afraid to show me how he really feels."

I turned around grinning up at Greg, who was looking down on me with awe and excitement. I took his hand and began to lead him towards the packhouse. I motioned for Zenah to follow closely behind. She followed in silence with her eyes on the ground. I heard Daniel scream in agony as our bond snapped, he fell to his knees holding his chest with tears streaming down his face. It took every fibre of my being not to let the pain show and keep the smirk on my face like I was enjoying his pain and suffering. Lana was now howling in my head, she had broken through the block, flooding me with guilt and sadness. Olivia looked at me with daggers in her gaze. This broke my heart as much as hurting Daniel, but I needed her to think I was serious at that very moment. Deep down I hoped she knew me well enough to know this was all a ploy to help them get away. Before Greg and I reached the front door of the packhouse, he turned and ordered everyone off his land. A shock wave of power flowed from him and all our wolves seemed unable to do anything but turn and walk towards the border. I saw Olivia and Justin help pull Daniel to his feet, they had to half drag, half carry him. He looked at me one last time with the most broken eyes I'd ever seen.

"AMBER! I will crawl if I have to, I will climb a hundred walls if I need to. I will do whatever it takes to make you mine again. You and I are meant to be together. I need you, you're my other half! Please don't lose hope. This isn't you, he had you brainwashed."

My heart twisted in knots at his words. Why couldn't he have been this passionate and said these things to me two days ago? Maybe things would have turned out differently. For now, I had to keep my ruse going, not only for their safety, but for my own and the rest of the packs. So I did what I had to and that was laugh. I laughed hysterically, I told Greg loudly how pathetic Daniel was and that he needed to just move on. I would never be his. With one last firm look, Greg and I entered the packhouse and closed the door. I prayed to the Moon Goddess that my plan would work. I needed it to work. There was no way in hell I was spending the rest of my life with this psychopath.

"So, what shall we do now, my spicy little Luna?" I didn't have time to respond as Greg pushed me up against the wall and tried to kiss me passionately again, while running his hands all over my body. I had to find a way to keep him at bay. He would never be having his way with me as long as I lived. Zenah was like the answer to my prayers as she cleared her throat and suggested to Greg that he go check out his new office and settle himself in. Thankfully, he agreed and let me go. "There will be plenty of time for me to show you my appreciation later."

He winked at me and waltzed upstairs to go find the office. I looked at Zenah with relief as I slid down to the floor shaking. One lone tear rolled down my cheek. What had I gotten myself into?

Chapter Twenty-One

Chapter 21

Olivia

Never in a million years would I have expected Amber to do that to my brother or our pack. How the hell could she reject Daniel for that monster? It didn't make any sense, Daniel must have been on to something when he said she had been brainwashed. I had to find a way to get back into the packhouse and confront Amber.

"I don't think that's a good idea, Olivia. You will risk Amber's life. I don't believe for a second that what she did was real. She had a method to her madness, we're just missing a piece to the puzzle. Trust your best friend."

"Do you really believe that, Evie? It hurts my heart to think she could be that cruel. Maybe you are right and there is a piece to the puzzle we are missing. We need to find out what that is very soon."

"We will, Liv, don't worry. Let's just get out of harm's way and figure out our next move."

Evie's confidence that it would work out gave me a small glimmer of hope. This wasn't going to be solved immediately, but we were a good team. With some determination and patience, we'd get the answers we needed. I looked over to Daniel as we carried him away from Amber. He had his head bent to the ground with tears streaming down his face. Justin and I were bracing most of his weight, his feet were dragging behind him.

We were reaching the border when we saw Alpha Arnold and the few men from Daniel's old pack. The concerned shadow that passed over Arnold's face did not go unnoticed. I motioned him to the side and told Justin to hold Daniel fully. I walked over to Arnold and told him what had gone down with Greg. He looked completely shell shocked and devastated for Daniel.

"He's been through so much in such a short period of time, I'm worried this may be what breaks him. I've never seen him this despondent."

"Let's get him back to your pack and maybe he'll come back to us. He needs time to process all of this bullshit."

Alpha Arnold agreed, but I can tell he's skeptical about Daniel being OK. I wanted to dive into it more with him, but now wasn't the time nor the place. I walked back over to where Justin was standing, holding Daniel awkwardly and slung his arm over my shoulder to help lighten the load on Justin. We nodded at each other and followed Alpha Arnold and his men. We were silent for the first half hour. Until Justin broke the silence, in a full panicked tone that startled me out of my thoughts.

"Holy Shit! Melissa and Logan!! They're stuck in Onyx Crescent with that psychopath. I swear to the Goddess if he hurts my sweet mate or my best friend, I will personally see to his extinction."

Justin's wolf was trying to surface and I could see him struggling to keep him at bay. My anxiety instantly spiked and Evie began to whine. I couldn't believe, with everything going on, I had forgotten about Logan. I felt like such an idiot. What if he tried to confront Amber, and Greg killed him? I began to spiral and couldn't catch my breath. I stopped and dropped down onto one knee.

"Olivia? I am so sorry, I didn't mean to make you panic. I was just having my own freak out, close your eyes and take a deep breath."

I could hear Justin coaching me through the fog in my mind, Evie jumped in and sent calming waves through me. I took one last long deep breath and stood back up.

"It's OK, Justin, I just let my anxiety take me to a dark place for a moment. I'm back now! Melissa and Logan are both strong and cunning, they will be perfectly fine. I wholeheartedly believe that. Let's get back to Blood Viper and come up with a plan to get this fucker out of my pack and my best friend back. The quicker we can come up with a plan, the faster we will get our mates back in our arms."

From that point, we picked up the pace and made it back to Blood Viper quicker than expected. We were met at the door of Alpha Arnolds' house by his mate Julie. She took one look at Daniel and let out a sob, running over to him with tears in her eyes. "My poor sweet boy, what happened to you?"

Arnold walked over and whispered in her ear for a moment. Her eyes widened and anger blazed in her eyes. "Oh, like hell, we're going to let that fucking bastard win! I know he's insane, but we will find a way to take him down and get your mate back, Daniel. I promise you that."

For the first time since crossing our border, Daniel gave us a sign of life. He sucked in a deep breath and choked back a sob, he looked up at Julie with broken eyes and shocked all of us by speaking in a hoarse, quiet voice. "I gave her to him, Julie, on a silver platter. I don't blame Amber for rejecting me, I deserved it."

"What the hell are you talking about, Daniel, how did you give her to him?" Julie looked from Daniel to Justin to myself. We waited to see if Daniel would answer her but he just hung his head low again and shut down once more.

"Are any of you going to tell me what is going on?" Julie was getting agitated. Arnold wrapped his arms around her and told her we'd explain everything, but let us get Daniel inside to rest.

She agreed and led us into the house. She showed us which room was Daniel's and we gently placed him on the bed. He instantly curled up into a ball. I asked him if he was going to be OK. He looked up at me without actually seeing me. I knew he was looking through me as if he were far away.

"Will it ever be OK, again?"

I sighed heavily and told him to get some sleep and we'd figure something out once he was in a better headspace. Julie, Justin and I left the room, closing the door behind us and followed Julie down to Arnold's office. We barely made it through the door before Julie spun on us and demanded we tell her what happened. As his sister, I knew it was my job to tell her everything. As I told her the story I watched Julie's face fall more and more, the further I went into it.

"My poor Daniel, so he thinks he gave her to Greg by making her think she wasn't worthy? Daniel can be oblivious sometimes, but I know he was falling deeply in love with her. We spoke two days after the challenge and he couldn't stop gushing about Amber. I knew then and there, that he was done for. I know they could work it out if given a chance."

I let Julie know I agreed with her, we just needed to figure out what Greg had done to brainwash her. Julie asked if there was a small possibility she wasn't brainwashed and truly had fallen for him? I let out a mournful laugh, and told her I truly hoped not, my best friend was better than that. I wanted to believe that with all my heart. Before we could speak anymore, Justin's phone rang. I was surprised he still had his phone after his shift, mine had gone flying with my shredded clothes and I hadn't had the time to go find it. He understood the look on my face and told me he had seen it under a bush while getting the shorts we were wearing, so he grabbed it.

Justin answered the phone and his face broke out into a huge relieved grin. It was Melissa. He spoke with her for a few minutes, listening to her tell him that she and Logan were safely back at Jade Moon with Gabriella. I froze at the mention of Gabriella, I had completely forgotten about her with all the insanity. Justin told Melissa we were safe and sound at Blood Viper, and would be staying there until we came up with a plan. He told her how much he loved her and hung up, looking around the room as if he had big news.

"Melissa told me that Margot insisted she and Logan take Gabriella and your mother back to Jade Moon. That way Greg wouldn't hurt them, since they have your and Daniel's scent on them. Margot stayed behind at Onyx Crescent to help Amber, she refused to leave with them."

I couldn't believe my aunt sacrificed herself like that. I was eternally grateful to her that she was willing to stay and help Amber, as well as impressed that she had the forethought to save our mates, Gabriella and my mother. I knew my aunt well enough to know she had a plan and would reach out to us as soon as she could. We just needed to sit tight for a bit and wait for her instructions.

Amber

I felt like I was in a daze, rejecting Daniel took a huge toll on me. Lana wasn't at her full strength to begin with and by rejecting Xander it weakened her more. She was currently curled up in the back of my mind and refusing to speak with me. I had never felt so alone. I was beginning to question if my decision was worth the hell I was putting everyone through. The hatred I saw in Olivia's eyes after I rejected Daniel broke my heart, almost as much as the look on Daniel's face. I was too far into it now to abandon my plan. Everyone's safety depended on my success. I just needed to find a way to let Olivia know that I wasn't the enemy and I was going to get rid of Greg. I just had to be very careful. I was worried about it so much and had no one to confide in. I wanted to go see if Gabriella was OK but didn't dare go near her room. If Greg found out about her he would surely kill her. I was startled out of my thoughts by a light knocking on my door. Zenah gently pushed the door open and gave me a small smile. She came in and closed the door behind her.

"Alpha Greg has summoned you for supper. He asked me to have you dressed formally, since you are celebrating his victory and your mating."

My stomach pitched at her mentioning the word mating. What the fuck was I thinking about going down the seduction route? Could I keep my emotions in check long enough to get this plan done?

"You don't have a choice now! You rejected our mates, you've ruined our happiness. So you better suck it up and work this plan through to the end." Lana's angry answer shocked me slightly. I knew she was mad at me, but I didn't think she would be quite that bitter. She knew I didn't do what I did lightly, it was our best chance to save everyone - especially Daniel. I would have to give her time, she would come

around eventually as she was my other half, or at least I hoped with all my heart.

As I absentmindedly tried to pick out an outfit for supper, I noticed Zenah staring at me oddly. "Do I have something on my face?"

"Oh, no, sorry." She blushed furiously. "I just had an odd encounter with an omega on the way up here, and I was trying to figure out how to bring it to your attention."

I cocked my head at her and urged her to continue, she had piqued my interest. "The omega said to tell you that Charlotte would be waiting for you, in the Jade section of the library, after dinner for your evening poetry session."

My breath hitched and my jaw dropped at what Zenah had just said. I needed to know who this omega was. She just let me know that Gabriella was safe at Jade Moon and the person wanted to meet me in the library after supper. It would be risky to say the least, but I would figure something out to throw Greg off.

"Zenah, who told you this message, it's very important that I know."

"She did not introduce herself, Luna Amber. Please forgive me. She was the same height as myself with what looked like green eyes. She was standing in the shadows of the hallway so I couldn't really see properly."

Zenah didn't need to say anymore, I knew exactly who had sent me that message. Margot!!

Chapter Twenty-Two

Amber

I got dressed as fast as possible for dinner, in a fancy low cut dress that I had hoped to one day wear on a date with Daniel. I didn't want to dress up, hell, I didn't even want to go down to dinner. I had to though. I had a role to play and if my plan was going to work I needed to be a hundred percent committed. Zenah was clear what Greg expected from me, and I needed him to believe that I was unequivocally his.

"Wow, Luna Amber, you look absolutely beautiful. The Alpha will surely agree and be very pleased."

An involuntary shudder coursed through my body and sent a wave of nausea through me. I gave Zenah a tight smile and a nod of thanks. I saw her face fall and felt instantly guilty for coming off so rude. She wasn't intentionally trying to trigger me. I let out a heavy sigh and looked Zenah in the eyes with an apology.

"I'm sorry if that came off rude. I know you were just trying to pay me a compliment."

"No, no, please don't apologise, Luna. I'm the one who needs to say sorry, I shouldn't have added the part about the Alpha. I know very well this is all a ruse."

"Indeed it is, but please we must never mention that again. Sometimes the walls have ears and I don't know what Greg's abilities as a hybrid are yet. I would rather be safe than sorry."

Zenah nodded in agreement and suggested we make our way down for supper. Keeping Greg waiting was never a good thing. We made our way to the dining room in silence. I was lost in thought. I just needed to get through this supper relatively quickly and then retire for the night. I would then detour to the library and meet with Margot. As we got to the door of the dining room, the quiet chatter I'd heard completely stopped; the whole room went silent with everyone's eyes suddenly on me, and all I heard was Greg.

"Ah, there she is! The lady of the hour, my beautiful little Luna."

My cheeks heated up instantly and started to burn from the embarrassment of his introduction. I looked at the faces of our pack members. I saw anger, disgust, curiosity, indifference. The wide variety broke my heart more than I cared to admit, everyone thought it was real and hated me for it. Greg motioned for me to join him at the head of the Alpha's table. As I walked by the other tables I heard the whispers of my pack members. "She is an opportunist", "she never loved Alpha Daniel", "she ran away to bring this monster back to the pack." The harsh whispers I heard kept getting worse, I wanted to turn on my heels and run out of there so fast. However, it was too late. I had reached Greg and he had already wrapped his arms around me and pulled me in for a hug.

"Since they already think so little of you, Amber, why not give them a show? That's what you wanted right?" Lana's icy bitter tone really hit a nerve. I had to steel myself not to burst into tears. I didn't let her know she had hurt me. I chose to fight back and solidify my ruse.

"You're right! I will give them a great show, thanks for the pep talk, it's showtime!"

I blocked Lana and instead of letting Greg hug me, I went up on my toes and wrapped my arms around his neck. I pressed my body fully against his and gave him a deep kiss. He responded instantly by bombarding my mouth with his tongue, it snaked in and took over mine, making me gag slightly. I covered it up by throwing in a moan for good measure. I regretted that as I felt Greg grow hard against my stomach. I tried to pull back slowly but Greg went to sit and pulled me down with him, our lips still locked together. I ended up straddling him on his chair, he grabbed my hips and my ass in his big hands, pushing me down onto his hardness as he ground his hips upwards. He let out a loud moan. I knew exactly what this fucker was doing, and I wanted to vomit in his mouth. I could feel his aura had expanded. Greg was holding all our pack members hostage with his power, forcing them to watch this disgusting display of him staking his claim on me.

I moaned again, hoping he would let my mouth go, which actually worked that time. He started kissing my neck like a starving man. I took this chance to gently but firmly push his chest back. He stopped and let a low growl rumble through his chest.

"Playing hard to get my little Luna? I'll have you know that's an even bigger turn on."

"No, I'm actually starving, I haven't eaten anything today."

"That is true. You're making a smart move. You will need energy for later!" Greg winked at me and let me slip off his lap. As I turned to take my own seat, he slapped my ass with a giant hand. The sound of his spanking reverberated around the dining room. I let out a squeak and rubbed my ass. I sat down quickly before he had the chance to smack the other side. He smirked at me and let out a hearty chuckle, I wanted to throat punch him so badly.

Supper passed without further incident. I spent most of the time trying to work out how I was going to get away from Greg to speak with Margot. I didn't have to wonder much longer, as it seemed she had everything worked out for me. As the omegas were clearing the table, Claudia came over to me and announced loud enough for Greg to hear, that my evening 'Goddess prayer session' was set up and waiting for me in the library. She gave me a firm nod and turned on her heels.

I held my breath waiting for Greg to comment and he didn't disappoint, he fell for the set-up hook, line and sinker.

"'Goddess prayer session'? You don't strike me as the devout type, my little Luna."

"Oh, I am very serious when it comes to properly praising our wonderful Moon Goddess. I follow all her teachings."

"All her teachings? I saw Greg's eyebrows reach his hairline. I knew which one he was most likely thinking of and I was going to use this to my advantage. This was going to be my ticket to make sure he didn't do anything before our ceremony.

"Yes, ALL her teachings, my Alpha! I have been saving myself for my mate."

I saw with dismay this caused Greg to get excited once more, his cock pulsing in his pants. I should have known he would enjoy the thought of deflowering a woman. Regardless of how excited he got, I would use this as my excuse to push for no sexual contact and he would have to obey; or at least I was really hoping that would be the case. Greg gave me an amused smile and nodded at me.

"Very well, my little Luna, go on and say your prayers to your Goddess. I will be waiting for you in our bed."

The wink he gave me made my skin crawl. I didn't waste any time getting up and making my way to the library with Zenah following behind me. When we reached the library, Zenah stood beside the door and told me to go in. She would stay outside and guard in case Greg decided to make an appearance. I thanked her and went into the library quickly. The lights were low, so it took me a moment to focus and spot the dark figure sitting in the back corner of the library. I walked over to Margot and threw my arms around her. A small sob escaped me as I hugged her tight.

"It's OK, Amber, I'm here now, you're not alone. Please tell me that it's not true though. Tell me you didn't reject Daniel for that psychopath?"

I choked on another sob as my eyes welled up with tears. I couldn't lie to Margot. I was hoping that if I explained the reasoning behind my choices she would understand, and not hate me for rejecting her nephew. I swallowed the lump in my throat and wiped away the tears that had spilled down my cheeks. I squared my shoulders and looked her straight in the eyes.

"Yes, I rejected Daniel in favour of Greg. However, not for the reasons you may think, or what people are whispering about."

Margot looked shocked at my answer but urged me to continue my explanation. She looked at me with kindness and curiosity, instead of anger and judgement, which gave me hope that she wouldn't hate me once all was said and done. I told her the entire sordid tale, and how I came to my choice of rejecting Daniel. It was to save his life. I desperately wanted to try and work things out once we took care of Greg. Margot looked relieved at my confession, she had feared that I had been brainwashed and would go through actually mating with Greg.

"Never in a million years would I dare to take that psycho as my mate, I can assure you that."

Margot gave me a huge hug and said she was going to help me get my plan solidified. I told her at that point that Greg was a hybrid wolf/witch. Her jaw hit the floor, I couldn't help but giggle a little at her reaction. She looked pensive for a moment before telling me she had a friend that had helped her years ago who was a witch. She would ask her if she had any ideas about how to block his powers, in order to give us a level playing field.

"He's large and strong, but nothing you can't handle, Amber. It's his magic that is the danger. If my friend can give us any ideas, I will let you know as soon as possible. We will meet like this again tomorrow. You've been here longer than the Goddess prayers usually take. Go back to Greg so he doesn't get suspicious!"

I looked at my watch and saw that she was correct. I would just tell Greg that I needed extra healing time after the rejection. I thanked Margot for not giving up on me and bid her good night. I left the library feeling lighter and more at peace, knowing that someone understood my decisions and was willing to help me get rid of Greg. Zenah was waiting patiently for me outside the library. She didn't ask me any questions. She simply nodded and followed me back up to my room, wishing me a good night outside my door. I took a deep breath knowing I was going to need all the strength I could muster in order to survive the night with Greg.

Daniel

After being put to bed by Olivia and Justin, I just stayed curled up in a ball for hours in silence. Xander wasn't talking to me, he was too hurt by the rejection. At some point I fell asleep and woke up in a familiar place. I felt instantly calm and at peace, a feeling I never thought I'd feel again after Amber rejected me. I looked around the meadow and saw Selene sitting by the small stream. She looked at me with sad eyes and beckoned me to come sit with her. I walked over to her slowly, admiring the beauty of my surroundings. As I reached her she patted the ground next to her, I sat down and she reached for my hand. Her small hands were warm and soft; they felt like life itself came from them. I looked up into her eyes and saw tears shimmering, I was confused why she would cry. She was a Goddess with ultimate power, so I gently asked her what was wrong.

"I am so sad that one of my children could be this evil and that you were affected by his evilness, so soon after having your whole world turned upside down."

"It's fine, I deserved what I got Selene. I took Amber for granted and pushed her away, right into his waiting arms."

Selene squeezed my hand in sympathy, I gave her a half smile that didn't reach my eyes. She gave me a pointed look that I wasn't understanding.

"You didn't push Amber into Greg's arms. She rejected you to save your life! She loved you so much she sacrificed herself to make sure you lived for Gabriella."

I was shell shocked by that revelation. "What do you mean she sacrificed herself? Are you telling me she wasn't brainwashed by that freak?"

Selene shook her head solemnly. "No, she wasn't brainwashed Daniel, she made a split second decision to put herself in harm's way to save you, by pretending to want Greg."

I was thankful to be sitting at that moment, I felt like I was drowning. Amber loved me enough to fake wanting that insane Alpha so I could live. I thought back to earlier and realized that she had begged Greg not to kill us as a favour to her. I couldn't believe she did that, and I couldn't tell if I loved her more or if I was even more angry at her for pulling such a dangerous stunt. Selene could read my mind and told me not to be angry with Amber, she had done all she could under the circumstances.

"At this point, does it even really matter? She rejected me, so we no longer have a chance."

"Well...not quite, you see...I didn't let the bond break!"

"What are you talking about, Selene? I felt the bond snap, it was very real!"

"I'm happy to hear my powers are that convincing!" Selene could barely conceal her smile and giggled.

"Am I to believe that you faked our mate-bond ending?" I looked at her incredulously.

"Yes, Daniel, you would believe correctly. I needed you to think it was real, it was the only way to protect Amber and all of you. The bond can be restored if Amber is able to defeat Greg, which by the way she has to figure out on her own! Getting rid of Greg without your physical help will empower her and help her heal from this whole ordeal. You can help from behind the scenes, but she needs to be the one who executes saving the world from my mistake."

"How can it be restored by Greg being taken out? I'm not sure I understand, Selene."

"Once Greg is gone you will be able to reconnect with Amber. She will feel more powerful that you trusted her decision making. If you both want to be together and you work as the team I know you are. The bond will return once you mate and mark her, it will snap back into place."

I couldn't believe what I was hearing, I was getting a second chance at making everything right. I couldn't believe my good fortune, a lone tear slid down my cheek. Selene patted me on the back for comfort.

"May I stay here for a little while longer and just enjoy the peaceful feeling this meadow gives me?"

"Of course, take the time you need to regroup. The fight won't be easy, but Amber is strong, fearless and highly intelligent. I believe in her and I know your belief in her will help her confidence soar."

I had no words so I just nodded and let out a deep breath. My mind was going a mile a minute, but I silenced it to soak in the peace of the meadow with our Moon Goddess sitting close by. I must have fallen asleep because when I opened my eyes I was back in my old room in Alpha Arnold's house. I took a moment to reflect on what Selene told me and then bounced out of bed and ran downstairs to find everyone. I had no idea what time it was but I hoped it was time to plan. We needed to help Amber get rid of Greg so I could prove to her how amazing she was and seal the deal with my mate.

"It's about damn time you woke up and smelled reality, human! Now, are you going to do things my way or what?"

"Welcome back, Xander, let's go get our mate!"

Chapter Twenty-Three

*O*livia

We sat in Alpha Arnold's office, tossing around some ideas of how we could go back and help Amber and Margot, when the phone rang, startling us all. Arnold answered and a relieved look crossed his face instantly.

"Margot! It's so great to hear your voice. Yes, Olivia is right here, one moment please."

I jumped up and practically yanked the phone out of Arnold's hand. I was so excited and relieved to hear Margot's voice that tears welled up in my eyes. I thanked her for taking care of everything and asked her if she had seen Amber.

"I have spoken with Amber this evening, she is holding up for now, but she's got quite a long road ahead."

"What do you mean, a long road ahead, Margot?"

"Oh, my sweet girl, Amber sacrificed herself to save Daniel and the rest of you!"

"How? She was either brain washed or chose Greg willingly." The second the words left my mouth I regretted it, I sounded so angry and petty, like I needed to punish Amber. Margot caught my tone and scoffed at me before putting me in my place.

"Well, Olivia, you need to understand, Amber did not choose Greg willingly nor was she brainwashed. She saw Daniel about to be killed and sprung into action by faking her attraction to Greg. She wanted to save Daniel and buy you all time to get away, she had a plan. It will take a bit of time to get all the pieces in place but ultimately should work at getting rid of Greg. I've asked a witch friend of mine for help with part of this plan to make it safer for her."

Margot went on to tell me the rest of the conversation she and Amber had, as well as the news that Greg was a powerful hybrid witch/wolf. That explained why she needed the help of her witchy friend. I saw what he had done earlier but didn't realise he was the one with the power, to say I was shocked and slightly nervous was an understatement. It's one thing to fight a strong alpha wolf that I was evenly matched with, but it was a completely another thing to fight a strong alpha wolf with unknown powers. I thought over what Margot had just told me; one thing was still bothering me about the whole scenario.

"Are you sure she's telling you the truth, Margot? I want to believe her but her rejecting Daniel was very much real and intentional."

"Olivia, she knew she had to do it to make Greg believe she was serious, she didn't want to reject Daniel. In order to put her plan into action it was needed."

I didn't get a chance to respond to what Margot had just said, because Daniel came bursting into the office. "THE REJECTION WASN'T REAL!"

We all stared at him slack jawed as he looked at all of us with wild eyes. I was suddenly worried his mind had snapped from the rejection and he was starting a psychotic episode. Margot asked me to put her on speaker phone, which I obliged. She couldn't see Daniel but I figured she had an idea that he looked half crazed from the sound of his voice. She gently asked Daniel to explain what he meant by the rejection wasn't real.

"The Moon Goddess came to me in my dreams, and told me that Amber only rejected me to save my life from Greg. She needed that psycho to truly believe her intentions with him were real. She told me that once Greg is gone, if Amber and I work together and get back to a place where we mate and mark, our bond will snap back into place. Selene didn't allow the bond to break as a reward for Amber's quick thinking to save me."

Margot cleared her throat on the other end of the phone, and I knew that it was aimed at me, I already felt the shame washing over me. How could I think the worst of my best friend? I spoke up and apologized, letting her know she was right. This earned me a strange look from Daniel which I just waved off. I asked Daniel if the Moon Goddess had said anything else of importance, and he then told us that she said Amber had to be the one to ultimately get rid of Greg. She was going to need our help though and we would know when the time was right.

"When Amber and I spoke she told me she was aiming to get rid of him the day of their ceremony, she needs time to figure out how to take him down. I'm waiting for an answer from my witch friend, who can hopefully help her. Once we get word back we can come up with a plan of our own to work in conjunction with Amber's."

We all agreed we would sit tight, as hard as that was and wait for answers from Margot's friend. Daniel asked Margot to tell Amber that he would never give up on her, and they would be together in the end. Margot agreed and bid us all good night. I asked her to be careful which she laughed at as she hung up. "Where's the fun in that?!"

Amber

Walking into my bedroom, after my meeting with Margot took the wind out of my sails. Greg was lying on the bed in what I assumed he thought was a seductive pose. I was internally gagging, talking myself down from actually throwing up all over myself. I did a good job of keeping my face neutral and even managed a playful smile. Greg patted the bed and I shook my head at him, his expression changed instantly to one of annoyance with anger boiling up under the surface.

"This isn't optional, my little Luna, you will join me on the bed right now."

"Alpha, I was just praying to the Moon Goddess, I made a vow which I fully intend to keep!"

"You may believe in that bullshit, but I don't! If I say I want you now, it's now!"

I bit the bullet and knew I'd have to give him a crumb to make him back off. I gave him my big sad doe eyes and sashayed over to him on the bed. I crawled over to him seductively and sat on my knees in front of him. I placed one hand on his bare chest and the other on his cheek, bending down I gave him a sweet deep kiss. He moaned which made me shudder in disgust, which luckily he took for pleasure. I gently pushed away and with my doe eyes let him know how it was going to be.

"You may not believe in that bullshit, my sexy Alpha, but I do! I want to keep my vow until our ceremony. Our first time is going to be the best night of my life. Mating and marking the most powerful Alpha isn't a small affair. When you take me it has to be perfect!"

I saw his expression soften and I knew I had him, I thanked the Moon Goddess for giving me such incredible acting skills. I would possibly believe myself, if I wasn't so nauseated by every word I spoke. He gently cupped my cheek and ran his thumb over my bottom lip.

"Very well, my little Luna, I will behave! But know this, the night of our ceremony all bets are off and I will be taking you long and hard. Over and over and over again. When I'm done with you, I will be the new god you worship for the rest of your life."

"I look forward to that night my Alpha, I bid you goodnight, for now."

I moved over to the other side of the bed and urged myself to fall asleep. Sleep was merciful and took me quickly. When I woke up Greg was already gone. I sighed in relief but was startled by a knock on the door. I went to answer and found Zenah on the other side with breakfast.

"Good Morning, Luna Amber, Alpha Greg asked me to bring you breakfast. He would like you to join him in his office once you're done."

"Thank you, Zenah, please come in and put the tray on the table by the window and the book shelves. I'll just change quickly and be right out, you will stay won't you?"

Zenah agreed and came into my room with the tray, closing the door behind her. I ran off to the bathroom to freshen up and changed in my closet. Five minutes later I was sitting next to Zenah at my small corner table, offering to share my breakfast with her.

"Zenah, can I ask you why you serve Greg but are supposedly on my side? You've helped me quite a bit but how do I know I can trust you? I'm sorry if that is rude of me."

She looked slightly crestfallen, but nodded her head in silent agreement. she cleared her throat and stared ahead at one of my bookshelves with a far away look on her face.

"You and I are more similar than you know, Luna Amber. I too am just acting my part! Greg has deemed me a lowly omega, but a loyal one. Or so he thinks, it's all part of the ruse. I only follow his orders to make him trust me. My ultimate goal is to kill the bastard."

Such a simple statement but one I wasn't expecting the mild mannered Zenah to make. I was taken aback by what she said and was trying to think of reasons why she would want to kill Greg, besides the obvious - being a tyrannical psychopath.

"May I ask what he has done to you for you to have that response?"

"Of course you may ask. I wasn't born an omega, my father was the Beta of our pack. He had served Greg's father loyally for more than thirty years. When Greg's father had his Luna burned at the stake for speaking ill against Greg, my father stood up and tried to stop it from happening. Sadly he wasn't successful and was quite vocal in his disgust over the situation."

Zenah paused and took a deep breath looking me in the eyes. I didn't like where this was going.

"The former Alpha killed my father, he slit his throat with Greg and I in the room. I was only two years old, Greg was eight. I will never forget the glee in Greg's eyes as he watched my father bleed out. Even at a young age I could see what true evil was. I knew I wanted to hurt the Alpha for what he did and as I grew older I vowed to kill him for what he had done. As I told you yesterday it was poetic justice that Greg murdered his father in cold blood those few years later. Since I never got to avenge my father by taking out my former Alpha I moved my vendetta to Greg. He is a sick individual who took great pleasure in watching my father suffer as he died. Then, once he became Alpha he made me an omega and treated me like shit. So, death is coming for him."

I sat there with my mouth wide open in shock, this mild, sweet woman was more than she appeared to be. She wasn't as young as I first thought and she has been carrying this torch against Greg for much longer. I made the snap decision that Zenah would help me take out Greg on the night of the ceremony. I told her what I was planning and asked her to help me rid the world of him. A beautiful smile lit up her face.

"I was hoping you would ask!"

Chapter Twenty-Four

Chapter 24

Greg

As I was sitting alone for breakfast I looked around the dining room at my new pack as they nervously rushed around looking down at their feet. I appreciated that these wolves knew who their new master was and they understood their places in the pack. I felt like this pack was given to me by fate. It was as if it was tailor made for me, just like Amber was the perfect addition to my life. I sighed happily to myself, last night didn't go exactly the way I wanted it, but I had my sweet little Luna exactly where I wanted her. I couldn't wait for our ceremony, I was going to take her to bed and fuck her for a week straight. I didn't get to sit in that glorious thought for too long; Samson had to insert himself and ruin my visions.

"Do you really think she wanted you? You can't be that stupid Greg can you?"

"What the hell are you going on about mutt? Of course she wanted me! Were you not there last night, the way she kissed me, and how she told me she couldn't wait to be marked and mated by me?"

"You know people can fake their actions and words right? I don't trust her! She jumped into your arms too quickly. I think if you looked deeper or questioned her motives you would be able to see through her as well."

"I think you're completely wrong Sam and I no longer wish to have that conversation with you. Do I make myself clear?"

Samson mumbled something about me being blind and demented, but stopped arguing and left me alone. I shook my head. I knew my wolf could be a pain in the ass sometimes, so I took what he was saying with a grain of salt and went about my day. I had to make some important calls so I informed my little Luna I couldn't meet with her after breakfast and in the end I didn't have time to have supper with her either. I only got to our room that night after Amber had already gotten back from her prayer session. I didn't want to try my luck since the night before I promised I wouldn't push her, but I really wanted to prove my point to Samson. I figured it wouldn't hurt to at least kiss her a little and see where that went. Amber was sitting on a chair in the corner of her room reading, so I went over and scooped her up, placing her on my lap and hoped for the best.

Amber

I had such a wonderful Greg free day, I couldn't believe how lucky I had been to not have to deal with that man all day. Margot also had fantastic news for me, her witchy friend was able to help us. The only downside was; I needed to fill a glass bottle with Greg's blood, and get it back to Margot as quickly as possible. We had already decided I would leave the bottle in a specific hiding spot in my bathroom, and Margot would have it picked up the next day, while an omega would be cleaning my room. I was excited to get the final details falling into place, the only down side was how to get the blood out of Greg. I was sitting in a chair reading a book when Greg came into the room, I pretended to not notice him. He scooped me up and put me on his lap where I felt his cock instantly poking my ass. It was unbelievable to me that after he promised me last night he wouldn't try anything with me, here he was ready to try again. It was OK, I was going to use this as the way I got the blood. I decided right there, we were going to get a little too hot and heavy, to the point I would scratch his back.

"I don't like that idea, Amber, there has to be another way?"

"I'm sorry, Lana, there really isn't one. I'm not going to let him go all the way, don't worry."

Lana blocked me, and I was just as disgusted as her but had to press on. I turned to straddle Greg and coyly asked him if he was happy to see me. His hooded gaze told me everything I needed to know, he leaned in for a kiss which I accepted. I kissed him and swivled my hips, grinding myself against his erection which earned me a loud moan from Greg. He was so damn loud it was annoying. I broke our kiss and took his shirt off; I was going to need easy access to his skin. I went back to kissing him and ran my regular nails along his back which made him shiver. He in turn took my top off which I didn't protest because I needed him to think we were getting heated. I ground my hips into him again and jumped slightly when his hands went under my skirt and cupped my ass. I guess I chose the right day to wear a skirt.

Greg stood up suddenly and made his way to my bed. He dropped me gently and started to untie his belt, but I stopped him by spreading my legs and running my foot along his chest, up to his shoulder while giving him a pleading look. He seemed to get the hint as his eyes darkened and he kissed down my leg towards my pussy. I didn't want this at all but knew I had no choice. It was too close to the end game now, I needed to do what needed to be done. I shuddered in disgust as he removed my panties, he of course thought it was in pleasure so it worked out for me.

Greg licked me once from the back to the front of my pussy, he looked up to me and I nodded for him to continue, but begged him to be gentle as it was my first time. I heard Lana laughing at my lie in the back of my mind, I told her to hush and get ready to elongate her claws when I gave the word.

"Oh, I'll gladly claw the shit out of that fucker."

"You have to be gentle enough that he thinks we're in the throes of passion, and not that we're trying to hurt him."

Lana grumbled but agreed she'd do as I asked, that was progress at least on her part. Greg was not good at going down on a woman, I felt like I was being licked by a starved dog who wasn't sure where the food was. I had to pretend it was the best thing since sliced bread, so I put on a show of moaning and writhing around on the bed, begging him not to stop. After a solid five minutes I'd had enough and told Greg not to stop, because I was SO close to my release, starting to shake my legs. NOW! I told Lana and she elongated our claws scratching deeply up Greg's back, filling our claws with his blood. I cried out my fake orgasm and squeezed his head tightly between my thighs for good measure, before jumping out of bed, rushing to the bathroom while sobbing and crying. I slammed the door and locked it, leaving Greg on the bed, bleeding and perplexed. I could hear him cursing and yelling at me that I clawed him too deeply. I rushed over to my vanity and got the bottle out of its spot and emptied my nails into it. I got mostly a full bottle as it wasn't very big. I was glad my sacrifice was worth it at least. I was washing my hands when I heard Lana cursing at me.

"I can't believe you let that fucking psycho go down on us like that, and he was absolutely terrible!"

"It was either that, Lana, or we would have had to take his cock in our mouth, and then what would we have done for the blood?"

"I would have bit it off, plenty of blood then!" Lana growled before retreating to the back of my mind once again. I braced myself against the sink and shook my head, she would have to forgive me one day. Lana was being so stubborn and acting as if I was enjoying any of that bullshit, I wanted to shower so badly but I knew I couldn't leave Greg alone after that little outburst. I had to go out and do damage control. I washed my hands for a second time to make sure all the blood was out of my nails before I stashed the bottle in its pouch and hid it where Margot had told me to. I took a deep cleansing breath, brought tears back into my eyes and put a sheepish look on my face as I slowly went back into my bedroom.

"There you are my little Luna, what the fuck was all that about? You clawed me really deep!"

Greg's tone held a mix of anger, concern and suspicion, so I really needed to sell this story for all it was worth. I forced a blush onto my cheeks and looked up at Greg bashfully through my eyelashes.

"Ummm...well...I...I've...I've...I have..."

"Are you going to spit it out this century, little Luna? I'm not understanding you right now."

I could sense the anger rising in Greg and figured I needed to ramp up my performance. I hung my head low and started to cry again for a minute before I looked up at him with broken eyes.

"I'm so sorry I hurt you, I've never orgasmed before Greg! It felt so good and was so intense I scratched you, then I realised I had just broken my vow to the Goddess and became really upset and burst into tears. I'm just overwhelmed, over stimulated and embarrassed as hell about it. That's why I ran to the bathroom. I also wish that I could have waited until our ceremony."

"Oh, shit, I'm a fool! I got so carried away I forgot you didn't have a clue what an orgasm felt like."

Greg face palmed himself and looked remorsefully at me. I wrapped my arms protectively around myself and shrugged away from him. I looked back down at the floor so I hadn't noticed when he stepped forward and wrapped me in a strong hug. This made me stiffen immediately which resulted in Greg hugging me tighter.

"Don't be that way, little Luna. Can you forgive me? I didn't mean to make you break your vow to your stupid Goddess, besides we didn't have sex so she'll forgive you! Think of it as a test of the operating system; you have that, and so much more to look forward to, once we've had our ceremony."

"Wow, this one's a real winner, Amber. Great choice!" Lana pushed forward to scoff at me.

"Lana, you know damn well he isn't a choice I wanted! This is the only way we can save ourselves, Daniel and the pack. Stop this shit right now, we need to work as a team or we're never getting away from this fucker."

"OK, OK, I'll be nicer...as long as you know I hate this shit with a passion and you owe me one after he's dead."

I rolled my eyes at my wolf and told her we'd talk once we were psycho free; for now she needed to trust me and give me back-up without attitude when I asked. This was all getting to be too much for me and if I was going to make it to the ceremony I needed my other half to show me some compassion. I was startled out of my argument with Lana when I heard Greg clear his throat, I had forgotten to answer him.

"Of course I forgive you, my sexy Alpha, I was just caught off guard that's all. I was also swept up in the passionate moment, so it's not all your fault if I broke a tiny piece of my vow. Your big strong arms wrapped around me have given me the space I needed to calm down and see reason."

"Well then, I'm glad I could be of service to my lady."

"I've got to say Greg, if that was a small taste of what's to come I don't think the pack will see us much!"

I let a small giggle out and gave Greg my most seductive smile, I regretted that instantly as he growled hungrily at me and picked me up. I gasped as he held me walking towards the bed, I looked at him with panic.

"Don't worry, little Luna, I'm only bringing you to bed and tucking you in. I promise I won't do anything until our ceremony in a few weeks."

"Thank you, I appreciate that."

Greg placed me gently in bed and tucked me in as he said he would, then went to the other side of the bed and stayed on his side. I fell asleep dreaming of Daniel being there instead, and holding me; I slept like a baby.

I woke up the next morning to a knock on my door and an empty bed. I sighed in relief that I could enjoy my morning Greg free again andI yelled at the person to come in. I assumed it was Zenah but was surprised to see the young omega Claudia come into the room. She bowed to me and told me she was here to collect my towels for the wash. I understood at that moment, she had been sent by Margot to collect the bottle of blood. I nodded at her and bid her to go right ahead, they were where they needed to be, Claudia smiled nervously and went swiftly into the bathroom. She emerged a few moments later with a few random towels and the pouch tucked into the end of one of the towels. She gave me a nod and wished me a good day before leaving the room as quickly as she had come.

I sent a quick prayer to the Moon Goddess that Margot's witch friend could process that quickly, and we could get this show on the road. I didn't want to keep this up for another week or two, it was exhausting and I was so worried I'd slip up and give myself away. Greg had seemed so suspicious the night before, he must have had a slight doubt. I needed to be extremely careful from there on out.

I got out of bed, went to shower and put the water much hotter than I usually do, needing to burn the feeling of Greg's touches off my body. After my shower I felt a lot better and decided to take my chances and go down for a late breakfast. I had taken an extra long shower of over an hour, that left me hope that Greg would already be off doing other things so I could eat in peace. I ran into Zenah in the hall on my way down to the dining room, she gave me a genuine smile and we walked together in happy silence. Just before we reached the dining room door Zenah leaned over to fix the collar on my shirt, whispering in my ear that Margot had already given the blood to her witch friend, and would have the potion back in time for our meeting that evening. She backed away as if she hadn't said a word and loudly announced.

"There you go, my Luna, now your collar is where it should be and you are looking good for Alpha." She winked at me as I gave her a genuine smile, grateful for her impeccable timing, when Greg suddenly appeared at the door on his way out.

"Well, the omega is correct, you do look fantastic this morning, my little Luna. I hope you slept well?"

"Oh, I did, my sexy Alpha, thanks to you!" I gave him a little playful wink which made him chuckle. Hearing this threw me off guard. Greg wasn't the type of man to chuckle, it was off-putting. I kept my facial expression neutral, however, and asked him where he was off to.

He said he would be going to look around the perimeter of the pack to work out a new patrol schedule. I told him to have fun as he gave me a chaste kiss, smiled and went on my way into the dinning room with Zenah hot on my heels. I sat down at the closest table and was served very quickly by Claudia. As she placed my plate down I noticed a piece of paper sticking out slightly from under the plate. I slid it out and put it on my lap under the table where I was able to read it.

Make sure to have 4 large glasses of wine tonight with your supper, Claudia will serve you and it will be grape juice. No actual alcohol! Try and act as drunk as possible, all will be explained later.

Margot

I nodded to myself, slid the note back under my plate and began to eat my breakfast as if nothing happened. I looked up to see Zenah smirking at me. I got the feeling she knew what the note meant, but as per my own instructions we weren't talking about it. Once I was done Claudia came and took everything away. Zenah and I went for a walk at that point, she told me Greg had given her a long list of things to do and he wasn't going to be around much today. I wished her luck and watched her head for the kitchen where all the other omegas were busy working.

I wasn't sure what to do with myself so I went back to my room and chose to read for a bit. I couldn't concentrate very well, so instead did a bit of strategizing for how to take Greg down. By mid afternoon I was getting bored when my phone pinged, it startled me as my phone had been silent since Greg took over the pack. I completely lost my composure when I read the message, it was from Daniel.

> Amber, I was a fool for taking your feelings for granted, I will spend the rest of my life making it up to you, once we are reunited. Stay strong, I believe in you and I know you are going to beat Greg. I am proud to call you my mate, and thank the Goddess for your quick thinking. Thank you for saving my life.

> I love you!

> Yours always, Daniel xxxx

I couldn't help the tears that came hard and fast; my phone screen disappearing for a solid two minutes before I got the tears under control. I re-read the last line about a hundred times, smiling through my tears, then did the smart thing and deleted the message from my phone. I triple checked it was completely gone, just in case Greg decided to check my phone. Daniel took a huge risk sending me that message, I wish I could answer it but I didn't want to put myself in more danger.

Daniel's message sparked a new-found fire in my belly and I decided to change and go down to train for a few hours before supper. I needed to be in top fighting form if I was going to go up against Greg and win. The afternoon flew by and before I knew it I was sitting down for supper with Greg, who was quite interested in my afternoon training session. I sensed the suspicion again so I smiled brightly and answered him, as if it was a totally normal occurrence.

"I was feeling sluggish. Before meeting you I was training to be the pack's Beta; I needed to be in peak form, so I became a gym rat. I missed the feeling of stretching my muscles and, after last night, I realised I'm going to need to have some pretty good stamina."

I giggled and winked at him, which seemed to work as Greg's eyes darkened and I could smell his arousal instantly. I wanted to vomit so badly at that moment but had to keep my happy charade up.

"Good call, my little Luna! I'd hate to hurt you, so maybe daily training until our ceremony is a good idea."

I was so happy he believed me that I thanked him for the good idea, and saw my chance for stage two of the plan for the night. As Claudia was serving me my supper I grabbed her arm before she walked away.

"Omega, bring me and my sexy Alpha a glass of wine! We are celebrating tonight, make sure it's a good size glass too."

"Yes, my Luna." Claudia played the meek, scared little omega role perfectly. She scurried off to the kitchen and came back a few moments later with two glasses of wine for Greg and I. The look Claudia gave me told me mine really was grape juice, as the note had said.

I raised my glass and proposed a toast to 'us', which Greg happily went along with, both of us took sips to try the wine. Greg liked the vintage of whatever wine they had given him, while I began chugging my grape juice happily as if it were the wine asking for refills, just like Margot had advised.

"Whoa, slow down there my little Luna or you will become a drunk Luna." Greg looked a little shocked at how fast I was downing the wine but then an amused smile spread across his face, I could only guess what disgusting thoughts were going through his mind.

"Don't worry aboot meeee, my soxy Alpa." I made sure to slur my words so he believed I was getting tipsy, his amused look grew into chuckles so I guess I was believable. As I took the last sip of my wine Claudia appeared to clear the table, and let me know that my 'Goddess prayer session' was all set up in the library when I was ready. I smiled up at Greg and told him my Goddess called. He rolled his eyes at me and told me to go. I got up, tripped over to him, gave him a sloppy kiss then turned on seemingly wobbly legs and zigzagged out of the dining room. I met up with Zenah in the hall, who gave me a smirk which I returned with a wink. I knew I was being extra at that moment, but Margot had told me to be a convincing drunk. I think I had succeeded, but only time would tell.

I walked into the dimly lit library and went to the back, where Margot was hiding in the shadows. She came and gave me a hug. "You've done a great job, Amber! The amount of blood was perfect, my friend was able to make what we needed."

"That is amazing news! What do I have to do, now?"

Margot produced two small vials, from her pocket, full of a clear liquid and carefully handed them to me. "Tomorrow, you need to make sure Greg drinks both of these vials. One in the morning and one at supper. The potion takes two days to work, it will siphon all his magic out of his body without him noticing at all. You just have to make sure he doesn't need to use any during that time."

"Fabulous, no pressure!" I rolled my eyes.

"I know, Amber, I'm sorry. We're practically at the finish line, just hang in there. After supper on the second day you will be able to fight a completely normal alpha male. No added power."

"I like the sound of that, I'm ready for this nightmare to be over. Margot, why did you want me to drink so much wine?"

"Oh, that! Hahahaha, well you're going to go back to your room right now, and say the Goddess spoke to you and you must do the ceremony in two days, instead of two weeks. If you're drunk he won't argue with you and will think the change in ceremony time is perfect. He knows sober you wanted all the extra time to prepare to be Luna."

"That makes good sense, thank you for thinking about that! If I were to just change my mind on a whim would make him suspicious, which he already seems to be. Drunk, silly me, he'll believe wants to move it."

Margot gave me the vials and told me to go, she wished me luck. Before I turned to leave I asked Margot if she could let Daniel know I got his text, and I would be holding him to his promise. Margot lifted an eyebrow but asked no questions, she simply agreed to deliver the message and bid me good night.

I left the library and discreetly gave the vials to Zenah at the door. I whispered that one full vial needed to be in a coffee the Alpha would drink at breakfast, and asked her to bring the coffee to our room; I'd keep him busy. Zenah nodded, let me know she had spoken with Margot and knew what needed to be done. I smiled and wished her a good night as I speed-walked to my room.

Before opening the door I hyped myself up for the final big performance. I burst through the door of my room and fell on my face giggling. Greg ran over to help me up with a concerned look on his face. I waved him off with a laugh as he tried to steady me but I just kept swaying side to side.

"Are you OK, my little Luna? You busted into the room like the devil was chasing you."

"I am AMUZNG...I had the bost prayer sesssshin with the Goddesssssssssss."

"Oh? Do tell." Greg looked at me with interest.

"The Moon Goddesssssss came to me and tolds me she things we need to mate soon! She said she knowssssssssss I thing you're sooooooo sexyyyy and I won't be ablllllle to hold on much longer. She toooold me to pick a day and mate you. Can we mate Friyay? I love friyay...it's my favurit day."

Greg looked momentarily taken aback, but then a slow cheshire-cat grin spread across his face. "This Friday? Two days from now? That's not too soon for you, my little Luna?"

"Nooooooo, I wanna maaaate, my soxy strooongggg Alpha!"

"Your wish is my command, my pet. I guess our ceremony is now Friday!"

"Oh, my Gawdess. Thank you SOOOOOOOOOOOOO much! I can wait!" I hiccuped and fell forward for good measure, at which Greg thankfully caught me. He picked me up and told me I needed to get to bed and sleep off all that wine. I snuggled into him and mumbled a thank you and pretended to pass out. He tucked me in and then turned out the lights. All I heard was Lana's voice as I drifted off to sleep. *"Checkmate Motherfucker!"*

Chapter Twenty-Five

Amber

I woke up with a pep in my step that I hadn't expected. The knowledge that my plan was coming to fruition, and the hell I was putting up with was nearly over, made me giddy. I woke up before Greg, I decided to go down to the kitchen and get him his coffee and add the first potion to it as instructed. I slipped out of bed silently and went downstairs, as usual Zenah met me in the hall.

"You're up early, Luna Amber, is everything OK?"

"Yes, Zenah, everything is great! I wanted to bring the Alpha his coffee this morning as a surprise." I winked at her and she nodded while patting her pocket, letting me know she had the vial on her. I rewarded her with a bright smile as I practically skipped down the stairs. We walked into the kitchen to find the omegas working on breakfast. Claudia and Margot were at one counter chopping fruit, so I walked over and bid them good morning. Margot smiled at me and Claudia shyly bid me a good morning. I went over to the coffee station and poured out Greg's coffee. I noticed he liked to drink it with six sugars and one cream. My stomach rolled as I added the excessive amount of sugar to the cup. I added the cream then looked at Zenah for the special ingredient, she was reaching into her pocket when Lana screamed at me.

"NO, don't put the potion in this cup!"

"Why not, Lana? What's the problem?"

"He's been suspicious of us, and you've never brought him coffee before. He won't drink this cup, I have a very strong feeling. The potion will be wasted, please bring him this one and you'll see."

"Lana, don't you think you're being a bit paranoid?! I agree he has been a smidge suspicious but do you really think he won't drink coffee?"

"Please, Amber, I need you to believe me. I can't keep living like this and if he wastes the potion we're fucked, literally!! I can't do it and won't do it!"

"OK, OK, you don't need to be so dramatic."

I sighed heavily, scrubbed my hands down my face and motioned to Zenah to hang onto the vial. She looked at me confused and concerned. I told her in hushed tones what Lana had said and she nodded in understanding.

"Your wolf does make a good point, Luna Amber. Greg doesn't trust anyone usually. If he were to dump the first cup we will be prepared with a second cup. It will contain the secret ingredient don't worry."

"And, what if he doesn't dump this cup? Then what? I'll have to figure out a way to get the damn potion into him."

"Oh, he will dump it, Amber, trust me!" Lana was so smug with her response I wish I could have punched her, but I knew how crazy I would look punching myself so I refrained. I clenched my fists, picked up the coffee I had made and headed back upstairs. I advised Zenah and Margot to be on standby, in case I needed the second cup.

Greg

I woke up with a huge smile on my face, Amber had decided to move our ceremony up to Friday in two days. I was finally going to get to fuck that little Luna of mine. I rolled over to grab Amber but was dismayed to find the bed empty. Where could she have gone? I got up and went to check the bathroom, thinking maybe she was taking a soak in the tub before starting her day. The bathroom was dark and empty, I started to get pissed off. Where the fuck was she?

"Now will you believe that she's off plotting against us?"

"Listen mutt, I think you're completely off base with that accusation. Maybe she went to train early?!"

"Sure, Greg, tell yourself that! For such a strong, ruthless Alpha, you sure are being dumb as fuck right now."

I put up a wall instantly, it was too bloody early to be told off by my wolf. Samson was really being a dick, but could he be right though? I scrubbed my hands over my face in frustration. I was about to scream out a stream of obscenities when the door to the room opened and Amber waltzed in. She looked momentarily taken aback that I was standing in the middle of the room. There was something else in her eyes that I couldn't quite place.

"Guilt, that look is guilt, Greg. She's up to something, I can feel it to the tip of my tail." Samson had pushed through the wall I'd put up and was angry as hell. For the first time since he said something I had a

gnawing pit in my stomach. I watched as that odd look disappeared from her face and was replaced with an instant cheery smile, as if nothing was amiss. I narrowed my eyes to really look at her as she walked closer holding a mug in her hand.

"I was so excited about what we decided last night, I wanted to surprise you with coffee in bed. Breakfast wasn't ready yet."

"That was kind of you, my little Luna, you've never brought me coffee before!"

"No, I haven't and I'm sorry. I've been slacking! My sexy Alpha deserves to be treated like the king he is."

I puffed out my chest at her praise, damn straight! This woman was going to worship the ground I walked on. I decided to humour Samson and took a dig at Amber. "You looked a little shell-shocked when you walked into the room, why was that, little Luna?"

"I wasn't expecting you to be awake and I wanted to surprise you. I was sad I may have woken you up, that's all."

"She's lying, Greg, I can smell it wafting off of her."

"Easy, Sam, she seemed sincere, but I will be cautious."

"Here's your morning coffee, Alpha, just as you like it; six sugars and a splash of cream."

"Oh wow, you know how I like it?" I was stunned that she had been that observant with regards to what I liked. My heart squeezed with pride and the knot in my stomach loosened slightly. Samson was wrong, she really did care for me. He'd see soon enough on Friday when we were marking our mate.

"DO NOT DRINK THAT COFFEE YOU STUBBORN ASS-HOLE!"

"Are you for real, right now?"

"I won't say it again, human, drink that coffee and I will push forward and rip her throat out."

"Fuck you Samson! You wouldn't dare!?"

"Don't fuck around, Greg, or you will find out really quick that I'm very serious."

"Fine! I will drop the cup and prove to you there was nothing wrong with the damn coffee." I reached out my hand for Amber to transfer the cup over to me, when she started to let go of the cup I moved my hand back a few inches. The handoff was missed and the cup clattered to the floor, smashing into pieces and splashing coffee everywhere. There was a look of horror on Amber's face. I couldn't tell though if she was upset she missed her shot at harming me, or if it was because she was now covered in hot coffee.

"Oh, my Goddess, Alpha, I am so sorry I missed the handoff. I thought you had the cup secured. Please don't be mad at me." She looked up at me with frightened eyes. There was my answer, she was scared I'd be mad at her for dropping coffee everywhere. Samson had me acting crazy.

I assured her it wasn't all her fault and I wasn't mad. I bent down and started picking up the pieces. I did one last test to appease Samson and sniffed the pieces of coffee covered ceramic in my hands. He had no choice but to agree it didn't smell tampered with. He cursed heavily and retreated into the back of my mind, blocking me. Stupid mutt was going to make me ruin everything, I decided at that moment I wasn't going to listen to his insanity anymore. Until Amber and I were marked and mated, Samson didn't exist.

A light knock was heard and I bid her to come in, I had summoned that omega Zenah to the room to clean up and bring me fresh coffee. "We had a small accident, Zenah, clean this up quickly! Where is my fresh coffee?"

"Yes, Alpha, I will have it cleaned quickly. Your fresh coffee is coming in a moment, we are waiting for a fresh pot. Breakfast started for the rest of the pack and we ran out."

I nodded in annoyance at the omega and dumped the handful of broken cup back on the floor. I went to wash my hands in the bathroom and when I came out there was another knock on the door. When the door opened it was the young nervous omega with my new mug of coffee.

"Here is your fresh coffee, Alpha, as you requested." She smiled slightly and bowed after she handed me the coffee. I did not drop it this time, took a long sniff and enjoyed the rich creamy scent. I was overdue for that caffeine hit it was about to provide me with. Samson let a growl loose which set me off.

"What the fuck is wrong with you? This omega works for us, dumbass! We have her mother in our dungeon back at the other pack. She knows better than to cross us. Enough now, I don't want to hear from you again until I need you to mark Amber on Friday."

Samson went completely silent as I chugged my coffee, today was going to be a good day.

Amber

I couldn't believe Lana had been right, I owed her an apology.

"It's OK, Amber, we all have our days where we're wrong. Today is your day!!" Her laughter echoed through my head; it was going to be a long day! Until he had both doses of potion I was going to be a nervous wreck. Lana's boasting was annoying as hell, but at least it was keeping me from over thinking. Zenah made brief eye contact with me while

Greg was enjoying his coffee, and winked, which I took as her letting me know that he was drinking the potion.

"It's going to work out, one down one to go!!"

Chapter 26

Justin

We had received great news that morning from Margot. She let us know that Greg had been given the two doses of potion successfully the day before. We now had two days to wait for it to do its thing, I wasn't quite sure what that thing was; I needed to ask Olivia. Margot had told us Amber moved her Luna ceremony to Friday and that would be when she would end Greg's reign of terror. I had thought since we had time to kill that we could maybe go back to Jade Moon and see our mates. I missed Melissa terribly and Mason had been hounding me to get back to her as well. He was a persistent bastard so I decided to bring it up with Olivia and Daniel.

"Olivia, what is the potion that Amber gave Greg going to do?"

Olivia looked up from her breakfast and nodded at me as she swallowed the bite of food she had in her mouth.

"The potion was made with Greg's own blood, the witch was able to isolate Greg's power in his blood and made an antidote of sorts.

Now that he has ingested the potion it is going to syphon his power over the next two days."

"How?" I cocked my eyebrow at her in confusion.

"Honestly, I'm not sure of the mechanics of the spell. From what I understood his power will essentially leak out of his pores and evaporate back into the universe."

"Well, that's different!" I had to chuckle at how absurd it sounded.

"I know, it's wild! The things witches can do is very impressive. I want to be there and help Amber dispose of Greg. Early Friday morning I will be sneaking back into the pack to speak with Amber. Margot already gave me the best route so I won't get caught."

"Would you like to see Logan one more time before going into battle? I know he would love to be with you and probably accompany you."

"What do you have in mind, Justin?" She looked at me with an excited smile.

"Well, there's a full day before anyone needs to get back to Onyx Crescent to kick the bad guy's ass. What would you think if you, Daniel and myself left now and went to Jade Moon? Daniel can see Gabriella and we, our mates."

Before Olivia could answer me Daniel perked up instantly, and shouted "Yes"! Seeing Gabriella was just what he needed to get himself out of the funk he was in. Olivia agreed and we finished breakfast at a quicker pace. Daniel went to let Alpha Arnold know that we were heading out until Friday. Mason was bouncing around my head excitedly at the prospect of holding our mate within the hour.

"Well done, human! I can't wait to hold mate in our arms, and then have a little fun."

"Easy, Mason, we have some work to do before we can have our way with our mate. We need to advise the pack that our father perished in the fight with Greg."

"OK, fine, we do the bare minimum then it's time for 'sexy time' with mate."

"Deal!!!!"

It didn't take us long to get back to Jade Moon, and when we pulled up Melissa was waiting for us on the front steps with Logan. Daniel looked around anxiously for Gabriella, she wasn't with them, but Logan showed Daniel on the monitor attached to his belt buckle that she was napping. I saw Olivia's face and it made me giggle; she practically swooned at the sight of a domesticated Logan. If I listened close enough I could hear her ovaries singing. Olivia jumped up and wrapped herself around Logan like a koala, making us all laugh. My laughter was short lived though as Melissa launched herself into my arms and clung to me, equally like a koala, kissing me desperately.

"Easy my sweet...I will have my way with you soon...I've missed you..." I was only able to get out those few words in between her frantic kisses. I was happy to see I wasn't the only one who was missing my mate so badly. I gently put her down and told her we needed to go to the Alpha office and speak with Richard. We needed to 'put in motion' the demise of my father and announce to the pack who their new Alpha and Luna were. This caught Melissa's attention and she stopped to give me the brightest smile.

"This is really happening? You haven't changed your mind?"

It was my turn to kiss her senseless. "I will NEVER change my mind. You are my entire world, and today I get to shout it from the rooftops."

"Well then, what are we waiting for? Let's get to the office! I linked Richard and told him you requested he meet us there."

"That's my good girl," I growled

I watched as Melissa squeezed her thighs together for friction. She loved when I called her my good girl. I needed to get this meeting over with quickly so I could get Melissa into bed and finally mark my mate. She didn't know this was what I had planned so I hoped it was well received.

I told Olivia, Logan and Daniel to make themselves at home while I took care of Alpha duties. They all told me to go have fun playing Alpha which made me cackle, as I grabbed Melissa's hand and we sprinted up to the office leaving our friends behind. We got to the office at the same time as Richard, who looked tired as usual but had a spark of hope that his Alpha was finally home so he could rest. I hated to burst his bubble but it had to be done. I ushered him into the office and didn't even wait for him to sit before I hit him with the news.

"My father is dead, I am the new Alpha as of today!"

"I...ugh...WHAT?"

Watching Richard sputter was comical, to say he was shell shocked would have been an understatement.

"Alpha Renato Watson is no longer in the land of the living and I, as his heir, am now the acting Alpha in charge. I will be addressing the pack later this afternoon. Right now Richard I need you to contact the council and let them know about my father's death, and that I am taking over officially."

Richard just sat and stared blankly at me for what seemed like an eternity before he snapped out of the trance he had been in. He narrowed his eyes at me as if seeing me for the first time, he nodded at me slowly and bared his neck to me in submission.

"Yes, Alpha! May I know what happened to your father so I can tell the council?"

I told Richard what happened with Greg kidnapping the Onyx Crescent's new Luna, and how he attacked Daniel's pack. I told the tale of how my father bravely stood up to the enemy, but was cut down quickly since Greg was a hybrid. Richard looked shocked and slightly incredulous that my father would actually help anyone other than himself. He went with my story anyway and offered his condolences. I thanked him and asked him to go to his office and make the call to the council, then prepare the pack for an assembly at four o'clock. He agreed without issue and rushed out of the office to do as he was tasked. I followed Richard to the door and locked it as soon as it closed. When I turned to face Melissa she raised an eyebrow at me and smirked.

"Oh! I see how this is going to be...hehehehe."

The sound of her giggles stirred something inside me and made me harden instantly. I wanted to make this last as long as possible, but being away from her even if just for two days made me a very hungry man.

"I am hungry, my sexy little omega, what are you going to do to satisfy your Alpha's hunger?"

"Hmmmm, I have one idea but you will need to come closer."

"Beware of the hungry wolf, my sweet omega." As I walked closer to Melissa she locked eyes with me and started to unbutton her jeans, slowly pushing them past her hips. Her gaze never leaving mine, the lower her pants slipped the more heated her gaze got. When I got about a foot or so away she hopped up on my desk and made a come hither motion with her index finger. She didn't need to ask me twice. I sat on my desk chair and rolled up to her, spreading her knees in the process.

"How did you know I was in the mood for an all I can eat buffet?" I growled gruffly and watched goosebumps travel up her entire body. I leaned into her pussy and ran my nose along her slit, taking in her amazing scent. Mason was getting all worked up in my head, I had to calm him down before I went any further as he was trying to come forward now and claim Melissa.

"Mason, you need to chill buddy! I want to make her cum a few times before we mark her."

"Hurry up, human, I want to make her mine!" He kindly retreated so I could concentrate on Melissa.

I turned my attention back to her gorgeous pussy that was glistening with her excitement through her panties. I grabbed them with my teeth and ripped them off. "You won't be needing those."

Melissa moaned out. "Oh, Alpha, I need you to eat me! I can't have you going hungry."

That's all it took for me to lose my resolve and dive in face first, my tongue made quick work of her juices and worked its way to her clit. She fell backwards on the desk and arched her back as I swirled my tongue around her sensitive bud. I worked two fingers into her tight pussy and started pumping a quick but steady rhythm. Melissa was moaning and writhing around my desk, I would never get sick of seeing that sight. I could feel her getting closer to falling off the edge, I doubled my efforts on her clit. I sucked it into my mouth and growled deeply causing a wicked vibration to surround her clit. This was my golden ticket, as Melissa screamed out her orgasm, her pussy clenched hard around my fingers and she soaked the top of my desk with her sweet juices. I licked up every last drop that was in her as she came down from her high. Melissa tried to sit up but I gently pushed her back down.

"That was just my first course, my naughty omega, I still want my second course and dessert."

"It's my pleasure to serve you, my sexy Alpha."

I made quick work of taking my pants off, they hit the floor with a thud. My eager cock sprang up ready to make Melissa scream some more. I gripped myself at the base and ran my tip along Melissa's wet slit, I loved watching her shudder in anticipation. I slowly pushed myself into her gorgeous pussy, watching happily as her eyes rolled back into her head, enjoying the feeling of my rock hard cock stretching and filling her. Melissa must have thought I was going too slow because she began to move her hips eagerly trying to get more of me inside her quicker. I couldn't leave her to suffer so in one swift motion I pushed myself in, up to the hilt. The sound that came out of Melissa's mouth was like music to my ears.

I lifted her legs over my shoulders which gave me a much deeper penetration. Pounding into her with hard deep strokes, the desk was moving across the floor I was fucking her so hard. Melissa took everything I was giving her with enthusiasm, as she met all my strokes head on.

"My Alpha, I'm not going to last much longer like this."

She was panting and barely able to get the words out, I could feel her walls starting to squeeze my cock a little tighter. I wanted to make her last a little longer so I could mark her and make it one hell of an orgasm. I abruptly pulled out leaving her with an empty feeling, she cried out in disappointment as I reached down pulling her into a sitting position by the back of her head. I silenced her protests by kissing her deeply, she moaned as I pushed my tongue into her mouth, tangling our tongues together. We kissed until we ran out of air, pushing away slightly, both of us dizzy. I trailed kisses down Melissa's beautiful neck, and sucked on her marking spot, making her shudder uncontrollably with pleasure. I continued down and gave her perfect breasts the attention they deserved.

"Alpha, I need you inside of me! The emptiness is too much."

I went back up to her sinfully delicious mouth and kissed her stupid again, all the while I was dragging her closer to the edge of the desk. Before she could fall off the edge I grabbed her ass roughly in my hands and lifted her off the desk as I sat back into my office chair, pulling her into my lap. I spanked both of her sexy round ass cheeks leaving my mark on her smooth skin and rubbed out the sting as I lifted her up enough to slip my hard throbbing cock back into her waiting pussy. Melssa slid all the way down my cock to the base and instantly started bouncing up and down happily. I wrapped her hair around my hand and pulled it forcefully, earning me a moan and a pussy squeeze. My cock throbbed in response, I wasn't going to last long like this. Melissa was bouncing and twisting her hips vigorously.

"You love taking all of my cock, don't you? My good girl."

"Your cock is the best part of my day, Alpha, I want it anyway you'll give it to me."

"It's always going to be yours for the taking!" I let our role play slip as now was the time. I kissed her neck and called Mason forward, our canines elongated and I bit into her marking spot. Melissa screamed out and orgasmed harder than I had ever seen in all the years we've been together. I licked the mark closed and went to admire my handy work, but didn't have time as Melissa lunged forward and bit into my marking spot, claiming me as hers.

I had never felt anything so intense in my life, my cock felt like it was blowing off my body. I grabbed Melissa's hips and held her tightly so I wouldn't lose her as I shot my load deep inside her. All I could see was white light and stars, and I'm sure if I listened closely enough I think I heard angels singing. When Melissa licked her mark sealing the wound, I felt like I just started breathing again. We both slumped against the back of the chair breathing heavily. I gently ran my hand over Melissa's head and kissed her forehead gently.

"My Luna, for now and forever! We did it, my love."

Chapter Twenty-Seven

Amber

I woke up feeling like I had been thrown off a cliff or dragged behind a car for a few miles. I had barely slept. I was so nervous about the potion not working out. Margot had gotten word to me that both potions had been given without issue, but I couldn't bring myself to be positive about the news. So much had gone wrong recently I just couldn't dare to hope. I struggled to sit up and instantly regretted my life choices as the room spun wildly around me. Drinking those two bottles of actual wine the night before had not been one of the best choices I've ever made. At that moment being so insanely stressed out it seemed like a good idea. That proved to be false, I was busy telling myself off when there was a light knock on the door. I groaned and croaked out a barely audible "Come in". My mouth was as dry as the Sahara desert, I closed my eyes for a moment to centre myself and push away the nausea. When I opened my eyes I saw a blurry Zenah who was staring at me with concern etched on her face.

"Luna Amber, are you OK? It's close to noon!"

"Not really, Zenah, I feel like I've been beaten if I'm being honest."

"What can I do for you?"

"Nothing much to do really, may I please have breakfast, a strong coffee and some Tylenol for this headache? I'm going to take a shower while you're gone."

"Not a problem Luna, I'll be back as quick as possible."

Before she left the room Zenah helped me to my feet and waited while I steadied myself, before she left me to take a shower. I truly appreciated this woman, she was so strong and resilient. I'm not sure I could have ever waited that long to avenge someone I loved. I was lucky to have her in my corner and helping me as much as she had been. I slowly made my way to the shower and turned the water on nice and hot, the way I loved it. The water felt amazing as it cascaded over my sore body, I could feel my muscles ease, to my relief. When I got out of the shower I felt like a new woman, ready to hash out the details of how I was going to take out Greg Friday. I dried off and donned a plush robe I had hanging in my bathroom. I went back into my bedroom and found Zenah setting up my breakfast at the table by the window.

"Zenah, you are a true blessing from the Goddess herself. Thank you for being so wonderful."

I watched as her cheeks got rosy and she thanked me again for being so kind to her. I couldn't even begin to understand what her life must have been like stuck under Greg's thumb. I ate quickly and then we turned to the most important part of why I wanted her to stay with me. We needed to run through how we were going to end Greg on Friday and Zenah had a few ideas which I really liked.

The options would depend on what happened first and how Greg would react. In the end we decided I would start it off by stabbing Greg with the ceremonial knife when he would try and get my blood for the chalice. This would weaken him, then Zenah and I would tire him out. I promised her she could deliver the final blow, she earned it for the years of hell he put her through. We finished our planning just in time as Greg barged into the room less than a minute later carrying something.

"Oh, my little Luna, I'm glad you're here. I brought you a present."

"A present for me? You're so sweet, my sexy Alpha, you didn't have to."

"Of course I did! I wanted to make sure my little Luna looks fabulous for our ceremony. I went back to my old pack and got you this dress, my ex mate had been saving it for a special occasion but it never came."

"Oh, wow, that's lovely...thank you so much." It took every fibre of my being not to sound sarcastic, I couldn't believe this asshole was giving me another hand me down. His ex mate was bigger than me so this dress was going to fit like a potato sack. I plastered a realistic fake smile on my face and came closer to look at the dress. To my dismay it was truly hideous, I was internally cringing.

"Oh, Alpha, it's too perfect, I have no words."

"Thank you, works! I can't wait to slip this little number off your sexy body and have my way with you." Greg was panting as he leaned forward and planted a kiss on me, I kissed him back and threw in a moan for good measure. What I really wanted to do was rip his throat out.

"Did he really just say, thank you would work?" Lana scoffed.

Greg hung the dress up on a rack and turned to leave the room. He said he had some work to catch up on and he would see me at supper. I smiled and waved him out of the room. I turned around to see Zenah trying to suppress her laughter.

"Oh, stop it! That hideous thing is not being worn tomorrow I can promise you that." We both burst out laughing, we really needed that release before tomorrow.

Olivia

We left Melissa and Justin to deal with his Alpha duties. Logan took us to Melissa's room where there was a crib for Gabriella. We walked in and, as if she knew her daddy was there, she woke up instantly and gave Daniel the most dazzling smile I had ever seen on a baby. Daniel rushed to her side and picked her up with a small cry, he hugged her gently but firmly against his chest. The poor man looked haunted, like he was terrified she'd be snatched out of his arms at any second. I walked up behind him and patted his back for comfort.

"It's going to be OK, Daniel, no one will take Gabriella away."

"Thank you, Liv, I'm just so worried about Amber. I know her and Gabriella had a strong bond and I can't imagine them never being together again."

A sob caught in his throat, which instantly brought tears to my eyes. I was worried about my best friend also and hoped everything worked out tomorrow. I didn't know if she had a plan but I was going to be there to help in any way I could. I felt Logan slip his arm around my waist for comfort, sending sparks shooting through my entire body. I shivered without realizing and felt his smile on the back of my neck where he kissed me. I cleared my throat lightly.

"Amber is strong, Daniel. I know my best friend, she won't rest until Greg is removed from this earth. I promise you I will be there to help her send that evil fuck back to Hell where he came from."

Daniel wasn't able to form any words, so he just nodded as he rocked Gabriella back and forth for comfort. I suggested he stay in the room and spend time with Gabby. He liked that idea. We told him we'd see him later at supper, but he said he'd see how he felt later. I didn't want to argue with him so Logan and I just left the room without another word.

Once out in the hall, Logan wrapped his arms around me, hugging me long and hard. I really needed that and was thankful I had agreed to Justin's plan.

"Mate smells so good! I would like to lick him from head to toe." Evie purred loudly.

"Maybe later Evie, he does smell good and I'm starving. We need fuel if we're going to get freaky." She agreed we needed a proper meal before turning Logan into our dessert. I mentioned to Logan that I was hungry and he said we were in time to catch lunch.

We headed down to the dining room, other pack members looked at us happily and continued their conversations. It was like night and day from the last time I had been there. You could really tell the difference not having Alpha Renato around made to these people. He really was a piece of shit Alpha, the pack was going to be so much better off with Justin in charge. As we ate and talked, I noticed a beautiful redhead walk into the dining room. I watched as her eyes landed directly on Logan. Normally I would have been jealous but I knew how much Logan loved me and this woman was absolutely stunning. She piqued both mine and Evie's interest instantly. After grabbing her lunch the woman walked over to our table giving Logan and I a shy smile.

"Hi Logan, it's been awhile since we've seen each other. I just got back from visiting family in Europe for the past three months. I heard you found your mate?!"

Logan's face instantly lit up and he smiled at me before looking at her for the first time. He had been looking down at the table uncomfortably for the entirety of their exchange up to that point. I assumed it was due to him thinking I'd be jealous or angry at him for talking to a beautiful woman. I rubbed his back reassuringly, as he grabbed my thigh and squeezed it lovingly.

"Yes, this is my beautiful mate, Olivia Stevens! Olivia, this is Leora Sanderson, we grew up together in the pack."

"It's a pleasure to meet you Leora!" I extended my hand with a big smile on my face.

Leora took my hand gently in hers and shook it firmly. An electric shock went through our palms and made us laugh as we recoiled slightly.

"The pleasure is mine, Olivia, it's not every day I get to meet the future Alpha of our neighbouring pack."

I couldn't help the laughter that burst out of my mouth. "Oh, girl, that is a whole story in and of itself. I'm actually not the future Alpha anymore, it seems I have a long lost brother. He's the new Alpha."

The look on Leora's face was comical. I felt bad leaving her hanging, so I invited her to sit with us and I'd explain. She looked regretful but declined my offer; I couldn't say why but that made me sad she wasn't staying. "I'd love to sit with you at supper and hear the whole story, could we do that? I promised my mother I'd have lunch with her and tell her all about her family who I visited."

"Not a problem, we would love that! You might even get to meet my brother if he decides to join us for supper."

Leora left us with a smile, and went across the dining room to sit with another woman, who was for sure her mother - they were almost twins. I turned to Logan and asked him to tell me all about Leora. He told me they grew up together, and he was more than certain that she had a huge crush on him. I asked him if he ever reciprocated the feelings? He admitted he thought she was gorgeous and that she was a very kind soul, but he only ever wanted his mate so never did anything. They knew at eighteen they weren't mates so they stayed friends. As I listened to Logan, I noticed Leora kept looking over at us from under her eyelashes as she spoke with her mother. I felt Evie panting in my head.

"Evie, is everything alright?"

"Everything is great, Liv! I want that wolf, you must convince her to join us."

"I like the way you're thinking, my friend. Should we tell Logan what we're planning, so we don't freak him out?"

"Let's surprise him, Liv, he knows you're freaky like that. You told him about your wild times in college with other girls and the couple of threesomes you had. I believe he'll be OK *with it once the shock wears off."* I licked my lips thinking of Evie's proposal. I had to admit I was intrigued to find out what this stunning, shy she-wolf would be like behind closed doors.

"It's always the quiet ones you need to watch out for," Evie chuckled.

"You're not quiet, though, so what can you say to that?" I laughed hysterically as I saw Evie's face drop in my mind.

"Very funny, human, make sure you get her into our bed or I will block your orgasms for the next month."

"You wouldn't dare!?!?!" I saw Evie turn around and saunter to the back of my mind. Damn crazy wolf, I was praying to the Goddess this would be an easy ask. Logan had finished talking by that point and was looking at me with a slightly worried expression on his face. I felt bad for him so I tossed him a bone.

"Don't worry Logan, I'm not mad or jealous. She's a beautiful woman, and I believe she meant nothing romantically to you. I know you are mine and I am yours." I kissed him gently before leaning over and whispering in his ear. "I'd like to have you as my dessert! Run up to your room and I'll be right behind you. I just need to check on something."

He didn't even hesitate, he got up quickly with an eager look on his face as he practically did sprint from the room. I chuckled to myself as I got up to approach Leora and her mother. They both stopped talking and looked up at me as I approached.

"I'm so sorry, ladies, for interrupting your lunch, I needed to speak with Leora privately, if possible?" Leora looked at her mother with a bit of fear in her eyes. The poor girl probably thought I was jealous and wanted to threaten her. She was in for quite a shock, I suspected. Her mother nervously patted her hand and said she needed to get back to work anyways, and to enjoy our chat. I waved her off and sat down in her now empty seat. As I opened my mouth, Leora nervously tried to tell me there was nothing between her and Logan. I put my hand up to stop her.

"I didn't come over here to cause trouble. Logan is my mate and I am secure in that knowledge as we are marked. I wanted to ask you if you would be comfortable joining us."

She cocked her eyebrow at me, "I said I would join you for supper! Why would I need to be comfortable?"

I giggled at her naiveté. "No, no, not joining us for supper, Leora." I gave her a pointed look. "Joining Logan and I in the bedroom."

Leora's eyes grew quite large and she drew in a sharp breath. She stammered a bit before she closed her eyes and took a few deep breaths to calm herself. I felt bad I had caused her that shock but it was also super cute and turned me on. I was really hoping she said yes, I wanted to get my hands on her so badly.

"What did you have in mind?" She asked with a shy, curious smile.

I didn't want to get my hopes up just yet, but it had to be a good sign she was asking questions and not just shutting me down.

"Well, whatever you're comfortable with really. Logan doesn't know, this will be a surprise for him. We can double team him and you can do whatever you like with him."

Leora's cheeks turned a deep pink and she looked down at the table bashfully. A thought then crossed my mind suddenly.

"Leora, have you ever slept with anyone before?"

I hoped that wasn't an insulting question as she was my age, but I didn't want to take that away from her.

"Oh, Goddess, yes! I've been with my fair share of men. Never been with a woman though, so that would be new for me. I'm intrigued and would like to take you up on the offer."

It was my turn to be shocked, was this for real? I was so excited, I couldn't wait to get upstairs. I told Leora that Logan was already waiting upstairs for me, I said I was going to go in and handcuff him to the bed. I needed five minutes, then she could knock and come in. She agreed and we went upstairs, happily giggling with each other.

I walked into Logan's room and he was sitting on the bed waiting anxiously for me, he gave me his thousand watt smile that turned my insides to liquid. I walked up to him and straddled him while deeply kissing him. He grabbed my ass, starting to knead it and I let out a little moan. Goddess this man had amazing hands, among other amazing things. I reached down and pulled his shirt over his head, momentarily breaking our kiss apart.

"My sweet sex kitten is eager today!"

"Oh, you have NO idea, baby!" I dropped to my knees and undid his pants smoothly in one swift motion, freeing his delicious cock. I kissed up his length and swirled my tongue around the tip for good measure. I was rewarded by my hair being wrapped around Logan's fist tightly, and a hearty moan as he slid his hard cock down my throat. I took it all in as if I were starving, moaning the whole way to cause vibrations in my throat that I knew drove Logan wild. I felt Logan's cock spasm a few times, I needed to back off before he blew his load too soon. I let his cock slide out of my mouth and he looked devastated at the loss of suction. I smiled coyly at him and told him he had a bigger surprise coming. He raised his eyebrows at me as I ordered him to get on the bed. I grabbed his shirt that I had taken off and used it to tie his wrists to the bed.

"Oh, it's play time is it?" He was practically vibrating with excitement.

"You'll have to wait and see my love." I winked at him as I reached over and secured my knot around his wrists. I just finished when there was a knock on the door.

Logan shouted "Please come back later, I'm busy."

"That's not very polite Logan, I'll see who's there."

"Liv what are you doing? Don't answer the door, whoever it is will see me."

"That's the point." Logan didn't get a chance to say anything else as I flung the door open for Leora and greeted her with a big smile. "Right on time, come on in."

"Liv? What the hell is this? I'm naked!" Logan was trying desperately to get free and cover himself up.

"Yes, you need to be naked to be fucked, Logan! I invited Leora to join us. Surprise!"

Shell-shocked was putting it too lightly, poor Logan looked like his soul left his body, and Leora was looking anywhere but at naked Logan.

"Liv, do something before she leaves!" Evie sounded desperate.

I walked over to Leora and lifted her chin to look at me, I smiled and leaned in kissing her softly. At first she was frozen, but within a few seconds I had gotten her to open for me and our tongues were gently dancing together. She was a fabulous kisser and I moaned in appreciation, I stepped forward grabbing the back of her head and deepening the kiss. That earned me a moan from Leora in return. Evie was purring up a storm in my head and Logan just stared at us with his mouth wide open. I ended our kiss as we both needed air, we both looked at each other hungrily.

"I knew she was going to be a wild one, Liv!" I laughed at Evie but then turned my attention back to Leora. I whispered to her that if she was uncomfortable with anything to let me know and I would stop. She nodded and then took me by surprise, leaning in and kissing me hungrily. I reached out and cupped her left breast kneading it and rolling her nipple between my fingers through her thin shirt and bra. I felt her shift as she pressed her thighs together for friction, I could smell her arousal and it made my own desire heighten. I saw Logan out of my peripherals writhing around on the bed excitedly watching the show. I lifted Leora's shirt over her head and removed her bra at a fast pace.

"You won't need that." I purred as I bent down to suck on her perfect little nipples. Leora ran her hands through my hair and held me in place as I sucked and licked her nipples to stiff peaks. I ran my hands down her curves to the hem of her jeans which I slowly unzipped. I heard Leora's breath hitch, but she didn't ask to stop so I continued with the removal of her pants. She delicately stepped out of her jeans and stood there in all her sexy glory wearing nothing but a baby pink lace g-string. Her skin was creamy white which set off her fiery red hair, she had a set of perfect perky breasts covered in the cutest freckles.

"You're too dressed for this party, Olivia, let me help you." Leora's voice had become husky and I was instantly dripping as she walked over to me and took off my shirt. She made sure to show each of my breasts some love, just as I had done for her. I was too excited and took my own pants and thong off. Leora licked her lips and ran her fingers up my thigh and gently through my folds. My knees slightly buckled from her actions, it wasn't all about me so I motioned her to the bed. "Let's go show Logan some attention, shall we? You have carte blanche, enjoy yourself."

We sashayed over to the bed much to Logan's delight. When we reached the edge of the bed we both climbed up onto the bed and crawled seductively towards him. Leora was the first to reach him, she hesitated for a moment but then decided to let go and enjoy herself. She kissed up his leg and thigh until she got to his balls. She licked his sack all the way up to the tip of his cock that hardened more. I saw him shiver in pleasure and it made my heart happy to see him enjoying himself. Leora started sucking his cock expertly, I had to stop and admire her technique.

I didn't last long before I was crawling under her and lying on my back. I guided her hip down so she was sitting on my face. I licked her sweet juicy pussy and made her moan loudly. That was all the encouragement I needed as I made my way to her clit and slowly played with her little bundle of nerves. She seemed to like what I was doing as she started grinding herself into my tongue. I swirled lightly and stuck one finger into her tight pussy, she twisted her hips for this and I could feel her walls squeezing my fingers. Logan was moaning like a beast above me, he sounded like he was thoroughly enjoying the experience. I added a finger and picked up the pace, I also added suction to my tongue action, this proved to be the magic combination as not too long after Leora came like a freight train. Her sweet juices gushed out of her tight pussy and I cleaned every drop not leaving any to waste. She was panting but continued to suck Logan off until he came down her throat with a loud cry. Leora was impressive, she swallowed it all like a champ.

"Be a good girl and untie me, Liv! I want to fuck that tight little pussy and return the favor for the incredible blow job."

I obliged and released Logan from his bindings. He sprang forward, pinning me to the bed and kissing me deeply. He picked me up and put me against the pillows, Leora crawled between my legs and gave me a sly smile. "My turn!"

She didn't hesitate as she bent down and planted kisses all along my folds to my slit, dipping her tongue into my tunnel. I arched my back at the glorious feeling, as she snaked her tongue up to my clit and began sucking and licking it with gusto. Logan had positioned himself behind Leora stroking his cock back to rock hard and ran it along the seam of her pussy. He pulled her hips up so he had a better angle and dove into her tight pussy causing her to yell out. The momentary loss of her tongue on my clit made me grab her by the hair and grind myself into her face. I was rewarded with two fingers inserted into my tight snatch. She pumped her fingers expertly and continued to suck on my clit. I could feel my orgasm building. Logan was pounding away at Leora's pussy which caused her to smash her face into my cunt, heightening the sensations. "I'm not going to last much longer, I'm going to cum Leora, please don't stop."

"I'm not far behind myself," she panted out before continuing suction on my clit.

One little nip on my clit was all it took to throw me off the cliff, and I came hard. Leora tried to suck up all my juices but Logan had wrapped her hair around his fist and pulled her hair back as he pounded into her and threw her over the cliff as well. He pulled out and came all over her back and ass. My love for Logan was already at an all time high but he surprised me by spanking Leora. I swear I came again instantly at that moment. Leora was taken aback but asked him to do it again on her other cheek. I felt like I was dreaming, this couldn't be my life could it? Leora rolled onto her back panting and catching her breath as Logan came over to me and rubbed his cock on my lips. I opened for him and sucked the combination of Leora's juices and his cum from his cock. Soon it was ready to go again, so he rolled on his back and told me to hop on. I didn't need any more incentive as I lowered myself onto his gorgeous rock hard dick.

"Fuck! I love your cock Logan, it's perfect!" I leaned forward offering him my breasts to suck on, he took my right breast and showed my nipple some good love. Leaning over caused my ass to lift into the air which Logan took full advantage of and spanked me good. I moaned and lowered myself all the way to the base of his cock. He groaned and gripped my hips, letting me twist and bounce to my heart's content.

"Leora, sit on my face!" He panted.

She didn't wait and crawled onto Logan's face, we were now sitting facing each other as he ate her out, we moaned in sync as he sucked her clit and slammed my pussy hard at the same time. I reached forward and grabbed her for a kiss; we were deeply kissing and I was playing with her nipples. The sensations were too much for all of us and we all came within seconds of each other, filling the room with the sounds of our pleasured screams. We all collapsed on the bed panting, I looked up at Leora with a huge smile on my face, one that she returned.

"You must play with us again, next time we visit the pack, Leora. That was fucking amazing."

Logan agreed and Leora blushed bright red, but agreed that it was the best sex she had ever had and would love to join us again. No matter what happened tomorrow I knew I lived my best life today, and that was what mattered at this moment.

Chapter 28

Justin

Four o'clock rolled around Melissa and I were standing on the steps of the pack house with everyone looking at us curiously. I cleared my throat and looked to Melissa for reassurance; she smiled at me and squeezed my hand.

"Members of Jade Moon, it is with great sadness that I announce the death of our Alpha. My father Renato Watson was murdered while defending the Luna of Onyx Crescent."

I paused for dramatic effect and looked around at all the pack members. No one really seemed bothered by the news, in fact, I dare even say I saw excitement and hope on most of the pack members faces. Honestly, I couldn't blame them, my father was a complete asshole and treated everyone in the pack like shit. I was his son and was the happiest one of all that he was gone.

"As my father's only heir, I proudly announce that I am the new Alpha of Jade Moon. My Luna Melissa and I have marked and mated.

We will have an Alpha ceremony once things settle down but today we pledge to you all that we will protect and serve this pack until our last breaths." A great cheer erupted from the crowd, the cheering turned into a loud, long howl, then everyone bared their necks to Melissa and me. She looked at me lovingly with tears shining in her eyes. I leaned over and kissed her hard and passionately.

"They are howling for you, my sweet Luna! We can finally be together out in the open, today our lives officially begin." Melissa jumped into my arms with a squeal of joy and I spun her around laughing with her. I looked over and saw Logan beaming at us, and Olivia smiling through happy tears. We had waited for so many years in the shadows and now being out together made me the happiest wolf on the planet. I looked past Olivia and saw Daniel holding Gabriella and half smiling. I knew he was happy for us but everything going on in his life was weighing heavily on him. Melissa announced to the pack that we would have a celebratory supper and all were invited. The crowd cheered again and several of the omegas came running up to hug her and congratulate their new Luna. Melissa blushed slightly, but smiled brighter than the sun itself. As we started to make our way back into the packhouse Olivia motioned for me to move off to the side.

"Congratulations, Justin! I am so happy for you and Melissa, you both deserve this happiness and so much more. I just wanted to let you know I will be leaving right after supper, I want to get back to Onyx Crescent as soon as possible. Margot is waiting for me."

"Not a problem, Liv, I understand! What do you want us to do?"

"We will probably need back up at some point, but we don't know if Greg will have any of his men there. I'm also not sure what Amber has up her sleeve, Margot told me she has a plan but didn't elaborate. If you and a few men could be on standby near the pack, we will let you know how to proceed."

"No problem, Liv, we've got your back on this. Hopefully by this time tomorrow, Greg will be no longer and Amber will be free."

"We can only hope, Justin! I've missed my best friend so much and I know Daniel is suffering terribly. Amber has gone through so much in the last few days it's unbelievable. I only hope she beats Greg and we can move on with our lives."

I agreed and suggested we get inside to eat, so she linked arms with me and we walked into the packhouse, smiling. Logan and Melissa were waiting for us at the Alpha table. I was so happy that my best friend was officially my brother now, and his kick ass mate was my new sister. I raised a glass of wine and toasted to new beginnings, and supper passed quickly but pleasantly. Before we knew it, Olivia was kissing Logan goodbye and driving back to Onyx crescent. I knew Logan was worried but I reassured him that we would be there tomorrow to help Liv no matter what.

Olivia

I made it back to Onyx Crescent in less time than I had expected, and Margot met me where we had planned. I hugged her tightly and thanked her for helping all of us: she was putting herself at risk of being found by Greg. Margot assured me there was a very low risk to her safety and that she was more concerned for Amber, who was neck deep in her plot against Greg. The only solace I found was when Margot told me the woman who had accompanied Amber and Greg that day, was really an ally. She had a vendetta against Greg and was helping Amber.

"Margot, you have no idea how happy that makes me, to know she has someone else on her side. Did you tell her I was coming to help?"

"No, I didn't want to distract her or get her hopes up in case anything went wrong."

"That makes sense I guess, we weren't able to save her the other day. I can't imagine what that did to her. She had to save us!"

"She did what she had to do for her people, Olivia, that's why you're going to need to let her take care of Greg tomorrow."

"What the hell are you talking about, Margot? I'm here to help and plan on doing so!"

"Yes, yes, you can help her! But you can't take over and do it all. Amber was the one who put herself at risk for all of this, and she needs to see it through to the end for her own self worth. She is the Luna of this pack and thus needs to be the one to take care of it."

"I understand! I'm only here for backup and extra muscle, I will defer to whatever she says. As you say, she is my Luna." I felt slightly affronted by Margot, but I understood where she was coming from, so I kept my mouth shut and agreed to just be there for Amber.

"Oh, that's a first for you, Olivia, keeping your mouth shut, what's the occasion?"

"Really, Evie? Now's not the time for your snarky sass. Amber has always been known as my Beta and I as the Alpha. Reality is I'm not the Alpha and she is my Luna, so she needs to know she's in charge and doesn't need me to do everything."

"Sorry, Liv, I'm happy you're going to let Amber shine. You're a great friend."

I rolled my eyes at Evie, and chose to ignore her further. I turned to Margot and asked her where I would be staying the night. She brought me to an empty cottage on the far edge of the pack. I knew this would be perfect since not many people knew about this house. I went in, to find it was all set up for me, and thanked Margot for her help in sneaking me back into the pack. She let me know she would come to get me in the morning and bring me to Amber. I bid her goodnight, as the bed was calling my name. I changed into shorts and a loose shirt, crawling into the bed and passed out pretty much instantly. My dreams consisted of us kicking Greg's ass in so many different ways. It was a great sleep.

Amber

I woke up feeling terribly anxious but I also had a feeling of hope and excitement for what was to come later that afternoon. I rolled over and my smile faded instantly as I saw Greg still sleeping next to me. I had hoped he would have left early like most mornings, so I could have breakfast with Zenah and go over our plans one last time to make sure there were no holes.

"He really does ruin everything doesn't he? Can't we just rip his throat out, right now, Amber?"

"Lana! We have to wait for after six o'clock, that's when the full forty eight hours is up. We don't know if his powers are still active before then. We can't risk screwing this up with impatience, please just hold on a little longer."

"Fine! I don't like it but I'll behave for now. Once we have the go ahead, all bets are off. I can't wait to end this fucker."

"When the time comes, Lana he's all yours and Zenah's, don't forget she gets the final blow that will end him."

Lana agreed that she would honour the deal we had made with Zenah, she was a wolf of her word. I rolled over and yawned loudly, kicking out my legs nailing Greg in the ribs. He let out a puff of air and started to grumble as he rubbed the sleep out of his eyes.

"What the hell was that, little Luna?"

"I'm so sorry Greg, I'm used to you being gone by now so when I stretch I've got the whole bed. Are you OK?"

"Like you actually care!" Lana scoffed and laughed in my head.

I chuckled along with Lana in my head as Greg rubbed his ribs. To my dismay he seemed fine and reached out to pull me to his chest. I thought about resisting him but I was so close to the end I couldn't risk fucking it up. I allowed him to pull me on top of him as he wrapped his arms tightly around me. He kissed the top of my head and nuzzled his nose into my hair sniffing it like a creeper.

"You smell delicious this morning, my sweet little Luna, I can't wait to have my way with you tonight after the ceremony."

"Greg, you're such a sweet talker. It's me that can't wait to get my hands on you and sink my teeth into you." I winked at him and he growled playfully at me. I could feel his cock harden against my stomach and I internally shuddered. I couldn't wait to get off him and go shower, he made me feel so disgusting. Lana was still laughing hysterically in my head and it took everything in me to hold my outward composure.

"This chump has a reality check coming his way, when you really do sink your teeth into him later!" Lana was rolling around in my mind and I couldn't hold it in anymore, I ended up chuckling out loud. Greg cocked his head at me, I blushed knowing I had better come up with a good excuse quickly.

"I was just thinking of all the amazing things you're going to do to me and the positions I'd like to try with you later."

"Well, if you want we can start practising now little Luna." Greg started to roll us over, he was half on top of me when I pushed back on his chest to stop him. He looked annoyed at my interruption of his intentions.

"Greg, today is technically our wedding day and I shouldn't even be seeing you right now. We could start our union off on the wrong foot with bad luck. You need to head out so I can start my day, it takes hours to doll myself up." I pecked him on the tip of the nose and pushed him off me slowly. He hesitated at first but then agreed to leave me to start getting ready.

Greg got up, changed in the closet and as he headed out of the room, blew me a kiss at the door, saying he couldn't wait to see me later. I waved back and the moment the door clicked closed I jumped out of the bed and raced into the shower, I needed to get his scent off me.

"That could have ended badly, Lana, you can't distract me like that for the rest of the day. I need to be focused."

"Sorry, Amber, I promise I'll let you stay focused on the task at hand. You have to admit though it's pretty funny you told him it's bad luck to see each other today. You're going to kill him before the end of the day, I'd call that pretty terrible luck."

"He's going to get exactly what he deserves later today, and I can't wait to see the look on his face."

I took a nice long, excessively hot shower. When I felt that I had washed his touch off my skin I got out and wrapped myself in my fluffy robe. I stopped and looked at myself in the mirror, wondering if Daniel would ever forgive me for rejecting him. I shook my head, now wasn't the time to go down that rabbit hole. I'd cross that bridge once I took care of Greg. I walked out into my room and was greeted by Zenah who was setting up my breakfast by the window.

"Luna Amber, I've brought you a hearty breakfast. You will need all the nutrients for your big moment tonight."

"Thank you so much, Zenah, I'd be lost without you. Are you ready for what's coming later?"

"Absolutely!! I have been waiting for this day for so many years, I honestly can't believe it's actually here. I'm scared to believe it's really happening."

I reached over and squeezed her shoulder reassuringly, Greg was dying tonight! There were no ifs, buts or maybes about it. I shared my breakfast with Zenah and we went over all the details of how the evening would go. I felt relaxed and confident at that very moment. I knew things could shift instantly and we could face trouble, but I wanted to enjoy that moment of calm before the storm. The afternoon passed quickly enough and before I knew it there was a knock on the door.

"That should be your dress, Luna Amber. We knew how much you hated the hand me down dress, so Margot got you something more suitable." I opened the door and was faced by a tall omega with her head bowed.

"Dress delivery for Luna Amber Small." That voice, I knew that voice, but it couldn't be could it? As I was fighting with myself the omega stepped into my room and closed the door, locking it swiftly. She looked up with a smile, all I could do was screech and launch myself into her arms.

"Well, I'm happy to see you too, Cupcake!"

We were both laughing and crying, I couldn't believe Olivia was here. Did that mean Daniel was here too? I looked up at her with the question in my eyes which she understood and shook her head. "He wanted to be here but it would be too dangerous, he's with Gabriella right now at Jade Moon. He will be watching over us later from afar in case you need back up during the ceremony."

My heart squeezed at the mention of my sweet Gabriella, I missed her terribly but was glad to know Daniel was with her safe and sound. I finally let Olivia go after what seemed like forever, turned to Zenah while wiping the tears from my eyes and introduced the two women. Zenah bowed her head to Olivia, who walked over and gave her a giant hug that took Zenah by surprise, making all laugh.

"Thank you for helping my best friend and protecting her when I couldn't."

"You're welcome, Olivia, but it is my honour to help Luna Amber. She is a special woman and doesn't deserve to deal with Greg alone."

"So, who's going to fill me in on the plan for tonight while we get you ready?"

Olivia linked arms with both Zenah and myself walking towards my closet, where they were going to help me get ready. Zenah did my hair while Olivia did my makeup. I filled her in on how we were going to take Greg down. I apologised for not having a role for her and she told me I was being ridiculous since I didn't know she was coming. Olivia said the plan was great and she would be on standby to help if needed. I was so happy she was here but glad I was going to do something for myself without her taking charge. About an hour later I was dressed and ready to head outside to the ceremony site. Before we left my room Zenah turned to me and handed me a beautiful jewel encrusted dagger.

"This dagger belonged to my father's family, he carried it everywhere with him. I want you to have it and use it to make the first cut into Greg. I will then use it at the end to finish the job."

I took the knife from her gently, it was beautiful and had a nice weight to it. I sheathed the knife and nestled it perfectly between my breasts. For anyone who didn't know any better it looked like part of my dress, the perfect camouflage. Margot had picked out the best dress for me, it fit beautifully and wasn't too long so I could manoeuvre easily. Olivia left ahead of us since she needed to blend with the other pack members. Zenah and I both took deep breaths and left my room to finally end this nightmare.

Greg

I was waiting eagerly for Amber on the platform I'd built in the middle of the pack yard, for this joyous occasion. I watched as the pack members nervously gathered, all of them kept their heads down and refused to make eye contact. Just the way I liked it, I couldn't have been happier at that very moment.

"She's not coming, Greg! I feel something isn't right and you're going to regret your choices."

"Listen you dumb mutt, Amber wants me and she will be here any minute now. Women take a long time to make themselves look good. Seeing her in that dress will make the wait worth it."

"You're not listening, Greg, I feel off and weaker than usual."

"I am listening Samson, and all I hear is a bitchy wolf. You've been wrong this entire time, and look here Amber comes now! You were wrong once again, she's in it to be with me."

"Fine! She showed up great! In a completely different dress than the one you picked. Guess she doesn't care about your opinion or your feelings. That's a big fuck you, if you ask me."

"Well, I'm not asking you! So back the fuck off." I growled at Samson as I shoved him into the back of my mind. Amber wasn't wearing the dress I brought her but there had to be a good explanation as to why

that was. I put on a big smile for her and waited patiently as she got closer.

Amber

We followed the curve in the path and the platform Greg had built came into view, he was standing there in khaki pants and a fitted white cotton shirt. I gave Zenah a side glance which she returned, neither of us were impressed.

"So, you needed to dress up like the good little wifey, but he dresses like a slob? Wow, this guy is a real winner. Good thing we're killing him, save the oxygen for people who deserve it."

"Lana, I couldn't agree with you more! Please remember the plan, after I stab him we need to make sure he doesn't have his powers anymore. Zenah will shift and attack him, we will stand by as backup, so please don't shift right away, OK?"

Lana agreed to listen to me and I was glad she was finally on my side. I looked down the path and watched as Greg's face contorted in anger, then just as quickly he plastered a fake smile on his face. The closer I got the more I could tell how pissed off he was because his eye was twitching. I guessed he was pissed off because I wasn't wearing the dress he gave me, too bad for him. I took the final steps up onto the platform and Greg grabbed my hands tightly. I winced from the pain which he noticed and eased up a little bit on his grip. I plastered the biggest, most sickeningly sweet smile on my face as he asked the question I knew was coming.

"Why aren't you wearing the dress I brought you, little Luna?" He gritted out between clenched teeth.

"Oh, well, you see the omegas tried to make the dress fit me and accidentally ruined the dress, so they replaced it. Do you like it?" I looked up at him expectantly, knowing I was pushing his buttons but at this point I had no fucks left to give. I gave him large puppy eyes as I waited for his answer.

He cleared his throat uncomfortably and mumbled, "Sure it's beautiful", before turning to the pack and announcing that we were all there for my Luna ceremony. He spoke about how Onyx Crescent was going to be the most powerful pack now, because he was the Alpha. I decided at that moment it was show time, I nodded to Zenah before I went for it. I interrupted him mid sentence.

"You don't like my dress, do you? You hate it! You think I'm ugly." I held my breath hoping he'd take the bait. After the confusion cleared from his face I saw the anger spark as he turned toward me.

"You got the son of a bitch, Amber! Now stab him with everything you've got." Lana growled.

I turned my back on him and clutched the dagger hilt, pulling it out of my cleavage. I felt his rough hands on my shoulder trying to turn me towards him. I used his angry momentum against him and plunged the dagger into his chest full force as he twisted me around. I missed his heart by a few inches, but it had the desired effect. Greg fell to his knees looking up at me pained. "Little Luna...how could you do that to me?"

"Easily, Greg, you are a monster and I could never be with someone like you. You will pay for all your evil deeds." Greg was momentarily distracted as I saw him trying to call up his magical abilities with no luck.

I was relieved that the potion had worked, that was step one completed. Before he could fully register the terrible position he was now in, I yanked the dagger out of his chest and stabbed him again several times causing blood to gush out. The pack members watched on in shocked horror; no one tried to help Greg since they knew what an evil prick he was.

"I will make you pay for this, little Luna, and you aren't going to like it."

"Yeah, not likely to happen, Greg. You're not leaving this platform alive, but I appreciate your attempted threat." I went to stab him again but he managed to stagger backwards so I missed, and fell forward slightly. Greg took advantage of this even in his weakened state and punched me in the face. He was weak so it didn't hurt nearly as much as it should have, but it did make me slightly dizzy though and I fell backwards.

Before Greg could attack me further I was instantly covered by Zenah's beautiful gray wolf who had jumped up onto the platform snarling at Greg. She was ready to get her revenge on him. Greg was shouting obscenities at us as he shifted. He may have been weakened and was somewhat powerless but he was still an alpha wolf, and was bigger than Zenah and myself. I was thinking of shifting but before I had a chance Greg pounced at me bypassing Zenah and pushing me off the platform a good fifteen feet away. He pinned me to the ground with his giant paws stepping on my throat. My vision started to get spotted as I ran out of air. I tried to struggle free but he was too heavy for me to move alone. This was not an ideal situation.

Chapter Twenty-Nine

Olivia

I watched from the back of the pack as Amber got thrown from the platform. The sound of her body hitting the ground made me wince in pain for her. I didn't even have a chance to blink before that asshole Greg was on top of her pressing his giant paw on her throat. I started to move rapidly through the shocked pack members, but was stopped by Evie.

"*Remember what Margot told us, Liv, we need to let Amber deal with this on her own. We are the last resort.*"

"*He's going to kill her if we don't do anything.*"

"*Give her a chance! You know how strong and stubborn she is.*"

"*Yeah, you're right, Evie, she's nearly as stubborn as me.*"

Evie snorted before bursting out in laughter. She was right though, Amber was very strong and twice as stubborn. I watched as she struggled against Greg, I was holding my breath begging the Goddess to give her the strength she needed to gain the upper hand in this situation.

My prayers seemed to be falling on deaf ears as he continued to squeeze the life out of my best friend.

Amber's struggles seemed to last forever but in reality it had only been a little over a minute. My anxiety was rising by the second, until I noticed Zenah shake herself out of the state of shock she seemed to be in. The giant grey wolf snarled and hurled herself towards Greg, it took her mere seconds to reach them. Zenah speared Greg in the side, sending him flying off Amber, who instantly started to cough and sputter as air entered her lungs once more. It took Amber a few seconds to regain her normal breathing pattern and sit up, the entire time Zenah stood by her side snarling at Greg.

"See, they have it under control, Liv!"

My body relaxed slightly, knowing Amber made it out of that situation. I knew it wasn't close to being over but at least I could concentrate better. Just then, Greg howled and several rogue wolves appeared around the fringe of the pack, this was my time to shine. I let Evie take over and we shifted instantly, linking the pack and telling people to go and seek refuge in the pack house. Chaos erupted as panicking pack members tried to run for cover, with the rogue wolves going after them.

"Like hell any of these fleabags will be taking out our people today. Let's make mince meat out of them, Liv." I never argued with Evie when it came to fights, she knew what she needed to do, I always gave her full control of the reins.

We went after the closest set of rogues, I could see the glint in their eyes thinking they'd have an easy kill. I loved fucking with assholes like that, before reaching them I stopped and bowed low as if I wanted to play. They stopped dead in their tracks looking at each other in confusion, while they were distracted I lunged at the one on my right and tore his throat out. He died with a stunned look on his smug wolf face, his buddy enraged by my actions, growled loudly at me. Evie sneered at him and matched his evil glint as she turned and kicked him in the jaw. The guy's head snapped back, he hit the ground hard but bounced up quickly to come after us again. We didn't have any more time to fuck around with this guy, since there were more rogues going after my pack members, and it seemed like only Margot and myself were fighting them.

"We really need to get the warrior training set up after this, fucking bunch of pussies."

I, of course, agreed with Evie. I was mortified, but didn't have time to be pissed off at the moment. We dodged the rogue's attack easily, we hit him several more times before slashing his throat; watching him bleed out in front of us. Two down, and who knew how many others to go. Evie and I ran towards two young pack members who were being cornered by a pretty big rogue, one of the girls was bleeding and that pissed me off. We pounced on the guy from behind since he hadn't seen us coming, we latched onto the back of his neck and dug in as he thrashed around with us riding him like a bull. Had it not been such a shitty situation I would have found it funny as hell. We managed to hold on for quite a bit before he was able to swing us off. We took a parting gift with us, a giant chunk of his neck and shoulder blade, the rogue roared out in pain gaining the attention of nearby friends who came running.

"Ugh, that fucker tasted funny! Can we just slash throats moving forward? I'm going to need to eat a mint bush after all this is done, to get rid of their nasty taste."

"How we kill them is up to you Evie, I'm just along for the ride!"

"True!" Evie grinned as we looked at the new group that had formed, it was us versus four fresh rogues and the funky tasting fucker. Five against one wasn't really a fair fight but we never backed down

and right now we were pumped up. I glanced over and saw Margot to my right kicking two rogue's asses, then to my left I watched as Amber and Zenah were throwing Greg around like a rag doll. She was still in human form which I found impressive yet weird at the same time.

We had the situation more or less under control, me being the one who seemed to be most in trouble. I expanded my alpha aura and watched as the rogues flinched and shrivelled away from me, but unable to move away, because I had them rooted to the spot. Evie spun in a circle slicing all of them to bits, with a satisfied smirk on her face. She then kicked dirt onto the dead rogues, and pranced over to where Margot had just finished off her last rogue.

"Well, that was fun! Are you OK, Margot?"

Margot didn't have time to answer, as there was more howling coming from in the distance, we quickly readied ourselves for another fight. A group of six wolves came over the ridge making Evie begin to growl, hackles up, but she stopped abruptly as a sweet familiar scent of apple cinnamon hit our nose.

"MATE!! NORMAN." Evie yipped happily, taking off like lightning towards Norman and Logan. She pounced on him like a puppy, we ended up rolling down the hill in a giant happy ball of fur. Evie was licking Norman mercilessly and I had to force a shift to save him. Logan shifted as well and locked his arms around me instantly to protect me from prying eyes. I couldn't help but giggle at his possessive side, it was hot.

"I'm sorry we're late, Liv, are you alright? Those assholes didn't hurt you?"

"We're great. We had fun taking those fuckers out. What happened to you guys?"

"We got ambushed by what I'm assuming is the tail end of those asshole rogues, we managed to take care of them. Our six against fifteen of the bastards. I'm happy we stopped them from getting here! Was it just you and Margot fighting?" I saw the anger flash over his face before I answered.

"Yes, it was just Margot and I fighting. I took out seven, and it looks like Margot, the remaining five. Before you say it, don't worry, as soon as things get back to normal we're starting hardcore training for warriors. I'm not fucking impressed at all."

"You and I both, sweetheart! We will teach them together, I will never let you fight alone again."

I was about to give Logan a kiss when Daniel shifted, coming over quickly, concern etched all over his face. I turned to see what he was looking at, I already knew it had to do with Amber. She had just been kicked a few feet away by Greg and was winded.

"We need to go save her and end this monster." Daniel was frantic with worry.

"You can't help her Daniel, she needs to do this for herself and I know you know that already." Margot gave Daniel a pointed look, he looked down at the ground in shame and mumbled something to his feet. I looked between Margot and Daniel with a questioning look. Seeing this, Margot simply smiled and told me Daniel knew how things had to happen today and left it at that. I wasn't going to argue with her right now and figured I could get the information out of Daniel eventually. We all turned quickly when we heard a sharp pained howl, what we saw shocked us all.

"*YES!!!! That's our girl, hahaha. Woooooo, Amber!*" Evie was howling while jumping around my head cheering Amber on. I was shocked to see Greg dangling in mid air, Amber had caught him by the throat and had lifted him off the ground. She was yelling at him, then finished by smashing Greg's wolf into the ground. We all heard his bones crack and the air leave his body from the force of the slam.

Amber

As I felt my end nearing I could faintly hear Lana begging me not to give up. I apologised to her for not having the strength I needed to get this giant wolf off of me. All my planning and sacrifices had been for nothing. I was so tired it would only be a few more seconds before I would be reunited with my parents and get to meet our Goddess. The darkness didn't come though, instead fresh air was rushing into my lungs. I coughed and sputtered while struggling to sit up. I saw that Zenah had come to my rescue, just in time. She was standing over me protectively, growling menacingly at Greg. I leaned back, closing my eyes for a moment trying to compose myself and regain my strength.

As I struggled to my feet Greg let out a loud howl, and I looked up to see a group of rogues surround my pack members. I was worried but I knew Olivia and Margot would protect everyone, so glad she had come to help us. I stood strongly as Lana had healed me fully, now ready to rid the world of Greg, nodding at Zenah; we both knew what we needed to do. I stayed in human form for now so I could speak if need be. I sprinted towards Greg picking up my dagger that had gone flying when he speared me. I grabbed him by the tail and slammed the dagger into his tail pinning him to the ground, he howled out in pain spinning on me. Zenah was right there and caught him, she began to smack the hell out of him. Biting down hard she ripped off his left ear causing a pained whimper to leave his wolf. I removed the dagger and stabbed it into his left hind leg, all while Zenah was slashing his face. We were hitting him simultaneously, fast and hard, not letting up for even a second. We needed to wear him down so his wolf wouldn't have a chance to heal. Greg got tired of being stabbed and slashed at one point. He bit into Zenah's shoulder causing her to back up quickly in pain. Greg tried to run away but he wasn't too fast. I was able to jump on his back and continued to stab him furiously as he tried to buck me off. Zenah healed quickly and came back to help me. I jumped off Greg so she was able to grab him by the tail and fling him a few feet in front of us. I jogged over and kicked him in the ribs and in the head, we continued to kick and throw him about for several minutes.

I noticed at that point that Olivia was outnumbered by a group of rogues. I was scared for her but knew I couldn't leave Zenah. We needed to punish Greg together for everything he had done.

"Olivia will be perfectly fine, Amber, she's an alpha. Concentrate on our next steps with this asshole." Lana was right, I needed to focus and not worry about my alpha best friend.

I took my dagger and cut a chunk of Greg's tail off, this really pissed him off and seemed to give him renewed energy. He kicked me with his back paws, sending me flying back and taking the wind out of me. While I was down he went after Zenah which took her off guard. He got some good hits on her, leaving her injured and bleeding, he turned to face me again. Greg's wolf smirking like a deranged lunatic, he began stalking towards me. I was about to shift when Zenah bit down on his amputated tail and ripped it clean off. I had never heard a wolf make that sound before, he was about to rip her throat out when I felt a wave of power wash through me.

"Mate is near." I couldn't let myself think of what Lana had just said, I needed to save Zenah. I bolted over to them and grabbed Greg by the throat squeezing tightly as I lifted him off the ground. He struggled to no avail, while I started yelling at him about what a horrible human being he was, and that death wasn't even good enough for him. I finished by body slamming him hard into the ground, his bones

made a satisfying sound. If I hadn't broken every bone in his body I would be shocked, the sound of the air leaving his body was like music to my ears. Zenah shifted back to human form to allow her wolf, Yasmin, to heal her.

"Thank you, Luna, for saving me, I wasn't expecting him to get the better of me."

"Hey, I was returning the favour. You saved me earlier, twice. We make a pretty good team, you and I. I couldn't let him take that away." I smiled at Zenah gratefully, but noticed Greg slinking away towards the trees. Zenah noticed as well and began to panic that he was getting away, I looked up and made eye contact with Margot. She smiled and we nodded to each other.

"Don't worry, Zenah, stay here and heal for a moment longer. Margot and Olivia have a fun, little game planned for Greg. Come join us when you're ready."

"Where will you be?"

"Just follow the sounds of that fucker screaming."

Zenah blinked up at me and let out a chuckle as I ran over to where Margot and Olivia had stopped Greg. Margot held some ropes in her hands, Olivia stood next to her with Daniel and Justin. I couldn't bring myself to look at Daniel out of embarrassment, but he stood next to me quietly and squeezed my shoulder supportively. Greg snarled at everyone and tried to swipe at Olivia, but all three alphas expanded their aura. Normally this would affect me, but not today. Their auras gave me renewed strength, in unison we all commanded that Greg shift. He was weakened so he had no choice but to comply. His human form was mangled and I tried not to stare at our handy work. Margot wrapped the ropes around his neck tightly, and proceeded to hogtie Greg. It impressed the hell out of me, but Greg on the other hand was beyond pissed off. He was screaming and swearing at us and foaming at the mouth.

"This way, gentleman," Margot motioned for Daniel and Justin to pick Greg up and follow her. We walked a good five minutes further into the woods where there was a pit dug into the ground. Margot hadn't told me what she had planned, all she said was she needed Greg to be weakened and then we would torture him some more.

"Are we going to bury him alive, Margot?" I was curious about what was about to happen.

"Oh no, sweet girl, even better than that, come look."

I walked over to the edge of the pit and choked back a shriek, the pit was full of rats crawling all over each other. I looked up at Margot who had a sly smile on her face, nodding at me happily.

"String him up across the pit boys, and make sure he's dangling low. These rodents are nice and hungry!"

I was shocked at first, but the more I thought about it the more I liked this punishment for him. Greg started freaking out when he saw the rats and tried to bargain with us, but we ignored him. Once he was tied spreadeagle tightly across the pit, the rats started to crawl up his body, scratching him and biting. The fun really began when one rat took a nice big bite out of Greg's not so big cock. If I thought the scream that came out of him when Zenah ripped his tail off was bad, that scream held nothing to this one.

"So, what have I missed? This is certainly a different form of torture."

I turned to smile at Zenah as she walked up to the edge of the pit, then looked down at him and spat. She told Greg that he deserved so much more for all the vile things he had done to innocent people all his life. Greg was crying and babbling incoherently which pleased Zenah greatly. We let the rats snack on Greg for a solid hour. They had completely eaten his cock off; they had snacked down to the bone on his right arm and eaten his remaining ear.

By this time, Greg was a horrible mess, so the guys took him out of the pit and untied him. He was breathing heavily but not moving, Zenah and I shifted, we both began growling at him. He looked back at us and started to crawl away feebly. I was the first to pounce and latched onto his right leg tearing it off his body, he barely had any voice left to scream. I threw the leg into the pit for the rats, Zenah did the same thing to his left leg.

As Greg continued to crawl away, slowly due to his bleeding heavily, we took turns jumping on his back and shredding him to pieces. There wasn't much left of him at that point, Zenah decided to end it, she shifted back long enough to tell Greg off.

"I have been waiting over twenty years to serve this justice. You will no longer ruin anyone else's life. I truly hope the Goddess tortures you for the rest of eternity."

As Zenah was shifting back to Yasmin we heard Greg mutter quietly, "Tortuga, I'm coming my love." It was such an odd thing to say. We didn't have much time to think about it though because, with one guttural growl, Zenah ended it all by taking off Greg's head. It flew for a few feet before stopping. We both shifted back slightly in shock, since neither of us had ever had to do something like that.

Olivia brought us both spare clothes to cover up, while Margot had Justin, Logan and Daniel collecting Greg pieces to put in a pile. Her witch friend had suggested we burn the body to be safe since Greg was of powerful witch lineage. Margot said a few words that her friend had told her to say as she lit the pile of fire, we all stood there and watched it burn. I was numb at that point and fatigue was setting in heavily. The shock of everything that had happened to me, and that I had to do, came crashing down on me. I stumbled back without meaning to and saw Daniel run over and hold me up.

"I know I don't deserve to be in your presence, Amber, but please let me help you?"

"How can you help me?" I was so confused and growing weaker by the second. My heart was racing at being so close to Daniel, then he was reaching behind my knees and picking me up when I fell backwards a second time. He held me tightly against his chest, there were no sparks anymore but he was warm and felt safe. With my head on his chest I could hear his heart pounding quickly. The last thing I remembered hearing was Daniel.

"I've got you, Amber, I won't ever let you fall again."

Then the darkness took over.

Chapter Thirty

Chapter 30

Greg

I crawled as fast as I possibly could, the pain was nothing like I had ever felt before. Those fucking rats took my manhood and left me broken. Now I was being hunted for sport, I couldn't believe my sweet little Luna had turned on me. She had to have been brain washed by that fucking omega, I knew I should have disposed of her long before.

"I told you she was faking this whole thing, but you didn't want to fucking listen to me. Now look how pathetic you are."

"No, you're wrong, Samson, she did want me! She was poisoned by that cunt. I'll find a way for us to be together just watch."

I turned my head to look at Amber, hoping that if she saw the pain in my eyes she would stop this madness and help me get away to heal. My pleading look went unnoticed as she brutally ripped off my right leg, flinging it back into the rat pit. My screams were barely audible by this point. I was numb and couldn't believe my little Luna was this vicious. I had been going to worship her like a queen. Now I had nothing left in me, I felt my life slipping away as my left leg was ripped from my body.

"Samson, do something! We need our magic to help us speed heal. This wasn't the way it was supposed to be."

"NOW you want my help? It's too fucking late Greg, we have no magic anymore. Those conniving cunts found a way to take it away from us permanently."

"WHAT? I thought it was just a blocking poison on the dagger she stabbed me with. I thought it would wear off."

"You're a fool! You underestimated Amber, and didn't want to listen to me. I can't believe I was paired with such a dumbass human. You're getting what you deserve, I'm just pissed I'm being taken down with you."

Samson retreated at that moment, I truly felt alone and realised as I had been arguing with my wolf that I was being shredded to pieces. This really was the end, I couldn't believe I had been bested by lesser beings. My only comfort came as I realised I would get to see my one true love again. I yelled out for my sweet Tortuga, telling her how much I loved her and prayed to the Moon Goddess she'd be waiting for me when I arrived on the other side. I looked up in time to see the omega aiming for my neck with her claws drawn.

Daniel

Amber had fully passed out in my arms which made me panic, Olivia assured me she was OK. She was breathing but I still wasn't convinced, so I started jogging towards the packhouse. I needed to get

Amber to the doctor and make sure nothing bad had happened to her. The thought of losing Amber brought tears to my eyes as I sped up my jog.

"Mate will be OK, Daniel, I think she was just drained after all that fighting. Lana said she had been through so much and just needed to rest."

"I want to believe you, Xander, but I still need the doctor to tell me those words for sure."

Xander shook his head but didn't say anything else, he knew when I was panicking there was no getting through to me. The logical part of my brain was screaming, Amber's wolf told us she'd be fine, she was just tired. Yet here I was being dramatic, I didn't care though. I had fucked up so royally by not paying proper attention to my mate, I wasn't going to make that mistake a second time. I wanted our mate bond back, something that was possible but I needed to work for it. I hoped to the Goddess above that Amber could forgive me and wanted it back as well.

I had made it back to the packhouse with Olivia and Margot in hot pursuit, and I started yelling frantically for help. Our pack doctor came running and told me to bring Amber into the first room. I placed her gently on the hospital bed before being asked to step aside by the nurse who had joined us. Without meaning to, I let out a warning growl which earned me quite the look from the doctor.

"Alpha, if you want us to treat Luna Amber I'm going to need you to keep your anger in check. We need space to work, you're still in the room so be thankful."

"Yes sir." I bowed my head in shame, I knew I was being irrational so I stepped back and let the medical staff do what they needed to do. I heard Olivia's muffled laughter from behind me in the doorway.

"What's so funny?" I linked her.

"You being told off by the doctor, that's what."

"I'm scared for Amber, I didn't mean to growl."

"I know you are, I'm sorry I laughed at you Daniel. I know my Cupcake and she's going to be OK. The last week has been traumatic as hell for her, you're going to need to give her space."

"I already gave her space, too much in fact, that's what caused this whole debacle. If she will still have me I will never give her space again."

"Daniel? You know that sounds creepy and psychotic, right? Mate just got rid of one psycho, let's not become a new one."

Xander was right, I was sounding a tad unhinged and the look on Olivia's face told me the exact same thing. I quickly let Olivia know I was just kidding about never giving Amber space again, and promised to find a happy balance. Olivia just shook her head and chuckled at me as the doctor walked over to speak with me

"Alpha, our Luna will be just fine. She was slightly dehydrated so we've started an IV to help her out. She will be as good as new in the morning after a full night's sleep. She used every last drop of energy she had in today's fight. You would have been proud of our Luna over the last few days, she held her own against that mad man and took care of this pack."

"Thank you, doctor, I am immensely proud of my Luna."

The doctor nodded and motioned for the nurse to leave us. As he left the doctor told me to let him know if there were any changes and that he would be back later to check on Amber. Once they were gone Olivia and Margot said they were going to speak with the pack members and make sure everyone was okay. I thanked them for all their help and went to sit beside the bed.

I gazed lovingly at Amber and took her warm hand in mine, kissing her knuckles. I saw Amber shiver from my kiss, deep down I hoped it was the remnants of our bond fighting to get back. I refused to give up hope, I had already lost my chosen mate. I wasn't about to lose the one person who was meant to be mine by fate. I would fight for our love with every last ounce of strength in my body. I spoke out loud to Amber, promising her that I was going to work hard to be worthy of her love. I looked up at her in time to see the ghost of a smile pass on her beautiful lips. She'd heard me! Renewed determination sparked through my body; I was going to be the Alpha she deserved, and we were going to build a life we both loved. I laid my head down on my arms looking up at Amber lovingly and drifted off into dreams of our future, still holding her hand.

Chapter Thirty-One

Chapter 31

Amber

The last thing I remember was hearing the sound of Daniel's heart beat as he held me close to his chest. His warmth made me feel safe and then the darkness came. I began to stir, I could hear a faint beeping sound and wondered what that could be.

"Time to wake up, sleepy head! The beeping you hear is a heart monitor."

I frowned to myself, confused as to why there was a heart monitor in the forest.

"We're not outside anymore, Amber, you passed out from exhaustion and Daniel rushed you back to the pack hospital." Lana's words startled me, my eyes flew open and I looked around the room in a mild panic.

I saw that indeed I was in a hospital room, judging by the faint light filtering in through the windows it was early morning. I went to scrub the sleep from my eyes but realised one of my hands was weighed down. I looked over and saw Daniel holding my hand tightly, as though I was going to disappear if he didn't hold me there. He had his head down on his arm on the edge of my bed snoring lightly and I looked at him in awe, drinking in the sight of him. He looked scruffy and dishevelled, but oh so sexy. I couldn't help but smile to myself while looking down at Daniel.

"Mate hasn't left our side the entire time. He's been a wreck, thinking you were going to die and leave him."

"Lana, he isn't our mate anymore, remember? I had to reject him to save him from that psychotic fucker, Greg." Tears instantly sprang to my eyes which I wiped away quickly with my free hand. I had already shed tears over this, it was pointless to cry now. It was a done deal; I had to live with my decisions and pray to the Goddess that we would both be blessed with a second-chance mate one day.

"Ambe..." Lana started to say something but I blocked her, I didn't want to hear her pep talk at the moment. The subject of my mate was a sore subject, I had waited so long for my mate and losing him hurt deeply. Lost in thought, I was startled by a sharp intake of breath beside me. I turned my head to see Daniel staring at me with tears streaming down his cheeks.

"You're awake!! Oh, sweet Goddess, you're going to be OK."

I was taken aback by Daniel's tears, I had never known any man in my life to be so open with his emotions. He started kissing my hand fervently laughing and crying simultaneously and I started to worry he was having a psychotic break. I reached over and wiped the tears from his cheek with my free hand, which ended up being a bad move. Daniel caught my freehand and held it tightly in his warm hands. He looked up into my eyes with his gorgeous hazel coloured ones and the raw emotions I saw swimming in them took my breath away.

"I'm so sorry, Amber, I'm not trying to scare you, I know I look like a wreck. I was so worried about you, you've been asleep for three days.

The pack doctor couldn't tell me if you would ever wake up again, I haven't left your side the entire time."

"THREE DAYS!!!!" My jaw hit the floor hearing that news, how was that possible? I must have been truly drained. I suddenly felt extremely embarrassed. I pulled my hands away from Daniel and curled into a ball with my back to him. I needed a moment to process what had happened. Daniel's emotions were hitting me hard and causing me to be severely overwhelmed by anxiety.

Daniel

Seeing Amber awake hit me like a freight train, I was terrified she would never wake up again. I had so much I needed to tell her and so many apologies to make. I had been so foolish and it had cost me my amazing mate. Amber owned my heart and didn't even know it, no thanks to my stupidity. Her touch surprised me and lit a fire in my soul that had me soaring high, but then she wrenched her hands away and turned her back on me. I froze! What had I done wrong? Did she just realise that she hated me? I tried to touch her shoulder and turn her to face me but she shrugged me off.

"Give her a few minutes of space Daniel, Lana just told me she's overwhelmed and can't process everything. You shocked her when you told her she was asleep for three days."

"Shit shit shit, I am such an idiot, Xander! Please tell Lana to tell Amber, I'm sorry."

"Lana knows you didn't do it on purpose, just give her a bit of space."

I nodded to myself and cleared my throat. I told Amber I was going to step out and get the doctor to come check on her. I barely heard her response but she did whisper, "OK", which gave a small spark of hope that she didn't completely hate me. I left the room scrubbing my hands down my face in anguish. How could I be so stupid? She just woke up, it wasn't the time to lay all my emotions on her like that. I got to the nurses station and asked her to call the doctor over. She was happy to hear that Amber was awake. The doctor followed me back to the room talking about how excited he was that she woke up and he was sure she'd be perfectly fine.

"We have a very strong Luna, this pack is lucky to have her. We're glad to have you back as well, Alpha."

"Thank you, doctor! Amber truly is an amazing woman and Luna, I will wait out here while you go check on her." The doctor gave me a questioning look but said nothing as he nodded and walked into Amber's room.

He was in the room for a solid half hour, it took everything in my power not to barge into the room. Amber needed space and I needed to give it to her, even though it was torturing me. Xander helped keep my willpower strong, he was communicating with Lana which was saving my sanity. The doctor finally came out and I startled him as I sprang forward wanting answers.

"How is she? Can she leave the hospital?"

"Well, Luna Amber seems physically to be completely recovered. Emotionally, she's a bit of a mess; she has PTSD from everything that happened to her recently. She is going to need time to work through everything, but I believe with time and the right help she will make a full recovery. She is just waiting for a change of clothes and then she can leave."

"Thank you, doctor." I hung my head in defeat as the doctor walked away patting me on the back. PTSD, this was bad. What did that sick fuck do to my sweet mate? I started getting angry, feeling the rage swirling in my stomach and ended up punching a hole in the hallway wall.

"Daniel, are you OK? The doctor told me Amber was awake and needed a change of clothes, so I ran down as fast as I could." Olivia's concerned voice was behind me. I was leaning my head on the wall, panting angrily, with my fists clenching and unclenching. "Daniel?" Olivia touched my back and I flinched, turning towards her with broken shame-filled eyes.

"Amber has PTSD and it's all my fault. If I had only told her how I felt she would have never left and gotten taken by that psycho. Everything's a mess and it's all my fault."

"It's not all your fault, Daniel. I chose to run away and hide instead of staying and telling you how I felt."

Olivia and I whipped around at the sound of Amber's soft broken voice. Olivia gave a little cry and ran to Amber scooping her up in her arms, giving her the biggest hug. They both started to laugh and cry, as they hugged one another. I couldn't help but smile at both of them as they clung to one another. Olivia took Amber back into the room to change, they came out a few minutes later both looking a lot happier.

"Ask mate if you can walk her to her room."

"I don't think she would want that, Xander, she seemed pretty clear earlier."

I felt Xander smack me in the back of the head, I didn't want to fight so I did as he said. My mouth felt dry and my tongue suddenly heavy.

"Ummm, Amber? Could I walk you back to your room?" I braced myself for the rejection, but it never came. She smiled shyly up at me and agreed to let me walk her. Olivia smirked at me and winked as she walked away promising to go sit with Amber later. We headed out of the hospital together and towards the front doors of the pack house.

I was taken aback when I suddenly felt a small warm hand take mine, with a slight tremble.

"I'm sorry, I feel a bit weak, I hope you don't mind?" Amber looked up at me nervously.

I took her hand fully in mine and kissed her knuckles. I told her not to worry, that I'd hold her up and I saw her visibly relax with my answer. We walked in comfortable silence for a bit until Amber broke the silence.

"You know, I truly meant what I said before? The PTSD is not your fault, I made my fair share of choices in this whole debacle. The whole situation was fucked up and I don't want you taking all the blame."

"Thank you for saying that, Amber, I appreciate it, but it was my closed off emotional stance that started it all. I have so much to tell you."

"Ask her on a date!" Xander was right about the walk so I figured what the hell, what was the worst that could happen? I stopped and looked Amber in the eyes, then asked her if she would have a private supper with me, off pack grounds. She surprised me by lighting up like a Christmas tree.

"I would truly love that, Daniel, would it be possible to go tomorrow evening? I want to spend my day today getting back into a normal head space."

I agreed, tomorrow would be perfect. It would give me time to plan an epic date just for her. She deserved the moon and the stars, which I fully intended on giving her. We had made it up to her room at that point, so I opened the door, and did a quick walk around to make sure there wasn't anything lingering from Greg. I had tasked the omegas to deep clean the room, removing anything that belonged to that fucker and Amber seemed happy to see her room clean and clear of his presence. I asked if I could give her a hug before I left and she agreed. I gently took her in my arms and squeezed her tightly, not enough to hurt her but enough to convey how I felt about her. As we released the hug I almost passed out with shock when Amber reached up and kissed me softly on the cheek. I couldn't help the enormous smile that spread over my face.

"See you tomorrow, Daniel, I look forward to supper with you."

Chapter Thirty-Two

Chapter 32

Amber

When I closed the door behind Daniel I felt like a weight had been lifted off my shoulders. We had talked on the walk to my room, even if it was a bit awkward, at least we'd tried. What came as a surprise was he had asked me out for dinner. For a split second I had been about to decline his offer but I thought better of it, and accepted happily. I got bold and gave him a small kiss on the cheek which earned me the most dazzling, knee-weakening smile I had ever seen.

"Mate is so sexy, isn't he?"

"Lana, you need to stop calling him that, we let him go. You're killing me every time you say mate."

"Why can't he still be our mate? Sure we rejected him, but we could take him as a chosen mate."

"Chosen mate? Could we really do that Lana? That wouldn't be fair to Daniel if we kept him from finding his true second-chance mate."

"What if he wanted us just as badly as we wanted him? If you chose each other no one gets cheated out of their second-chance mate. You'd be each other's second chance."

That thought caught me off guard, was Lana right? Could we decide to be each other's second chance chosen mates? I had to sit down for a minute to think, my head had begun to swim with all the possibilities and I became overwhelmed. I heard the gentle knock on the door but was frozen where I sat. I tried to call out but couldn't move my mouth, no matter how hard I tried. The door opened slowly, I heard Zenah's soft spoken voice ask if she could come in. She gasped and ran over when she saw me sitting stuck in a panicked state on my bed. Zenah fell to her knees in front of me and took my hands in hers.

"Luna Amber, I need you to look at me. Good, that's really good. Now take a deep breath in through your nose and exhale from your mouth and count to three as you do it."

Zenah talked me through the panic and I felt my heart rate start to come down, my vision cleared up and became sharp again. I could clearly see the concern etched on my friend's face, I instantly felt guilty for scaring her.

"Thank you so much for helping me, Zenah, I am so sorry you had to see that. I didn't mean to scare you."

"What happened?"

"Lana and I were discussing something and I just got a little overwhelmed that's all."

Embarrassment began to overtake me, so I stood up quickly helping Zenah to her feet. I told her I was fine now and she had nothing to worry about. I changed the course of the conversation to ask her why she had come to see me. Zenah being the angel she was, took the hint and let go of any more questions she may have had.

"I came to tell you goodbye, Amber. Now that Greg is gone I need to go back to my pack and set everything right."

"Will you come back?" I was hit with immense sadness by this news. We hadn't known each other long but I felt a kinship with Zenah and would have liked her to stay in the pack. I couldn't force her to stay though, all I could do was offer her a place at Onyx Crescent and hope she would take it.

"I appreciate your offer, Amber, right now I'm not sure if I will come back. Give me a few days and I will let you know how I plan on proceeding."

I plastered on the best fake smile I could muster before telling her I would wait for her decision in a few days. I wished her a safe trip back and asked if she needed anything or anyone to go back with her. Zenah shook her head with a proud smile and said she was perfectly alright going back alone and needed nothing. She told me I had given her the biggest gift by helping her rid the world of Greg, then caught me off guard by wrapping her arms around me and hugging me tightly. I hugged her back equally as tightly, and told her no matter what she chose I would always consider her a friend. We let each other go and wiped away stray tears that we both had sliding down our cheeks. This broke the sadness and we laughed heartily at each other. Zenah left me moments later with a little wave and a sad smile. I could tell she didn't want to leave as much as I didn't want her to leave. I crossed my fingers and sent a small prayer up to the Moon Goddess that she would choose to come back and stay.

The panic attack and shock of emotions from finding out Zenah was leaving left me exhausted. I decided to take a nap for a short while to help regain my energy, but my quick nap ended up lasting for several hours. I missed lunch and supper according to Olivia, who came up to my room with some supper for me, a little concerned. I scrubbed the sleep from my eyes and sat up quickly with a touch of panic returning to my heart. I had so many things I wanted to do, and I had lost my entire day.

"Shit, I lost the entire day, Liv! I wanted to check on all the pack members and help them clean up and organise training schedules."

"Don't worry, Cupcake, everyone knew you were in need of a good rest. I helped the few pack members who had been mildly injured by the rogues. Daniel has been working hard all day as well, setting up schedules and a whole host of other projects."

"Oh, sounds like you both have everything handled and won't need me, then." I felt crestfallen and dejected hearing this and slumped my shoulders in defeat looking down at my feet.

"HELL, NO! I won't let you slip back down that road, Cupcake. We need you, all of us do. Daniel, myself and the pack. Onyx Crescent won't accept any other Luna, after that impressive show you put on the other day. You are our Warrior Luna, Amber."

I was pulled out of my pity party by the sharpness in Olivia's tone, she had never spoken to me like that before in all our years of friendship. I stared at her and blinked repeatedly. I couldn't decide if I wanted to cry or be happy because my best friend just told me everyone needed me. The tears won but I couldn't stop myself from chuckling lightly.

"Oh shit, Amber. I'm so sorry if I was too harsh with you. I just needed you to know how much you meant to all of us! Had you known before, maybe you wouldn't have run away."

Olivia was right, had I known how certain people felt about me I wouldn't have run. I was full of remorse for the pain I'd caused everyone with my snap decision. Had I not left like I did, Greg would not have had the chance to kidnap me.

"No you're right, Liv, had we all communicated, myself included, that entire terrible situation could have been avoided."

"Don't be hard on yourself, Amber, we found out Alpha Renato had offered up the pack to Greg in some fucked up deal. He was coming for us regardless, the only thing that would have changed in that whole ordeal would have been us. We would have all fought him together and he wouldn't have hurt you like he did."

That bit of news was startling and infuriating all in one shot. I couldn't say I was shocked to hear Renato was involved, that man was scum on earth. I was just glad all of the terrible people were now gone. Olivia coaxed me over to my small table where she had set my dinner, I sat down and started eating. I was hungrier than I thought and thanked her for thinking of me.

"You're my best friend, I'm always thinking of you! Thinking I could have lost you really hit me hard."

I looked at Olivia with guilty eyes and apologised for any harm I caused her, she smiled and told me not to worry. I was back and that was all that mattered. I smiled at her and continued to eat.

"So, did you and my brother have a chance to talk at all on your walk back here?"

I cleared my throat awkwardly. "Yes, we did, and he asked me out on a supper date." I whispered the last part, but of course being werewolves Olivia heard me.

"OMG! HE DID? EEEEEEEEEEEEEEEEEEEEEEEE!" Olivia squealed so loudly I think the Moon Goddess heard her; I tried to block my ears but it didn't work. She stopped suddenly and gave me a terrified look.

"You said yes, right?"

I couldn't help but laugh at her. "Yes, I accepted his date."

"Oh, thank the Goddess! That explains a lot. Daniel was making a lot of phone calls all afternoon and I was wondering what some were about. I am so excited for you both, you and Daniel deserve to be happy."

I decided to tell her what Lana had told me about becoming chosen mates, I asked her opinion on it and she thought about it seriously for quite awhile before answering me.

"Honestly, Cupcake, I think it's a great idea, you both deserve the chance to be with each other. See what could have been had Greg not come along and fucked everything up."

"I want to, Liv, but I'm terrified. What if one of our second-chance fated mates shows up one day? He would leave me for that wolf and I'd be heartbroken. Or my mate may not accept my rejection and take me away from Daniel, leaving him heartbroken."

"Amber, if you saw the way my brother acted when you passed out in his arms, you wouldn't have any worries. I had never seen anyone panic so hard and become so insanely protective like that. He took protectiveness to a whole new level and never left your side."

I couldn't help the blush that crept up my cheeks. I couldn't imagine him being that crazy over me. As I was about to tell Olivia I thought she was embellishing the whole thing there was a knock on my door. I went to answer it and there was a young omega holding a stunning green dress out to me, with a card and single red rose. She handed them to me with a smile and wished me a good night. I closed the door and turned back to Olivia with a confused look on my face. She walked over to inspect the dress, telling me excitedly to read the card it came with, for answers. I gently tore open the envelope and read the card.

I am counting down the minutes and the hours until I can be back by your side. Please be ready for supper tomorrow at six o'clock, and if it pleases you, wear this gift I chose especially for you.

With all my love,
Daniel XoXoX

My cheeks flared to a deep red. I couldn't believe he had bought me this stunning emerald green dress. This beautiful gesture made my heart flutter and soar, I hadn't seen something this stunning in a long time. I looked down at the dress in awe with a soft smile on my lips, meanwhile, Olivia grinned at me like the Cheshire cat.

"Well, looks like you're going to have one hell of a good supper date tomorrow, my sweet Cupcake."

All I could do was nod at her absent-mindedly, as my brain swirled with every possible scenario. All of them ended with Daniel and I together, which I wasn't mad about. The idea of us being chosen mates was growing on me, but I kept that close to my heart as I went to hang up the dress in my closet, until tomorrow.

Chapter Thirty-Three

Chapter 33

Daniel

I won't lie, I was nervous as hell about taking Amber out. As wolves we never really dated, we're given our mates by the Goddess and that's it. Annabelle and I had chosen each other, but even then we were friends first and never dated. So, to say I had no clue what I was doing would be an understatement, but I had to pull out all the stops to make Amber feel special. I had royally screwed up by not telling her how I felt and getting lost in all the Alpha work without including her. Xander insisted that I send Amber a dress for our date, with a personalised note and flower. I thought he was crazy, what woman wanted to be dressed by a clueless man? Apparently, I truly know nothing, not only did the omega who delivered the dress say that Amber looked stunned and very happy, but Lana reached out to Xander and told him how happy she was with our gift.

"I told you, human, we wolves know how to woo our women! Listen to me and we'll have our mate back by the end of the night."

"I don't know Xander, some of your ideas are great, others not so much."

"Had you listened to me from the start, we would have already had a marked mate and none of this shit would have happened. But what do I know right?"

I couldn't even argue with him because technically he was right, I probably should have listened to him. What happened was terrible, but, now in the past, I couldn't change any of the outcome even if I wanted to. All I could do was make the effort to put everything right again by showing Amber I respected her, appreciated her and loved her. I had spent most of the day before, doing research and talking with Olivia. Having Amber's best friend with intimate knowledge of her life, at my disposal, was a blessing. I wanted to make sure anything I chose to do on our date would hold meaning for Amber. She needed to get to know me and I needed to get to know her. I cheated a little by asking Olivia a few questions about her, so I could make the date extra special. She was excited to help me and I owed her one for all the insight she provided me with.

I had just finished the work I needed to do for the day when there was a knock on my office door. I knew who it was before they entered by her scent and I bid Olivia to come in.

She burst through the door excitedly. "Why are you still here working, brother? Shouldn't you be getting changed for your date?"

"I just finished my work and called two of the venues for tonight to confirm we're still good to go. Aren't you supposed to be helping Amber get dressed?"

"I'm on my way to her room now to help her, don't worry she'll be ready for you at six."

She winked at me as she walked towards the door, but before she stepped out of the office she paused and turned to me with a serious look on her face. "Daniel, be honest with her! She needs to see the real you and know you've got her back the same way she had yours. Also, if you hurt her again I swear to the Goddess I will kick your ass to within an inch of your life."

I gulped audibly, and blinked at Olivia, knowing full well she could and would make good on that promise. I cleared my throat and nodded at her.

"Understood! I have no intention of hurting her again. I will be an open book and show her exactly the kind of man I am. A man who truly does love and appreciate her, a man who will move mountains for her."

"Good! Have a great time, I can't wait to hear all about it from Amber tomorrow."

Olivia giggled and waved as she left my office letting the door close with a thud. I shook my head to myself as my nerves started to creep up on me. There was a lot riding on tonight and my confidence was waning with each passing moment.

"If you listen to me tonight, I promise you I will get our mate back for us. Please trust me."

I didn't have much fight left in me, Xander had managed to wear me down so I agreed to listen to him as much as I could. He seemed satisfied with my answer, prancing around in my head as I made my way to my room. I had enough time to take a power nap, shower and get ready to pick Amber up at her door for six. I had just about made it to my room when Justin walked up to me.

"Daniel! I've got the car you asked me to borrow for your date tonight."

"No shit? You really weren't kidding me about owning that model? Justin, I owe you one, my friend."

"I wouldn't tease you about something that important. I know what tonight means to you, Amber and even the pack." Here are the keys, I've parked her up front. Have a blast!"

I thanked Justin, and went into my room to get ready. I had a renewed sense of hope, now that I had the keys to Amber's favourite car in my possession. This was only the first of many surprises I had in store for her tonight. I prayed to the Goddess it would be enough to win my mate back.

Amber

I was a nervous wreck from the moment I opened my eyes, I had dreamed about Daniel all night long. Some of the dreams were good, some were great and then the last one before I woke up turned into a nightmare where Greg reappeared. I tried to clear my head all day telling myself they were just silly dreams and not to read into them too much. As much as I tried to relax I ended up spending my day in an anxious spiral, either pacing my room or staring blankly out the window. The latter was how Olivia found me when she came to help me get ready for my date. She was concerned for my mental health when she saw me, but I shook myself out of my stupor and explained what had me in such a mood. She understood how stressful all this was for me, but in the end she gave me the best possible advice.

"You are running this show! If you aren't feeling it then you come home and move on. No one is going to push you into anything you aren't ready for. Just let go and have fun!"

Olivia was right, all I had to do was go along for the ride and try to have fun. If I wasn't feeling it then I could say no. Her words helped me feel powerful again; I was able to bounce back and start to feel excited about the date again. I told her I needed to take a quick shower then I'd be ready for her to help me with my makeup.

"Take your time, Cupcake, make sure you shave everything." She gave me a naughty wink and grin.

I couldn't help but burst out laughing. Olivia was such a joker. I had to remind her I was going on a date with her brother, did she really want that visual? That reminder seemed to do the trick, because I had never seen a smirk wiped off someone's face so fast. I could always count on my best friend to lift my spirits when I was down, and I told her as much an hour later when I was finally sitting in front of my mirror. Olivia busied herself with prepping my skin for the makeup and then dove in, painting my face like a masterpiece. We talked and giggled while she worked her magic and once she was done I could barely recognise myself. I hadn't looked that good in a long time, if ever.

"Daniel may not recognise me, Liv!"

"Oh, he will, and he's going to be speechless, just wait."

I moved onto my hair next which I kept simple; down with light beachy waves. Olivia approved and went into my closet to get my new dress, then she walked out with the beautiful piece and helped me into it.

"Fits like a glove, Cupcake! Hot damn, Daniel will drop dead when he sees you."

"We'll see! He should be here any minute." I got a bit nervous at that realisation, but didn't have time to dwell on it because we heard the knock on my door. It was a few minutes before six and it was show time.

Olivia walked over to the door with me close behind her, opened and hid behind it, so I was the first and only thing Daniel saw. The moment we both saw each other you could feel the air sucked out of the space like we were in a vortex. The air became electrically charged and I think the whole pack house heard the audible gasps we both uttered. Daniel looked like a runway model in a sharp, black, tuxedo style suit and was carrying a beautiful bouquet of flowers for me. I was truly thankful my dress was long so he couldn't see my knees shaking and my thighs pressing together for friction. Although, undoubtedly he'd be able to smell my arousal which made my cheeks heat up. I looked up into his eyes and couldn't help but laugh out loud at his expression. His eyes were round like gold coins and his jaw was so wide open I could see down his throat.

"Are you OK, Daniel? You haven't blinked in a solid minute!"

Olivia's question and subsequent laugh broke us both out of the spell we were under. I saw Daniel shake his head and then he started to blink again. "Amber, you look absolutely stunning. I could never have imagined how beautiful you would look in that dress when I picked it for you. Here, these are for you."

He handed me the flowers and I couldn't help the blush that deepened at his kind words. Olivia took the flowers from me and told me she'd put them in water for me. She wished us both a great night as she squeezed by us in the doorway.

"Don't do anything I wouldn't do!" She gave us both a wink and we could hear her chuckling to herself all the way down the hall.

Daniel gave me a dazzling smile and asked if I was ready to have some fun. I said I was as he offered me his arm like a gentleman. I took his arm happily and smiled up at him as we walked towards the front door.

"So, what are we doing tonight?"

"The question is: what aren't we doing!"

I looked at him questioningly, but he just gave me a secretive smile and told me I'd see soon enough. We had made our way outside by this point and as we got to the bottom of the front steps I looked up, stopping dead in my tracks.

"Amber, are you OK?" Daniel asked with a concerned tone.

"Is that our ride for tonight? Where did you get it?"

"Yes, it is our car for the night and I borrowed it from a friend especially for our date. Is everything ok? You don't like it?"

"Like it? Daniel, I fucking LOVE it! The Aston Martin DB9 was mine and my father's favourite car. After my mom passed away dad had trouble connecting with me, except we both had a love of classic cars and especially Aston Martins. It's even the right colour of midnight blue, I can't believe we get to drive around in this tonight."

I wiped away a rogue tear that had slipped from the corner of my eye. I couldn't believe Daniel had done this for me. It was, surely, impossible for him to know how much this car would have meant to me. I had a sneaky suspicion my best friend had a hand in this, but I didn't mind at all. This earned Daniel major points, he had clearly listened to Liv, but how he was able to find the exact model of mine and my father's dreams was truly incredible.

"Shall we, my lady? We don't want to be late for supper."

He held open the door for me while bowing slightly, and I felt like a princess as he waited for me to slide in before closing the door gently. Daniel jumped into the drivers side and the car roared to life; the sound of the engine revving gave me chills. I couldn't help the giant smile that was plastered on my face as we started to roll forward and the smile was nothing compared to the even bigger smile and laugh I had moments later as the car stalled. Daniel swore under his breath and started the car again, slowly easing his foot off the clutch and unfortunately stalling it again.

"Daniel, have you ever driven a manual car before?"

His red cheeks told me everything I needed to know. "I watched a handful of videos yesterday and figured it wouldn't be too hard."

"I can't believe you tried to learn manual for me by watching videos, that is the kindest thing anyone has ever done for me. If you don't want to be late for supper do you mind if I drive?"

He sheepishly agreed to let me drive and we switched spots. I started the car again, revelling in the sound and feel of the car purring beneath me. I looked over and thanked Daniel for letting me drive, he smiled genuinely at me and kissed my hand which sent shivers up my arm. "I promise I will drive after supper." He was very matter of fact in his tone, I giggled and told him I looked forward to him driving after supper and proceeded to ask him where we were going. He would only tell me what street to head for in town but refused to tell me anything more. I didn't want to push so I told him to hang on tight, gunning that beautiful piece of machinery out of the driveway, with Daniel letting out a little shout. I had to admit if this was how our date was starting then the rest of the night was going to be a blast, no matter what he had planned.

Chapter Thirty-Four

Daniel

I couldn't believe I stalled the car, not once but twice. I sat there in the passenger seat wishing the earth would open up and swallow me whole.

"This worked out so much better, Daniel, mate thinks you're so cute and look at her face. She is SO happy to be driving this car."

"Yeah, I don't think so, Xander. She for sure thinks I'm a loser, the smile is for the car."

"Listen, human, you need to get your head out of your ass and let yourself enjoy this. Stop being self deprecating or she will pick up on it and not want anything to do with you. If you ruin this for us I will never forgive you."

"OK, fair enough, I will do my best to get out of my head. I promise."

"Good! Now compliment her on her driving."

I listened to Xander and turned to Amber with a smile on my face. She looked at me briefly and shot me a smirk. I told her she looked good driving the car and she let out a hearty laugh. She told me she wasn't so sure about that but she was enjoying driving the car. I returned her laugh, I told her I was glad my incompetence allowed her to do something she loved. She looked at me shyly and then reached over taking my hand into her small warm one. I looked down at our connected hands as an electric shock went through my body. Amber put my hand on the stick shift, covering my hand with hers. She then proceeded to let me shift the car while she clutched, patiently explaining how everything worked and making me listen to the engine when we shifted. I was in utter awe of this stunning woman, if I already wasn't in love with her I would have fallen deeply at that very moment. She was happily teaching me and I was enjoying her doing so.

"I hope you've been paying close attention, since you'll be driving us to our next destination as promised."

"Oh, but you seem so happy driving, I can't bear to take that away from you. I've already made a fool of myself, I couldn't bear any more humiliation tonight."

"Oh, come on now, you promised! It's not hard and I believe in you!"

Her words meant more to me than she would ever know and this is how she managed to convince me to drive to the next spot. We were pulling up to our dinner stop, once she parked I jumped out and ran around the car to open the door for her. I helped Amber out of the car, she gave me a beautiful smile as she thanked me. Her smile melted my heart as we walked the short block to our destination. I watched as her face recognized where we were going and then lit up in shock, disbelief and happiness, in that order.

"Are you for real right now, Daniel? This is really where we're eating?"

"Yes, this is where we're eating! Why do you know it?"

"Know it? I have a dish named after me there! That has been my favourite restaurant since I went to college not far from here. It's been a long time since I've gone there though and I can't believe you knew about it."

"Well, I heard it was a good restaurant, and Olivia said you would like it."

She wrapped her arms around me and gave a squeeze as she practically skipped through the front door of the restaurant. The older woman at the front of the restaurant instantly recognized Amber, and ran over to hug her. They exchanged chatter for a few minutes and Amber introduced us. The lady, who I found out later was the owner, gave me an appreciative once over and winked at Amber. They both giggled as I blushed, then she insisted on giving us the best table they had which was off in a quiet, private corner. The table was in front of a large window that looked out over a beautiful garden. As beautiful as the scenery was, I couldn't take my eyes off my beautiful mate. Her smile was electric and her eyes bright and happy. I hoped that this was helping to ease some of the trauma she had been through.

"I've got a confession to make, Amber. Please don't judge me or laugh at me."

Her expression changed to serious and concerned. "I could never judge you, Daniel, what do you need to tell me?"

"I've never had Persian food before, I feel so uncultured. Would you help me choose a dish please?"

"Absolutely!" She reached over the table and squeezed my hand gently, giving me a small smile. She ordered for me and when the food came it smelled delicious. There was so much of it and I couldn't wait to dig in. Amber had ordered us both a dish called Barg, which I came to find out was fillet mignon cubes, cooked over a charcoal grill, the meat was tender and flavourful. She looked pleased with herself every time I took a bite and my eyes rolled back in my head happily. We shared a dip called Mirza ghassemi with flatbread, the flavours were extraordinary, and I understood why she had made the restaurant her favourite.

While we ate we talked about all sorts of things, there was never a lull in conversation which made my heart happy. The owner had come over to check on us at the end of the meal and bring us tea, and once she left us I had something to give Amber, which I was a bit nervous to give her. I cleared my throat and placed a decent sized jewellery box on the table. Amber's eyes widened slightly as she looked up at me in surprise. I slid the box over to her and she opened it with shaking hands, gasping as the lid swung open. Inside the box there was a white gold charm bracelet. She took the bracelet out of the box to look at it closer, and turning it over she let out a small cry. Her eyes filled with tears, I felt terrible I had just blown everything.

"I'm so sorry, Amber, if you don't like it I will return it." I reached to put it away but she shot me a look that froze me in place.

"Don't you dare return this, I would never forgive you! I absolutely love it with my whole heart. This is the sweetest gift anyone has ever gotten me, Daniel. You've got my father there, and a charm of you and Gabriella together."

"It's not just a charm bracelet, it also doubles as a fidget if you get anxious at any point; see these beads?"

Amber looked at me with tears swimming in her eyes and mouthed a barely audible thank you. I stood up and went to her side, I took the bracelet gently from her and helped clasp it to her wrist. She admired it on her wrist before jumping up and throwing her arms around me. I was caught slightly off guard and stumbled backwards, landing on my ass with Amber on top of me. The laughter that came out of her made my heart soar.

"Well done, human, laughter is the best way to woo our girl."

I couldn't tell if Xander was being sarcastic or not, so I just ignored him and held Amber close, while we laughed like two fools on the floor of the restaurant. After a few moments we wiped away the tears of laughter and I stood up taking us both to our feet. Amber wasn't expecting that so she let out a little squeak and clung to my neck. I bent down and gave her a quick chaste kiss which made her cheeks instantly turn bright pink. I paid for our supper not long after and we left for our next adventure. Amber stopped and handed me the car keys, reminding me I had promised to drive. I laughed nervously but a promise was a promise. I knew where we had to go next wasn't far so I hyped myself up to be able to do it. I got Amber into the car and sent up a prayer to the Moon Goddess that I didn't fail again. I put the car into reverse and miraculously didn't stall it.

"So far so good, Daniel! I know you can do it."

Amber's belief in me bolstered my confidence, so when it was time to go forward I did what I needed to do and the car lurched forward. I had to admit a bit rougher than I would have liked, but I didn't stall so it was a win. Amber cheered for me which made my cheeks go rosy in the process. By the time we made it to our next destination I felt like a pro and couldn't stop smiling. We parked the car and headed into stop number two with a renewed sense of fun and hope.

Amber

I was so proud of Daniel for driving from the restaurant, he seemed so proud of himself as well, which gave the date a whole new sense of excitement. We left the car and walked towards a nondescript building, and when I looked at Daniel questioningly he only smiled and said you'll see. We walked in the front door and were instantly hit with the deliciously sweet scent of fresh cake.

"What is this place, Daniel? Are we getting dessert at a bakery?"

"You aren't far off the mark but not exactly." His vague answer peaked my interest even more, as we walked up to a burly man standing behind a counter.

"Ah! Bonjour, mes amis (Hello my friends), you must be Mr. Stevens and Ms. Small?"

"Yes, we are, you must be Mr. Bélanger?"

"Oui, oui je suis Monsieur Bélanger (yes, yes I am Mr. Belanger)."

"Excellent, we are so excited for your class tonight!"

"Parfait, suivez moi (perfect, follow me)."

I was now putting the pieces together, Daniel had brought me to a baking school. Olivia must have told him about my love for baking and I was internally swooning at this point.

"Mate really put a lot of effort into this date, didn't he?"

"Yes he did Lana and I'm really starting to fall for this man. He's trying to learn about me in my happy places."

As we followed the chef to the back of the school I slipped my hand into Daniel's. I felt him flinch in surprise but then his hand curled tightly around mine and gave it a gentle squeeze. My emotions were beginning to swirl, I could see us working as a couple having fun every day together. The guilt of possibly taking him away from his second-chance mate, though, was real and eating at me. I was confused about what to do.

"Just have fun, Amber, you don't need to analyse your feelings this second."

I thanked Lana and pushed the guilt down, as we had reached our destination. We walked into a large room with multiple kitchen stations set up in a horse shoe shape, there were couples at all the stations except the farthest one in the back that was empty. Mr. Bélanger pointed to the station and told us that it was ours for the evening. He went on to start the class and let everyone know that we would be baking cupcakes tonight. I couldn't help the giggle that left my lips, Daniel looked down at me and winked. I knew for sure now, Olivia definitely had a hand in helping with this date.

"Amber, I've got to tell you I'm a terrible baker. I've always burned anything I touch, this is your domain. I will be your sous chef, so tell me what to do and I will do it."

"Hahaha. OK, Daniel, no worries. Can you get me a large bowl and these ingredients?"

I pointed to a list that was on the counter top and he saluted smartly and dashed off to get what I needed from him. I couldn't wipe the silly grin off my face as I tied an apron around me to protect my beautiful dress.

The entire time we were making the batter we smiled and laughed, we were both relaxed and having a blast. Daniel had taken off his suit jacket and had his sleeves rolled up, and the sight before me made me press my thighs together as my imagination ran wild. Of course Lana was no help, she kept filling my mind with erotic thoughts. She was begging me to do naughty things to him. It got so bad that at one point I cracked an egg putting the shells in the bowl and the actual egg in the garbage. I ended up blocking Lana for my own sanity, with Daniel making me laugh while we worked.

He wasn't kidding when he said he was a terrible baker, I had asked him to measure out the flour and he ended up wearing it from head to toe. He was a disaster but an eager helper nonetheless, we got the batter made and I took care of making the ganache for the filling. I felt quite accomplished when we finally got the cupcakes in the oven and the chocolate ganache was cooling in the fridge. I went back to our station to start on the buttercream frosting. Daniel had offered to do the dishes which worked for me; I hated doing dishes with a passion.

"You compliment each other well and make a good team!"

"I won't argue that with you Lana, we do make a great team."

I still didn't want to get my hopes up so I busied myself making the frosting. I had just turned the mixer on to whip the butter, when I felt strong arms wrap around my waist and pull me tightly against a hard, defined chest. As if I had no will of my own, my body betrayed me by melting into Daniel's embrace. He began to gently rock me back and forth to the music playing from the ceiling speakers, to my surprise he started gently singing the song to me in my ear.

"...*if I could turn back the clock...I'd make sure the light defeated the dark...I'd spend every hour of every day keeping you safe...*"

My breath hitched in my throat as a lump formed, I loved this song. His hair tickled the back of my neck as he bent his head to plant a gentle kiss on my collar bone. This sent an involuntary shudder through my body and I felt him squeeze me a bit tighter as he continued to sing.

"*I'd climb every mountain...And swim every ocean...Just to be with you...And fix what I've broken...'cause I need you to see...That you are the reason.*"

I felt the two tears hit my shoulder before Daniel buried his face into the back of my neck breathing heavily. I felt he was trying to compose himself so I didn't want to say anything to embarrass him. A moment later his hot breath was tickling my ear.

"You are my reason for being here, Amber. You and Gabby are the only reason I want to get up every morning. You have made me realise

I need to work hard to be the mate you deserve, and not take anything for granted ever again."

I wanted to say something back but the lump in my throat was too thick and wouldn't let any sound pass. I tried to clear my throat and opened my mouth just as a fire alarm started to scream from across the kitchen.

"Fuck! The cupcakes!!"

Daniel let me go from the warm cocoon he had me in and I dashed over to the oven ripping it open to be met by a facefull of smoke. I coughed violently, waving my hands to try and disperse the smoke quickly. I was mortified, I hadn't burned any of my baking in years.

"You were happily distracted, it's OK!"

I didn't even want to answer Lana, I was too busy dealing with the smoke, watery eyes, never ending coughing and burned cupcakes, that I had been looking forward to having Daniel taste. To say I was bitterly disappointed in myself would be an understatement. The chef walked over and smirked at me, he told me not to feel bad, these were industrial ovens so not the same as at home. He told me it happens at least twice every class that people burn their baking. That made me feel a little better but not by much. I went and trashed the burned cakes and returned to see Daniel already measuring out a fresh batch of ingredients.

"Don't worry, Amber, we'll make them even better than the first batch. Plus this batch won't have a chance of egg shells in them."

He winked at me and I burst out laughing, my bad mood instantly disappeared.

We made quick work of the second batch and this time I sat by the oven and watched the cakes like a hawk. Our second attempt was a success and I was happier than before as I plated the final cupcakes for the presentation. Daniel was beaming at me as I walked over to show him our platter of cupcakes. Chef Bélanger came over with an impressed look on his face.

"Madame, ils sont formidables!" (Ma'am, they are great!)

"That's my girl!" Daniel whistled in appreciation as I blushed a deep red.

Both Mr. Bélanger and Daniel took a cupcake and bit into them, simultaneously. The noises they made would have been hysterical if I weren't so self conscious. I wanted the floor to open and swallow me, as all the other couples looked at our station.

"Amber, these are the best damn cupcakes I've ever had in my life."

"I agree. Ms. Small, you have a true gift for cakes. I would gladly buy your recipe if you would allow me to?"

I was shocked at what Mr. Bélanger had asked and shyly told him I'd gladly sell him the recipe. Daniel told the chef he'd give me his contact information and I'd be in touch when I had a free moment. I was grateful Daniel stepped in as I was beginning to become overwhelmed by the attention. We left the baking class not long after.

"Thank you, Daniel, for such a fun night! I really appreciate everything you've done."

"Well, the fun isn't over yet, my sweet, I've got one other thing planned for us."

I loved that he was so eager and had so much planned but I had become emotionally drained. I felt horrible asking to go home but I figured this would also be a good test to see if he respected my boundaries.

"Daniel, I'm so sorry but can we please head home? I got really overwhelmed at the end there and I can't do anymore. You deserve the best version of me and right now I can't offer you that anymore."

I saw a brief shadow of disappointment cross Daniel's face but it was gone as quickly as it came. He smiled down at me genuinely and with a bit of concern, he took my hand and kissed my knuckles.

"Of course, my sweet! If you're done for the night I will take you home, no issue. We can do the last part of the date tomorrow if you're up for it?"

"I would love that! Thank you so much."

We got back to the car and he helped me into the passenger side. I loved how he didn't even hesitate to get into the driver's seat this time. We drove home slowly and I watched him from the corner of my eye with a shy smile. I was using the bracelet to calm myself and it really helped. Soon I was yawning and Daniel reached over to take my hand and squeezed it gently.

"You can fall asleep, I've got you."

"Thank you, Daniel, I had an amazing night."

As I drifted off to sleep, Lana spoke up gently. *"What if that second batch of cupcakes was symbolic of your relationship, Amber? The first time around went up in flames, but you have a second chance to start from scratch and make it better than ever."*

Her words hit me like a freight train, what if this was our second chance? If we both wanted it, we most certainly could make this work. I thought about this all the way home with my eyes closed. When we pulled up to the packhouse Daniel thought I was sleeping, I felt cheeky so I pretended to be asleep to see what he would do. He surprised me by reaching over and petting my head then traced my face with the back of his hand.

I heard him whisper, "You are my other half, I promise I will protect your heart this time."

I had to be careful not to smile or he would know I wasn't really sleeping. He came around the car, scooped me out as if I didn't weigh anything and held me against him like I was a fragile piece of glass. We made it to my room quickly and I heard him whisper to someone that I had been tired and asked to come home. He thanked the person for coming to help get me out of my dress so I could sleep comfortably. The voice that answered was Olivia's. I was touched that he had asked Olivia to help me as I wasn't awake to consent to him undressing me.

Daniel made my heart soar as he gently placed me on my bed, he kissed my forehead and whispered in my ear. "Sweet dreams, my queen. You have every inch of my heart and you don't even know it, yet. Just wait, you will soon know what you truly mean to me."

I thanked the Goddess he turned around to leave at that moment as a tear rolled down my face. I tried to hold it back but I just couldn't anymore, Daniel had my heart bursting. I heard the door close softly, and Olivia walked back over to the bed. I felt the bed dip as she sat on the edge next to me.

"Alright, Cupcake, he's gone. Now spill! I know you aren't really sleeping."

Chapter 35

*A*mber

I should have known that Olivia would see right through my charade. I cracked open one eye in time to see a pillow coming straight at my face. I didn't have time to dodge so took the hit full on and my head smashed back into the other pillows. I quickly reached over to grab my own weapon and hit Olivia back, sending her sprawling across my bed in a fit of laughter.

"Bahahaha, you insane little Cupcake! Do you really think you can beat me in a pillow fight?"

"I'll die trying! Hahahaha."

We fought each other while laughing hysterically for a solid twenty minutes until we both flopped on my bed exhausted with no clear winner. We called it a draw and started to wind down from the insanity.

"So, are you going to tell me about how the date went and why you were pretending to be asleep?"

"Absolutely! Let me get out of this dress and my makeup first." I ran to change quickly and came back to find Olivia curled up in my bed snoring lightly. I couldn't help but giggle, she wanted to know everything but couldn't stay awake, typical Olivia. My best friend loved her sleep. I turned off my lights then climbed into the bed next to her and covered us both, wishing her sweet dreams.

My dreams that night were a mix of Daniel to start but ending with Greg telling me I would never get to be happy and he would have the last laugh. I woke up with a start, drenched in sweat and shaking uncontrollably. I reached for Olivia, but she wasn't there anymore. I noticed a note on the pillow and took it with shaking hands, trying to focus on the note so I could bring myself out of the panic attack that had hit me.

You owe me a story and a rematch, don't think you won just because I passed out! I had to be up early to start warrior training. See you at breakfast.

Love Olivia

I took a deep breath and talked myself down, the fucker was dead he couldn't hurt me anymore. I didn't understand why my brain wanted to continue punishing me but it would be fine, I would fight until I got back to normal. I jumped out of bed and made my way into an ice cold shower, it was painful but really helped centre me and ended the panic attack. I changed into a pretty blue romper that I thought Daniel may like, since he told me the night before he loved the colour blue. I threw on some makeup, did my hair and put my new bracelet on before heading down for breakfast. As I walked into the dining room I was greeted by a wonderful surprise, Zenah had come back and she was sitting at the Alpha table deep in conversation with Daniel. I ran over to her and threw my arms around her happily.

"Zenah!!!! I am so happy you're back! Is everything OK? You weren't gone for long."

"Ah, Luna Amber, I came back yes. I wanted to speak with you and Alpha Daniel."

I looked over to Daniel who was staring at me as if I were a steak dinner and he was a starving man who hadn't eaten in months. I blushed furiously when we made eye contact, his eyes didn't hide from me what he was feeling or thinking. He shook his head and cleared his throat realising we weren't the only people at the table or in the room for that matter.

"Good Morning, Amber, you look absolutely stunning! Please sit down and have breakfast with us, then we can go up to the Alpha office and discuss with Zenah what brought her back."

I agreed happily and sat down while Claudia brought me my breakfast with a large smile on her face. Everyone was so much happier now that Greg was long gone. I also noticed how Daniel had said Alpha office and not 'his' office. I wondered what that was all about but figured I could ask him after coffee and food. As I sipped my coffee I looked around the dining room at all the smiling wolves and to my surprise saw many faces I had never seen before. I looked over at Zenah and Daniel, Zenah looked at me shyly.

"That's why I came back so soon!"

I wanted to give her the proper space to speak freely so I nodded and continued to eat without asking anymore questions. I finished breakfast quickly and we went up to the Alpha's office. Daniel closed the door behind and we all took seats, as I was about to sit next to Zenah in front of the desk Daniel told me to go sit behind the desk. Zenah was my friend and she was here to discuss things with Luna

Amber. I was momentarily shocked but agreed and sat down in the Alpha's seat. I looked over to Zenah and gave her a smile before asking her what she needed to speak to me about.

"Luna Amber, the pack members were so relieved and grateful that we had disposed of Greg. No one wanted to take his place, there are too many terrible memories in that pack. Greg killed a lot of the pack members off over the years simply for breathing wrong."

I reached across the desk, taking Zenah's hands in mine and squeezed them in comfort. The sadness in her eyes was heartbreaking, especially knowing her father was a casualty of Greg's, and his father's, terrible nature. I urged her to continue what she had to say, so Zenah took a deep breath and forged ahead.

"Luna Amber, would you allow the few remaining pack members and myself to join Onyx Crescent?" Zenah bowed her head down to look at the floor with an anxious expression on her beautiful face.

"Zenah, would you give Alpha Daniel and I a moment, please?"

"Of course! I will be outside, please let me know when it's OK to come back in."

She got up quickly leaving the office and I turned to Daniel, who had a huge smile on his face. I was confused about what the look was for, since this wasn't something I considered to be a happy situation. I arched my eyebrow at his and blinked several times.

"What are you so happy about Daniel? This isn't something to be smiling over."

"You don't think so? I do! This woman could have gone back to her pack and claimed the title of Alpha since she killed the previous one. Instead she recognized how broken they all are and chose to turn to you, Amber. She is here today asking to be part of your pack and I am so proud of you. Your strength and compassion truly inspire me to be a better Alpha."

I hadn't thought of it that way, Daniel's words surprised me and made me blush deeply. I looked him dead in the eyes and saw nothing but love and pride shining in them. I had to shake my head to clear the haze of hope I had creeping up my spine; I had to think logically. I had no say if they joined this pack, I wasn't Luna and I told Daniel this.

"Well, you see, Amber, you really are the Luna of this pack. You just need to see it for yourself."

"We aren't mates anymore, how can I be Luna?"

Daniel stood up and walked towards me, eyes blazing with a look I couldn't quite place. He gently took my hands and lifted me out of my seat, cupping my face. He looked me deeply in the eyes and got within an inch of my face.

"You are my Luna, my heart only wants you. It has always been you and I won't rest until you believe me, Amber. We don't need to be fated mates for me to be happy, I chose you and will continue to choose you every day for the rest of our lives."

The tears sprang instantly to my eyes, my heart was squeezing painfully in my chest. How could he say those things to me after I rejected him? I was beginning to panic so I began to fidget with my bracelet to calm myself. Daniel saw what was happening, put his forehead to mine and walked me through a breathing exercise. This helped calm me, then he bent his head to kiss away the single tear that had slipped out of my eye and down my cheek. The feeling of his warm lips pressed against my cheek sent an electric current through my body. It was all too much for me and my knees gave out, Daniel caught me and took me to sit on the couch. I could feel his heart beating erratically as he carried me and couldn't help but wonder did I affect him that much?

"Yes, you do, Amber, he clearly loves you and wants to make this work. Please consider taking a leap of faith, I don't think he will ever hurt us again."

Lana was begging me to listen to reason, so I took a deep breath and promised her I would try to be more open. Daniel sat on the couch and placed me on his lap. I was feeling awkward at first but then I melted into him and placed my head on his chest. The rapid beating of his heart made me feel at peace. I took a deep breath and began to speak before I had a chance to think about what I was saying.

"Daniel, let's pretend we do decide to be chosen mates. What would my role as Luna look like to you?"

I felt him smile on the top of my head before he began to speak. "Amber, you are my equal. Hell, I'd even say you are better than me in every single way! When you decide to officially be my Luna we will run this pack together. There are no decisions that will be made without your input, there will be times I will need you to make the decisions without me. Today is a perfect example, you were the one who made the people feel safe so you decide if they stay."

I liked the sound of that, I wanted to run the pack together, so badly. Something snapped in me at that moment and I found myself looking up at Daniel seriously.

"OK, I will make the decision today! Can we do a trial period? I want to give us time to work together."

I had never seen anyone smile so brightly in my entire life. Daniel's smile was blinding as he agreed to my trial period. He surprised me by asking if he could kiss me, I blushed bright red, shocking myself by agreeing. Daniel wasted no time, obviously not wanting to risk me changing my mind. He gently cupped my cheek and tilted my head up to him, looking me in the eyes.

"I failed you before, Amber, and I won't ever forgive myself for that. I promise you right here, right now that you will always be my priority. I want to make you proud of your decision to choose me."

My breath hitched as he leaned down and gently kissed my lips, he didn't push me for more than I was willing to give. The kiss was gentle and tender, it lifted my soul out of the dark making me feel light and free. He broke the kiss and sweetly kissed the tip of my nose before sitting back and smiling at me.

"So, have you decided what you want to do with Zenah's request?"

"I have! I would like to offer her and the remaining pack members a place in our pack. I would also like to offer Zenah a position as my Gamma."

"I love that idea, I want you protected as often as humanly possible and I won't always be able to do it. Zenah is loyal, fierce and a skilled fighter. You have made a wise choice and I respect that."

It was my turn now to give Daniel a bright smile and asked him to let me up so we could go get Zenah, and finish our discussion. I rushed to the door and found her waiting patiently as she had said she would. We all sat back down and I took a deep breath before launching into a little speech, hoping it worked in my favour.

"Zenah, the Alpha and I have spoken and we would love to invite you and the remaining pack members to be part of Onyx Crescent. There is one condition to this though."

I said the last part very seriously and watched as the smile on Zenah's face fell slightly.

"What is the condition, Luna Amber? We don't have much to offer but we will do our best to meet your condition."

"Zenah, your friendship and loyalty were what got me through the days stuck with Greg. If you want to be part of Onyx Crescent I absolutely need you to be next to me as a ranked member. Will you be my Gamma?"

The look on Zenah's face was absolutely priceless, she was shocked to her core and speechless for a solid two minutes. Her mouth hung open and her eyes welled up with tears of joy.

"Yes, Luna Amber, Yes! It would be my pleasure to be your Gamma and protect you."

I was so excited I jumped out of my seat and threw my arms around her in a giant hug, thanking her for agreeing. After a small excited celebration between the three of us we sat down to talk about the new pack logistics.

Zenah told us there were thirty-four members who were moving into the pack. We figured out where they would be going once integrated into the pack. Zenah left about an hour later to tell her pack, and for them to go back and get their belongings. Daniel congratulated me on a job well done and asked me to join him in the garden for a celebratory drink. I agreed and we headed out of the office together.

Chapter 36

Daniel

I was in such a good mood, I couldn't believe Amber and I would be doing a trial period as a couple. I was floating on cloud nine, watching her be the Luna I knew she was meant to be. Amber agreeing to join me for a drink in the garden was the icing on the cake. I boldly took her hand as we walked out the back of the pack house and she didn't recoil which made me smile.

"Don't push your luck, human! You've somehow gotten lucky up to this point. Don't screw this up." I couldn't even be mad at Xander for his comment, it was true I didn't want to push my luck.

We walked through the garden and sat on one of the benches together. I started telling Amber about our last activity the night before that we didn't get to do, suddenly Olivia came bounding over to us like an over excited child.

"There you are, Cupcake, I was looking for you at breakfast and had just missed you." Olivia pouted her lip dramatically.

"Yes, sorry Liv, I had to speak with Daniel and Zenah, who came back. We ate pretty quickly."

"Perfect! More tea to tell me all about, since we missed out on our talk earlier." Olivia had a huge smile on her face, looking down at me with a pleading look in her eyes. I took the hint and stood up vacating my spot on the bench for her.

"Cock blocked by your own sister, ouch! I liked being an only child." Xander dramatically drawled.

"Easy buddy, she's Amber's best friend, she needs time with her friend. That will also give me time to do something special for her."

I excused myself from the ladies and went to my office. On my way out of the garden I linked Olivia, asking her to let me know when her talk was nearly over with Amber. I told her I had a letter I wanted Amber to read privately, she assured me she would let me know and have Amber stay in the garden to read. True to her word, two hours later, Olivia linked me and I sent Claudia to the garden with the envelope for Amber. I was happy that Claudia was now smiling and no longer nervous. Her mother had returned, and her evil uncle had been killed the same day as Greg, along with his other followers. As she was leaving I asked Claudia to watch Amber from afar and link me when she got to the last page in the envelope. She agreed and went on her way.

I sent a silent prayer to the Moon Goddess that my letter would be well received. A knock on my door a few minutes later startled me out of my thoughts, Olivia peeked her head in the door and gave me a smile.

"She got your envelope from Claudia and is reading it now, I hope whatever you wrote her works to solidify your relationship." Olivia winked at me and wished me luck as she closed the door. I let out a nervous laugh and dove into some paperwork to distract me while I waited.

Forty five minutes later I got a link from Claudia that Amber was on the last page of the letter. I high tailed it back to the garden and saw her sitting comfortably on the bench reading the last page of the letter I had written her. Her beauty took my breath away as she looked up at me with tears shining in her eyes.

"Did you mean everything you wrote in this letter?" The scared-hopeful look broke me.

"Yes, I meant every word, Amber, I was a fool to push you away and I will never do that again. I value you more than you could ever know." I caressed her cheek, which she leaned into and smiled.

She showed me the third page of my letter which was a drawing of her I had made. "Did you draw this, Daniel?" I nodded at her as she looked at me in awe, then told her that as part of the date the night before, we were meant to go on a moonlit walk then do a drawing class together. She looked surprised about a drawing class, I said it was something that I loved to do and I wanted to share the experience with her.

"Well, you're incredibly talented, Daniel, I don't think I've ever looked more beautiful than in this picture you sketched of me." She blushed and looked so adorable.

We sat in the garden for hours talking and laughing, we eventually noticed the time and had to go get ready for supper. Leaving each other seemed like a hard endeavour for the both of us; this was a happy moment for me and I just kept smiling like a fool. At dinner we announced to the pack that we would be having new pack members joining Onyx Crescent soon. The entire pack was receptive to the news about new members and the terms we had brokered with the new arrivals. Supper was a jovial affair and it didn't go unnoticed that a lot of the pack members were giving us curious looks the whole evening, as if trying to figure out what was going on between Amber and I.

We had a good chuckle about it as we made our way to our separate rooms later in the night. I kissed her on the cheek and bid her goodnight. We both walked away from one another with smiles on our faces.

Amber

The next few weeks flew by as if I were in a dream. I had fully invested myself in our trial relationship. I had to admit that it felt so natural and good, most days my fears were almost non-existent. Only if I let my mind wander did I have small panic episodes, but Daniel was wonderful at helping me through them. Having him and Gabriella around really made a difference and their love pushed me to be the best version of myself. Daniel and I spent every day in the Alpha office working on pack business together, then we'd finish at four and spend time with Gabriella until supper. When I allowed myself I could see us being a real family. Lana reminded me daily that I was the one who made the decisions, and if I wanted to be a family then make it happen.

It had been about a month since I told Daniel we could be a couple on a trial basis. I was scared to admit that I was wholly wishing it wasn't a trial anymore, I had real feelings for Daniel and he had proven to me that he really did care about me and valued my opinion. We had just put Gabriella to bed one night, and as we were creeping out of the room I tripped on the door frame and went careening towards the floor face first. I didn't make it far before I felt strong arms wrap around my waist and pull me against a hard chest.

"Thank you, so much!" I blushed up at Daniel completely embarrassed that I was so klutzy. My chest was heaving from the adrenaline rush and I realised his was as well. I did something I didn't think I had the guts to do. I reached up and planted a kiss on his open mouth. I started to pull back flustered but Daniel had other plans. He held the back of my head crashing his lips to mine, he ran his tongue along the seam of my lips for me to open for him; which I did. Our tongues danced together sensually, I couldn't help the moan that escaped my throat. My moan sent Daniel into a frenzy, he picked me up as if I weighed nothing, never breaking our kiss. I instantly wrapped my legs around his waist to anchor myself to him, I felt if I didn't I would float away. We ended up against the hallway wall, he pressed my back into the wall and I could feel his cock growing against my core as I was wrapped around his waist. I didn't know what came over me but I started twisting my hips against him causing him to moan animalistically. Daniel broke our kiss at that moment.

"Easy, my tasty little Cupcake, I'm not sure if I can control myself if you keep doing that."

I blushed at him calling me his tasty little cupcake but felt emboldened, so I reached down and rubbed his cock through his jeans. Daniel's eyes turned black, full of desire.

"Maybe I don't want you to control yourself." I breathed out seductively, I couldn't believe I had just said that. I was tired of playing it safe, and not taking what was mine; I wanted him as much as he wanted me. "Take me to our room?" I asked him flirtatiously.

It didn't take him more than three seconds to already be moving towards our room. I couldn't help but giggle at him, and felt his cock twitch with every one that came out of my mouth.

"You're going to be the end of me, my sweet seductress." He more or less sounded pained, then I realised his jeans must have been very tight. We closed the door to our room and I let myself slide down his body earning another seductive moan from my sexy mate. I grabbed his belt and started to undo it, but Daniel grabbed my hands and stopped me. I blinked up at him in confusion, he looked down at me with concern.

"Amber, I don't want you doing something you're not comfortable with or not ready for." He looked so sad as he said those words, all I could do was smile up at him.

"I want this Daniel, I want you more than anything. I'm tired of hiding my feelings, I want the whole package with you."

Daniel looked shocked as a bright smile played across his face, he let go of my hands and nodded to me. I continued my mission and this time succeeded in getting his belt and jeans undone. His pants fell with a thud to the floor, his cock springing up in my face. I couldn't help but lick my lips, his cock was a work of art. I had hit the jackpot and I wasn't even ashamed to admit it. Lana began to howl in my head.

"Thank you, Amber, I wanted mate so badly, you won't regret this decision."

I didn't answer Lana as I had a cock that needed some attention and looked up at Daniel through my eyelashes. I proceeded to lick the precum off the tip as he shuddered in pleasure. I didn't waste time taking him all the way down my throat, he cried out in surprise and grabbed the back of my head to steady himself. I swirled my tongue from the base to the tip of his shaft, enjoying his shaking knees. My powerful Alpha was putty in my hands. I tightened my grip on his gorgeous cock and pumped harder as I intensified the suction, the whole time never ending the swirling of my tongue. I knew Daniel was getting close to his end when I felt him getting rigid and his breath more ragged. I cupped his balls and lightly squeezed them and that was all it took, he let out a shout and released warm cum down my throat.

I swallowed every last drop as I backed away from him and looked up to see him in a complete daze.

"Amber! I have never climaxed that hard before. You are truly magical."

I couldn't help but blush and giggle at that, the moment the giggle left my mouth Daniel's cock sprang back to life. I couldn't believe my eyes, it truly was a sight to see. He looked down at me with a cocky wolfish grin on his face.

"My turn to return the favour!" He reached down and pulled me to my feet in one swift motion. Kissing me passionately he took my breath away, as we kissed he unzipped the sun dress I was wearing and let it fall down my arms and chest revealing my breasts. Daniel stopped our kiss long enough to knead both breasts together, pinching my growing nipples. "Beautiful!" he breathed out. By the time he was done giving my breasts attention my nipples were harder than rocks and begging to be sucked.

Daniel kissed down my neck, nipping my marking spot lightly causing me to shiver in delight. He made his way to my nipples and gave me sweet release by gently licking and sucking on each in their own time. Daniel surprised me by lifting me up and carrying me to the bed, he put me down carefully and gently pushed me back on the bed. I complied and watched as he kissed down my body, all the way to my feet and back up my thighs. As he got to my sweet spot he playfully nipped my inner thigh for me to open my legs. My legs fell open and I heard his breath quicken as he took a deep breath of my arousal. He slowly kissed my inner thigh until he reached his prize, where he didn't waste time and sucked my clit into his mouth, swirling his tongue around my sensitive bud. I arched my back off the bed and Daniel reached a strong arm over, pinning my hips to the bed, as he began to eat me like the ravenous wolf he was.

"Ahh, Daniel, I won't last long like this." I was writhing around the bed uncontrollably, and moaning like a psycho: his tongue game was seriously on point! I could feel my orgasm coiling in the pit of my stomach, then he sped my explosion along by inserting two fingers inside me and pumping in a steady rhythm. I came undone in no time, screaming out his name happily. Daniel lapped up all my juices eagerly, and I was a shaking mess for a solid minute while he started kissing his way back up my body. He kissed me and I tasted myself on his tongue, this was sexy and I wrapped my legs around his waist. He positioned himself at my entrance and slowly pushed himself in. I cried out at how thick and long he was, and Daniel stopped looking at me in concern.

"Please don't stop, I'll be fine! It's been awhile since I've been with anyone and you're the biggest I've ever had." I internally face palmed myself that I had just made that admission to him.

"Don't worry, Amber, mate is happy you said that, look how bright he smiles."

Lana had a point, it looked like he loved what I'd said, he had puffed out his chest and proceeded to push himself fully into me and start pounding at a swift pace. I went wild moaning his name, begging him not to stop. I had never felt that full and I wasn't going to last at the rate he was going.

I looked up at him and made a split second decision. "Mark me!" His eyes snapped to mine searching for the truth, and then nodded when he saw my feelings plainly visible. He bent his head down kissing and licking my marking spot, and I shivered uncontrollably until he bit down to mark me. I screamed out in agony and ecstasy as the white hot pain turned into a mind-blowing orgasm. He finished the mark and before he could move away Lana pushed forward and marked him, he screamed out in pain and pleasure as he emptied himself inside of me. I licked my bite and he looked at me in awe. Suddenly I felt tingles all over my body; his scent hit me full force. My head was swimming from all the sudden feelings, I felt something snap into place inside of me and couldn't believe it. I knew Daniel felt it too from the look on his face.

"Daniel, what just happened?" I was incredulous and needed to hear something from the man I loved.

"Hello, my sweet mate. The Goddess kept her end of the promise."

I blinked at him in confusion.

As Daniel rolled off me and pulled me into his arms, he proceeded to tell me about his dream with the Moon Goddess, and how she was going to give us our bond back, if and only if I wanted it. I couldn't believe what I was hearing, our Moon Goddess felt so bad about Greg that she gave me my mate back? I was shocked and had no words. Daniel asked me if I regretted my decision, but I was quick to tell him I could never regret getting to love him fully and get to have our souls connected as well.

"Thank you for loving me, Daniel, I promise you I will always put in the effort to make us work and not hide from you anymore." Daniel returned that promise and proceeded to get a towel to clean me up. We fell asleep peacefully in each other's arms.

The next morning Daniel and I took a shower together which caused us to be late for breakfast. I looked in the mirror at my mark as I got dressed and marvelled at its beauty. It was a beautiful wolf sitting in an onyx crescent moon, outlined in silver. The marks shone in the sunlight as we made our way to breakfast and I knew there would be some excitement about our fresh new marks. What I wasn't expecting was the sheer and utter chaos when Olivia squealed so loudly I thought all the windows in the pack house would shatter. Zenah rushed over, picked me up and spun me around happily - I was glad I hadn't eaten yet. Then, came all our pack members, excitedly congratulating us. By the time we sat down to eat I felt like I needed to sleep for a day, to recover.

"Still no regrets?" Daniel laughed through a mind-link.

"Don't tempt me to change my mind!" I replied and gave him a pointed look.

I couldn't be mad, the people we loved and cared about were just happy for us. Later that afternoon we made a formal announcement to the entire pack that we were in fact marked and mated. Daniel also told the pack that the Moon Goddess had blessed our union and given us back our mate bond. The crowd were taken aback but thrilled that they had a blessed Alpha and Luna. During the announcement we also took the time to introduce the pack to their new Betas: Olivia and Logan. The funny part was we hadn't asked them first, so they were completely floored by our choice. Olivia sobbed, and then punched Daniel for making her sob in front of the pack. Logan was just worried he wouldn't make a good Beta; we assured him he would after he saved Justin and his sister.

We had a lot of work to do if we wanted to bring the pack to glory after having such a terrible Alpha for so many years. We were well on our way to having a solid pack because we had an amazing team of friends and family surrounding us. I was happier than I had been in a long time and was excited for the first time with what the future held for us.

Justin

The day had finally arrived, it was time for our Alpha and Luna ceremony. In werewolf terms this was akin to a human marriage. I was getting ready in one of the guest suites with Logan and Daniel, who had come from Onyx Crescent for the occasion. I was happy to now count Daniel as a friend, and even happier to see that he and Amber had marked each other. Best part was, we found out that after they marked their mate bond was given back to them by our beloved Moon Goddess.

Packs, far and wide, were talking about the Goddess-favoured Alpha and Luna. Which made making allies very easy for them. No one wanted to run the risk of going up against Onyx Crescent if the Goddess was on their side. This worked out for me, seeing as Jade Moon was the closest pack for help. After all the Greg garbage we just needed peace and calm for a while.

"I'm so happy to have both of you here with us today. This ceremony was a long time coming, and having our chosen family here means the world to both of us."

I got a little misty eyed and Logan came over and gave me a hug. "I for one wouldn't want to be anywhere else. I am so happy my sister gets to marry my best friend."

Logan and I laughed and cried while we hugged for a minute before we finished suiting-up and headed down to the ceremony space. I was anxiously waiting for Melissa on the ceremony platform, when after what seemed like an eternity the music started suddenly. I looked to the back of the pack house and my breath hitched as I saw my beautiful mate walking out in the most stunning baby blue dress I had ever seen. Melissa was being flanked by Olivia and Amber, as she floated towards me much too slowly.

The whole pack turned towards my mate with awestruck expressions, there were whispered oohs and ahhs going through the crowd and she passed them. Everyone else melted away as she drew closer, until she was finally by my side on the platform. One of the elders on the council began to speak to us and the pack. I honestly heard nothing of what he said; I was too entranced with Melissa's beautiful blue eyes smiling into mine. I vaguely remember cutting our palms with the ceremonial knife and drinking our combined blood connecting us as the leaders of Jade Moon. I was brought out of my trance by hundreds of congratulations flowing into my head from all our pack members. I shook my head and threw a block up as quickly as I could. I looked at the elder sheepishly and he gave me a knowing smile.

"What can I say, my mate is mesmerising!" The blush spread across my face and down my neck. I coughed awkwardly, inviting the elder to continue on with the next part of the ceremony. We were now connected to our pack by our vows, but we had also planned a part for our personal vows. I turned to Melissa and took her hands in mine, unable to help myself, I went first.

"Melissa, from the moment we met as children I knew you were special. Even if at the time you were my best friend's annoying little sister who liked to follow us on our adventures." I watched as she blushed a beautiful rosy pink before continuing. "Truth be told, the more time we spent together the more I fell for you. You were strong, fierce, brave, kind, loving and funny. When we found out we were mates it took my breath away. I felt like I had won the lottery that day." Tears were shimmering in both our eyes as we gazed lovingly at each other.

"I know our happiness was short lived since we both knew my father would never accept our union. I will spend the rest of my life making up for all the hurt that man put you through, my love. Your devotion to our relationship and being mine in secret was awe inspiring." I reached out and wiped the tears that were falling freely from Melissa's eyes. "I want to spend the rest of eternity making you smile and laugh, you are the other half of my soul and we make the best team. I can't wait to spend everyday reminding you how amazing you truly are, and telling the world you're mine. No more hiding: I love you!"

Melissa took a deep breath trying to compose herself before saying her vows to me. I kissed her palms encouragingly as she began to speak. She was so nervous her vows were just a quiet whisper, a secret just for me. I knew that being werewolves the others on the platform could hear her but they pretended not to hear anything. The rest of the pack just sat there staring at us curiously. When Melissa was finished the elder turned to the pack and told everyone he was happy to pronounce us as mated for life, but before he could tell us to kiss, a loud bang caught everyone's attention. We all turned to look at the pack house, what I saw made me believe I was hallucinating; until an all too familiar voice boomed out.

"Well, well, well, what do we have here? A wedding? And, you didn't even think to invite your dear old mom? I'm hurt, Justin, I thought I raised you better!"

"Mom?? You're supposed to be dead!"

Manufactured by Amazon.ca
Bolton, ON